FOR
Love
OF
HONOR

Endorsement for Terri Neunaber Bentley

In *For Love of Family*, Terri Neunaber Bentley offers readers a rich, immersive setting with well developed, lovable characters.

Greta Picklesimer
Author of the *Love in the Kentucky Hills* series

TERRI NEUNABER BENTLEY

FOR Love OF HONOR

IN A LAND SO STRANGE   BOOK TWO

AMBASSADOR INTERNATIONAL
GREENVILLE, SOUTH CAROLINA & BELFAST, NORTHERN IRELAND

www.ambassador-international.com

For *Love* of Honor

©2025 Terri Neunaber Bentley

Paperback ISBN: 978-1-64960-634-1
eISBN: 978-1-64960-683-9

Cover design by Hannah Linder Designs
Interior Typesetting by Dentelle Design
Edited by Emily Caseres

Scripture taken from The Holy Bible, English Standard Version. ESV® Text Edition: 2016. Copyright © 2001 by Crossway Bibles, a publishing ministry of Good News Publishers.

AMBASSADOR INTERNATIONAL
Emerald House
411 University Ridge, Suite B14
Greenville, SC 29601
United States
www.ambassador-international.com

AMBASSADOR BOOKS
The Mount
2 Woodstock Link
Belfast, BT6 8DD
Northern Ireland, United Kingdom
www.ambassadormedia.co.uk

The colophon is a trademark of Ambassador, a Christian publishing company.

ACKNOWLEDGMENTS

Special thanks go to Christine Maconachy and her husband for being excellent tour guides of Gettysburg, Pennsylvania. The knowledge acquired there prompted a better understanding of battle conditions and placement for my Civil War characters.

I also received wonderful historical tips from Gail Chumbley. Her years teaching history provided many helpful historical insights.

Finally, I appreciated the musical guidance I gleaned from choir teacher Annette Mackey as to what songs an aspiring singer in the 1800s sang. The character of Maria could not have been developed without this assistance.

CHAPTER 1

Surely there is a future, and your hope will not be cut off.

Proverbs 23:18

NOVEMBER 1860

ALTON, ILLINOIS

"Lena! Lena! You won't believe this!" The door swung open in a gust as Karl blew in from the street, waving the *Daily Alton Telegraph* newspaper over his head.

Alarmed, Lena dashed out of the kitchen into the parlor. "What happened? Is the town on fire? Karl! You'll wake Johanna." Their daughter continued sleeping on the nearby couch without a stir.

"He won, Lena! Lincoln won!"

Relieved that Karl's news did not require her immediate attention, Lena turned back to chopping vegetables for dinner.

"Oh, Lena. Did you ever think that the man we saw debate here in Alton a few years ago would end up being President of the United States of America?" Karl's excitement thwarted his breathing. "We have our own man in the White House! A man who honors free men of all colors, not at all like Douglas. I was so upset when he wasn't elected to the statehouse after those thoughtful debates, but God must have saved him 'for such a time as this.'"[1]

Lena only half-listened to her raving husband. Karl reached out and spun her around the kitchen. "Lena, do you realize how wonderful this is?"

Lena's baby kicked, and she held her hand over her bulging stomach. Smiling up at her husband, she said, "Karl, I don't follow all this political stuff like you. But I can tell you think this is very important for us, so I am happy." He pulled her forward, arching beyond the swell of the babe and drank in a deep kiss.

"Oh, Lena. I couldn't be happier. I have you, the children, and now a president who will put all this slavery oppression to rest. God is so good."

Little Johanna stirred from her sleep and rubbed the back of her fists into her half-opened eyes. Karl scooped her up, and she giggled and came to delightful life at her father's attention.

"We have only great days ahead, my ladies." He spun both Lena and Johanna around in an impromptu dance. "We'll be able to raise our family here in peace and safety, Lena. They even moved the prison to Joliet this year. What more can go right?"

But as November passed and Christmas approached, Karl's hope for the future began to dim. The newspapers were reporting trouble was brewing. It seemed that not everyone was happy about the new president. Tensions were mounting, and Karl worried that his

---

1   Esther 4:14

home wouldn't be as safe. His work kept him busy, but his mind was distracted by impending doom.

Karl pushed open the front door as Johanna ran to her papa on chubby toddler legs. However, Karl's eyes remained on the newspaper he brought in with him.

"Papa! Papa!" Johanna pulled Karl from his newspaper momentarily, and he lifted the child with one arm without missing a paragraph of reading from the treasure in his other hand. Johanna cupped his face with her two small hands and turned him to her. "Papa?"

Karl's gaze landed on his cherub's rosy cheeks and dazzling sapphire eyes. Her blonde ringlets mimicked her father's, although his were shorn close to his ears and hers framed her impish face. She was her father's daughter—a keen observer of her world, she absorbed the adult energy around her. She peered into his face for a moment. "Papa sad?"

Realizing how his demeanor rubbed off on his little daughter, Karl pinched her cheeks and tickled her. "Nothing to worry your pretty, little head about." He started to put her down. "How was your day, princess?"

Johanna resisted his release and held tight to her father with a pleading grip. "No. I gots to tell you 'bout Christmas."

"Christmas, heh? What do you know about Christmas?" He put the paper down and let Johanna chatter on about all the wonders of the season she had learned.

"Mommy said it's Jesus' birf-day."

Chuckling at her pronunciations, Karl sat her on his lap and confirmed, "That's right. And we will celebrate by singing Christmas songs at church, too." How could anyone remain downcast when greeted at the door by this whimsical creature? He leaned close and whispered in the tot's ear, "If you are a good girl, you might get a new dolly, too."

She squealed and hugged her papa tight.

*L*ena left her kitchen duties for a moment to enjoy father and daughter snuggled together in the parlor. Their perfect little girl would soon have a baby sibling to accompany her as well. Karl was a doting father and husband. The Lord showered his blessings on them every day. But Lena could see the worry in Karl's brow. Every time he read the paper, his mood changed from her usually jovial husband.

Over dinner, while Johanna was busy building castles in her mashed potatoes, Karl shook his head toward Lena. "The world is about to explode, Lena. The *Telegraph* says South Carolina seceded from the Union."

Lena frowned. "What does that mean?"

"It means that those traitors are furious that Lincoln was elected president, and they want to leave the United States and become their own country."

"Can they do that?"

"Not if Lincoln can stop them."

"Isn't South Carolina far from us? I'm not sure why you should be so upset. Surely, we won't need to worry about something happening so far away."

"I don't want to worry you, Lena. I hope you are right; but if other states decide to follow their lead, this may turn into an awful problem—for everyone."

"I'll pray that doesn't happen, then." Lena cleared the dishes before cleaning up their potato-caked daughter. "Come on, little girl. Time to get ready for bed."

Johanna yawned. "But, Mama, I'm not tired."

Karl seemed to shake off his melancholy for a moment and chuckled at his stubborn child. "I think Mama's right. Come on with Papa by the fire. I'll read you a story while Mama cleans up the dishes."

Lena gave him a grateful smile and began carrying the plates into the kitchen. She hummed softly to herself, but her thoughts raced with the news Karl had shared with her. An uneasiness had settled in her chest, but she tried to shake it off. She laughed at herself. South Carolina was a long way from their home. They were safe from trouble here. At least, she hoped so.

$\mathcal{B}$y April, tensions had continued. News was beginning to spread that a civil war was on the horizon, but no one wanted to believe it.

Lena had more to deal with at home now that the baby had arrived. And with a toddler underfoot as well, she barely had time to listen to gossip that was spreading like wildfire around town. She busied herself now with picking up the toys strewn about and trying to keep her eye on the stew simmering on the stove.

She had finally been able to get Baby Dora down for her nap. This baby always had some disagreement with the world. She nursed fitfully; she slept restlessly; and she screamed often. Dora only settled when she was held, but keeping her bundled to her mother was wearisome and restrictive while completing daily housekeeping chores. Lena's home collected uninvited spring mud, and meals became a basic fare because of the demands of the newest family member. Nothing was getting done at home.

Lost in her thoughts, Lena jumped when the door flew open. The rain rushed in with the swing of the door as it slammed behind Karl and his damp *Telegraph*.

"Lena! They did it. Those scum actually did it. South Carolina attacked our troops at Fort Sumter, and now we'll have a war!" Spitting words in contempt, he stormed into the kitchen to show Lena the headlines that had turned him into a charging bull in his own household.

Lena gave the paper a cursory glance as she nudged past her raging husband to the now-squalling babe he had awakened from a fitful nap. "Karl! I've been trying to lull her to sleep all afternoon; then you come storming into the house like a mad man." Jostling the three-month-old to her shoulder, Lena cooed and hummed a soothing tune to her fussy infant daughter.

"Look . . . you scared Johanna, too."

Huddled on the couch, clutching her Christmas doll, Johanna sucked her thumb.

Karl softened at the sight of his cowering little girl. "Oh, honey, I'm so sorry. Papa's not mad at you. Come here." Lifting her off the couch, Karl tossed her in the air as she squealed in delight. "That's my girl. I knew you had a smile in there somewhere." Nestling Johanna on his lap, Karl spoke in softer tones over her head to Lena.

"Six more states have joined South Carolina in leaving the Union. Lincoln is calling for seventy-five thousand volunteers to join the Northern army."

Alarmed, Lena quit stirring the pot of stew on the stove. "You surely aren't thinking of joining the army!"

"No, I think I can help from here. There are rumblings about them opening the Alton prison again for the war effort. Plenty of legal work will be created right here, and I can contract with the military to do it without leaving you."

"I was afraid you were going to leave me here with the girls." Lena tried to soothe her own nerves as she tried to rock the fussing Dora back to sleep. "I couldn't bear that."

Placing Johanna down to scamper off with her doll, Karl kissed Lena on the forehead before she turned back to slicing some bread for dinner. "Don't worry. I plan to stay right here, and this war shouldn't last long at all."

CHAPTER 2

For my brothers and companions' sake I will say,
"Peace be within you!"

Psalm 122:8

PERRY COUNTY, MISSOURI

"Thomas! Get your nose out of that paper and help me with this fence post before the hogs run off again, or Papa is going to tan both our hides!"

Thomas rattled the newspaper he held in his hand. Across the ditch, his younger brother pushed against a leaning post, unsuccessfully trying to stand it upright. Thomas peered over the paper a moment and asked, "Don't you want to know what's going on in the world, Tobias? There is a war going on in our own country. Have you even heard about South Carolina?" He ignored his brother's tussle with the fence and returned to reading.

"Do you want a war with Papa? You always have your face in a book or newspaper. I need some help here," Tobias shot back at his older brother.

Thomas folded the *Anzeiger des Westens* and tucked it in his jacket pocket before shrugging the jacket off to assist his brother. Since the May sun had already burned off the morning mist, the jacket was

14

in the way. The previous day's rain had softened the ground where Tobias prodded the stubborn post. With the extra hands, the post succumbed to the will of the boys, and they stomped it into place before reconnecting the fencing wire to it.

With the animals corralled again and fed, Tobias beat Thomas back to the house for their noon meal. Mother waited with a ladle of hot lentil soup for each of them while their younger sister Stella set the steaming bowls on the table in front of her working brothers. The twins, Henry and Herman, sat—or rather squirmed—across from their older siblings.

The twins were the first in the family to be born in America and were husky, cornfed stalwarts at only six years old. They were more like brawling cubs than helpful farmhands at this stage, but their promising build and robust nature forecast a bright future for them on the Missouri farm. Stella had been a mere babe when the Krueger family had crossed the Atlantic for their new home in America and had no recollection of it, but Tobias and Thomas were old enough to remember the treacherous journey where they lost a brother at sea. They now settled on their own acreage south of St. Louis, where Germans had settled in Perry County as many as thirty-five years earlier. The rolling hills west of the Mississippi provided plentiful hunting grounds of deer, pheasant, and rabbit, while the fresh air invigorated adventurous young boys to roam and thrive.

Tobias, almost eleven, was a natural farmer. Crops flourished with his tutelage, and he relished dirty hands and grubby dungarees. It only frustrated him that his older brother by three years often disappeared as soon as he declared his portion of chores complete.

Thomas never labored over outdoor tasks any longer than necessary. He preferred soaking in everything he could read. His curiosity about the world beyond the farm beckoned him to faraway places.

"Papa, did you hear about what happened in St. Louis with General Lyon?" Thomas knew better than to talk politics at the table, but this was different. With the war started, it was important to share what was going on. The *Anzeiger des Westens* was a German newspaper, so Papa would have no trouble keeping up with the latest reports if he was so inclined.

"Thomas. We are far enough away from St. Louis to stay clear of any trouble in the city. Don't worry your brothers and sister."

"But, Papa, Governor Jackson refused to send militia to fight for President Lincoln and started training troops to join the Confederate forces. General Lyon had his Union troops surround them and force them to surrender—right in St. Louis. The conflict is almost at our doorstep. We need to be aware. Lyon calls his men the 'Wide Awakes.'"

Thomas' siblings hung on to his every word. Papa sent him a stern scowl.

Not heeding the warning, Thomas added, "And it says here"— pointing at the paper in his hand—"that General Lyon fired on some rioters, killing twenty-eight, and then marched the prisoners through the streets. We must be careful next time we go to the city, Papa."

"We have no reason to go to the city for a while. We have the fields planted, and the local store will supply what we need until this blows over. This war will not last long, and people will come back to their senses soon. For now, quit worrying the family about all this talk of attacks, riots, and prisoners and such. Understand me?" Papa shifted in his chair and leaned closer to Thomas with a frown.

Thomas relented and tucked the newspaper away where he could pore over it again later. This topic must be discussed further. Although Missouri allowed slaves, the Germans in Perry County did not abide by such practices; and Thomas was sure they would side with General Lyon against Governor C. F. Jackson's Confederates. Although Papa was well-informed about the happenings in their adopted country, he only discussed them with his adult friends and not with his wife and children.

In the afternoon, Thomas found his father alone sharpening some of his tools in the shed. "Papa?"

Papa continued spinning the whetstone without turning to face his eldest son. "What now, Thomas?"

"You said you thought this war would be over soon, but Colonel Franz Siegel is recruiting German Americans to help fight and . . . "

"What is that to you, young man?" He continued to work as his son pleaded his case.

"I think some of the boys around here will be joining up—"

"You get all thoughts of running off and fighting out of your head right now. You are only fourteen years old!"

"I'll be fifteen this s-s-summer," he stammered.

"Don't you dare think about it. You are too young to fight in the war." He continued, "Besides, as the oldest, you must help guide your little brothers set a good example." He turned and walked away as he punctuated his speech with, "And don't tell your mother about you wanting to be a soldier."

Spring rolled into summer. Thomas' fifteenth birthday passed, and he learned that the prisoners who marched through the streets in

St. Louis were held across the river in the Alton military prison. The Union had reactivated the prison for the Rebel prisoners after South Carolina had taken Fort Sumter. His mother mentioned offhand that they knew a woman in Alton—Lena—who had read stories to Thomas and his younger siblings on their voyage to America.

Thomas had not been much older than his twin brothers were now when his family had crossed the ocean, but her soothing voice had calmed him when the winds whipped the ship on the ocean. Her bold friend in a green jacket had also regaled them with stories about Native Americans and monsters as they continued their journey on a steamship up the Mississippi. Mama had learned through letters that her friend Lena was married to that man now. Did he still tell those great stories? Had he joined the Union effort? Thomas had no idea.

Many German immigrants had flocked to enlist after Lincoln had called for more Union soldiers. Boys only a little older than Thomas left their families to support the North each week. Sunday services consistently revealed another absent seat next to mothers and fathers who said *auf wiedersehen* to their eligible young fighting men. The community spoke with a combination of fear and pride when their sons joined to fight for the country they grew to love. The families left behind were sure that their sons' contribution guaranteed a quick end to this war.

"Don't worry. They'll be back soon," they all murmured.

A few months later, the Krueger family gathered their four boys and only daughter into the wagon to attend Sunday services in Altenburg. When they arrived, many were milling around in the August heat before venturing indoors. News was buzzing.

"What's got everyone worked up?" Papa asked Herr Needhaus.

"It's Willow Creek. Troops are fighting right here in Missouri."

Mama gasped as she helped Stella from the wagon. The twins had bounded out already and chased some boys their age around the side of the church. Tobias and Thomas absorbed the news and its implications, glancing first at each other, then back to the adults.

"Willow Creek? Is that near here?" Papa inquired.

"Not really. It's closer to Springfield. I think most of us thought the fighting would not touch us here. We are far away from places like South Carolina and Virginia."

Papa nodded as he mulled over the new development, careful not to glance at Mama or the boys. "Well. Right now, let's go to church. Thomas, get your brothers for worship."

Once seated in the family pew, the pastor's message from John 16:23-30 struggled to break into the minds of the preoccupied parishioners. The sermon focused on prayer. True, everyone was praying now. Praying for safety. Praying for the war to end soon. Praying for loved ones far from home. Praying that danger would not camp on their doorstep while mothers held their children closer.

The pastor emphasized praying with confidence, telling the congregation, "There is no greater art than to believe from the heart."

He continued reading from John 16:23-24: "'Truly, truly, I say to you, whatever you ask of the Father in my name, he will give it to you. Until now you have asked nothing in my name. Ask, and you will receive, that your joy may be full.'"

Thomas shifted in his seat and let the pastor's words rest on him. Was praying going to be enough to win a war? He preferred a God of action.

The congregation prayed fervently to be protected from all the issues war might bring them. Thomas prayed he might help by becoming a soldier before it was over.

The congregation dismissed to the familiar German recessional hymn, *Wer Nur Den Leiben Gott*. However, the hymn, "If Thou but Trust in God to Guide Thee," took on more significance this morning. The families filed out of the sanctuary with the verses ringing in their heads:

> *He'll give thee strength, whate'er betide thee,*
> *And bear thee through the evil days.*

Thomas prayed for personal strength to combat the evil that was befalling the country. God's love may be unchanging, but he hoped his father's resolve to keep him home for more years before joining the Union army changed. The war may be over before he could make his contribution to preserving the Union.

Leaving the confines of the darkened sanctuary, Thomas was momentarily blinded by the noonday August sun before his eyes could adjust. Humid steam rose from the grasses, casting a surreal haze over the dale. The busy morning robins already stilled to the promise of oppressive noonday heat. Loud talking directed his attention to Lieutenant Schlegel. The old Prussian Army veteran had gathered a crowd of men outside in the square.

"You've all heard about Willow Creek. War has come to us, dear people. We must defend ourselves. Every able-bodied man should take up arms against these Rebel forces, or this nation we have adopted as our own will fall to slave-owning debauchery."

"But the Union lost at Willow Creek!" someone shouted back at him.

"I read they killed General Lyon," added another. "Even more reason to throw our support to them. They need us. Many Germans have already taken up arms against the enemy. You may have read in the papers of Bavarian Nicholas Bouquet from Iowa, who fought with distinction at Willow Creek." Looking at the undecided faces, Schlegel continued, "'Fellow German Colonel Franz, who fought at Willow Creek, is gathering more Germans for the Union.' There are many strong backs here. Let's show this country that Germans will fight to keep it whole!"

His crescendo accented with his arm raised brought an exuberant cheer from the group. Then a stir rippled through the crowd, and several young men stepped forward to sign up.

Thomas and his family watched in dismay. Thomas was resigned to respect his father and wait until he was older but yearned to go with them.

Tobias shook his head at the commotion. "Who will farm the fields if all the 'strong backs' go off to war?"

"Not everyone will leave." Papa answered. Turning to see Mama's furrowed brow, he said, "We will be fine. There is no reason for anyone to attack us here. Come, children. It's time to go home."

CHAPTER 3

Sing praises to the Lord, O you his saints,
and give thanks to his holy name.

Psalm 30:4

FROHN, GERMANY

"Mama. Mama!" Maria flew through the front door in a whirl as Eva and their mother looked up from their kitchen preparations. Eva's dusting of flour on her forehead and apron swirled around in the light of Maria's disturbance. The older sister grimaced at her younger sister's unladylike entrance.

"Maria! Someone chasing you or something?" Eva returned to her bread-kneading without much concern for Maria's outburst.

Ignoring Eva's comment, Maria handed her mother an envelope she extracted from her pocket. "Look. A letter from Lena!" The bread-kneading could wait; both girls leaned in with interest as Mama read. A post from America warranted family excitement. They took so long to arrive that every tidbit of news was months old before reaching them, and they were eager for every word of it. The last time they had received one of Lena's letters, she had given birth to baby Dora. Maria could see how anxious her mama was to learn how her daughter and granddaughters were fairing as she took the envelope and gingerly opened it so as not to damage a precious word. Mama began to read out loud:

"*Dear Mama and Papa,*

I am sure you have heard about the war here in the United States. You need not worry about us. No battles are near us here in Illinois, and Karl has offered his services to help with legal matters at the military prison, which is right here in our town of Alton. So he will not need to fight, which brings me great relief.

Not only am I happy that the girls will have their father around, but we are also expecting again; and I will have my hands even fuller before long. I suspect I may be carrying twins this time since I am getting so large, and the doctor has guessed this is the case.

It pains me that you cannot see your grandchildren. Johanna is already reading the children's books on her own that Martin sent last Christmas. She tries to imitate her papa when he is poring over legal papers in the evening. Karl wear spectacles when he reads now, and Johanna has asked for her own pair. She insists they will make her read faster.

Little Dora adores her big sister and copies her every move. Johanna finds Dora to be simply a nuisance and in her way most of the time. Did I treat my sisters the same way? I don't remember. Dora's prized possession is a stuffed cat she totes around everywhere. Johanna teased her by saying we need to get a dog to chase her cat away. Dora only clutches the raggedy thing to herself tighter, so Johanna can't take it away. I assume Herman doesn't write home often, so I will include my brother's news for you, too. Herman and Dagmar's farm is thriving. You would be proud of the farmer he has become. I see them and the children when they bring produce to the prison or come into Alton for supplies.

Hans is almost as tall as his father now. He is a strong, athletic boy, who works beside his father. He prefers building things outdoors, rather than sitting in school but finished his eighth-grade studies this year with honors. Their Katie and our Johanna are inseparable when they come to visit. An outsider would think they are twins, since they were born the same week and resemble each other the way I remember Maria at a similar age. Their rosy high cheeks, steel blue eyes, and golden hair prompt both Herman and Karl to talk about keeping a shotgun handy to ward off the boys someday.

Dora, on the other hand, sports tight curls like her father, which are unruly to comb; and she still carries her toddler baby fat with her. She is adorable but in a different way than the other two.

I miss you all and hope we will be together again. Give everyone a hug for me. Write soon.

Your loving daughter,

Lena

Eva chuckled. "Boy, I remember Lena teasing us like that. It sounds like Johanna is just like her."

"I don't remember her teasing us," interjected Maria, still looking over Mama's shoulder at the letter held tightly in her hands.

"You were too little. You were barely in school when Lena left for America. Heidi and I are closer to Lena's age. We teased each other all the time."

"If you and Heidi don't find someone to marry soon, you will be old maids. Lena's not much older than you, and she is married and expecting for the third time already." Maria tossed her hair over her shoulder, turned with a flounce of her skirt, and headed out the door again leaving her sister to stare after her.

"*D*on't worry, Eva," Mama soothed. "Everything happens in the Lord's time."

"I don't need to marry. I can provide for myself. I'm learning so much at Frau Ziegler's bakery, I will be able to support myself with my own shop in time." She paused. "I don't know why everyone thinks a girl must wed to be happy. And I don't need to hear dispersions from my own sister." Sliding the re-kneaded bread into the oven, she wiped her hands on her apron and strode out the back door for some fresh air.

Moments later, Heidi walked through the front door. "Mmm. It smells good in here. Eva must be baking again." She sat her cloth bag down by the door and wandered into the kitchen to check the aroma source.

"You're right," Mama answered. "The fresh bread will complement dinner tonight. Will you help set the table please? Your father and Thomas will be here soon."

"Yes, but where is Maria? Isn't she supposed to set the table tonight?" Heidi placed the table settings for each family member. "After all, I'm sewing all day with seamstress Estel. What is Maria doing all day but looking at herself in a mirror?"

"She delivered the mail a while ago and sashayed back out again." Mama sighed and shook her head. "She lives in her own world, I think."

"That's true enough. She thinks she is going to live like royalty without lifting a finger. I think she is going to have a rude awakening soon, Mama, if you and Papa don't make her pull her own weight around here."

"She's still young, Heidi. There's plenty of time for her to grow up yet."

"You baby her too much. At Maria's age, we all had more work to do."

"Enough, Heidi. Let's have a peaceful meal."

At that moment, Papa and Thomas trounced through the door after a day of hunting. Thomas held up two pheasants for the whole family to admire and proclaimed, "Tomorrow's dinner!"

"You can clean them after we eat," Mama directed. "Right now, clean yourself up for supper."

"Mmm. Now that is a smell to come home to." Both hunters agreed as they discarded their guns at the door and cleaned up for the evening meal over a waiting basin of water.

Eva and Maria came in from different doors and met at the table to sit with the rest of the family. The parents sat at each end, and the four remaining children sat in birth order on opposite sides. With their brother Martin away at university and their two oldest children now living in America's Illinois, only these four children remained.

Bowing their heads, the family said grace together:

> *Komm, Herr Jesu; sei du unser Gast;*
> *und segne, was du uns bescheret hast.*
> *(Come, Lord Jesus, be our Guest.*
> *And let these gifts to us be blessed.)*

Mama looked across the table at her dwindling brood and produced the precious paper Maria had delivered earlier. "Papa, we have a letter from America."

Papa started to reach for it then. "My eyes aren't as good as they once were. Why don't you tell me what Lena says?"

"You know your children well, since you did not assume it was from Herman." Mama unfolded the creased paper and read it to the rest of the family.

"Twins?" Papa exclaimed. "My, my. Our family in America is growing so much."

"I wish I could go to America," Maria lamented.

"What would you do in America?" Eva and Heidi said in unison.

"Sing, of course." Maria flipped her blonde mane for it to bounce off her shoulders. "Everyone says I'm the best singer around here. I could entertain at concerts wherever I wanted to go."

"Now is not the time for anyone to be heading there. Lena tells of the war. I'm sure you are safer at home," Thomas added.

"But Lena also said there is no danger where she is."

"You are too young to be gallivanting around the world performing at concerts, young lady," Papa scolded. "Singing in church is fine enough."

"Oh, Papa. You are so old-fashioned. I am sure the Lord has more in store for me than only church singing. If He gave me such a fine voice, I am sure He would want me to use it."

"You need to be humbler, Maria. The only boasting you should be doing is in the Lord, not in yourself or in your voice," Mama scolded.

"But, Mama, God gave me this voice, didn't He? Why would He want me to be cooped up in this little town with it when I could glorify His name throughout the world?"

"Somehow, I doubt glorifying God is the reason you want to see the world, little sister." Heidi glowered at her sister. "A humble heart would not be sashaying herself all over the place. She should have a contrite spirit."

"I am the way God made me for a reason. Why my family cannot understand it is insulting." Maria rose to excuse herself from the table.

"Not before you help clear the dishes, Miss." Heidi stopped her in her tracks. "I set the table after a day of work. It's time you do your share."

Maria stormed to the sink and started scrubbing the dinnerware with a vengeance as the rest of the family gave her a wide berth.

CHAPTER 4

Everyone helps his neighbor and says to his brother, "Be strong!"

Isaiah 41:6

ALTON, ILLINOIS

Karl entered the town meeting with a folder of briefs under his arm. The room was already filled with contentious men and women squaring up on each side of the town argument. News was out that the previously abandoned state prison would now be a military post penitentiary during the war. Complaining against the government would not make any difference, but that did not stop a town meeting from voicing opposition.

Karl represented the Union prison authorities since his firm contracted their legal obligations. He straightened his collar and organized his papers on the narrow table before him for reference. Mayor Krum entered the room from a side door, followed by a burly assistant bodyguard who strained his chambray shirt against protesting front buttons.

Mayor Krum wore his gray tweed suit; his pocket watch chain draped from his vest pocket as he slid the timepiece away into its place upon his entrance. The puffy eyes gave evidence of little sleep, and he pounded his gavel for order as the buzz of the room wound down to a murmur.

When all eyes were on him, he began, "A reminder to the citizens gathered here: you do not speak unless you are called upon to do so. If there is an uproar, you will be ushered out of the room." He peered around the room before giving his assistant a side glance. "If you desire to speak to the issue, you should have left your name with Clerk Brown." He gestured to a thin man, whose eyeglasses slid down his beak-nose, seated near the doorway. "Mr. Brown, will you call the first person to the podium?"

"George Hanson."

A round man wearing his best patched overalls made his way to the front of the room. Others encouraged him as their designated spokesman. He retrieved a crumpled paper from his pocket and addressed the mayor. "Your Honor."

"I am not a judge, Mr. Hanson. Just speak your mind. It will be fine." With a weary sigh, the mayor gave the floor back to the nervous Mr. Hanson.

"Your . . . " Stopping himself before repeating his mistake, Hanson continued "Sir? We have been told the prison is to take in over thirteen hundred"—he looked at his notes for assurance—"yes, thirteen hundred Rebel prisoners. We"—he glanced back at his supporters, who nodded and whispered, "Yes!" before the mayor tossed them a stern look not to talk. "Our wives and children will not be safe if that happens. This prison will be a menace to the people here. What if anyone escapes? We have families here who must be protected." Mr. Hanson's voice rose to a higher pitch as he spoke, and many townspeople nodded in supportive agreement with a few exclamations of "That's right!" and "You know it!"

Krum's gavel beat again, and the room quieted. "I have warned you." Looking back at the red-faced man standing before him, he asked, "Do you have anything else, Mr. Hanson?"

"Well, no, sir. We just want you to put a stop to this invasion of Rebels to our fine town. We already suffer the pro-slavery raids from across the river looking for runaways. We don't need any more trouble."

"Thank you, Mr. Hanson. You may return to your seat." Turning back to Mr. Brown, Krum said, "Next name, please."

Others came forward. Some disputed Hanson's numbers. Most were fearful for the safety of their loved ones, too. No one wanted the war knocking at their door. It was bad enough that outside St. Louis, Camp Jackson had suffered a massacre where twenty-eight civilians were killed. No one wanted to be involved in a similar event in Alton.

Karl shook his head. If only these folks knew how much Alton was already involved, they might not feel so snug in their beds at night. The fact was, Alton had secretly received twenty-one thousand rifles from St. Louis to keep them from falling into Rebel hands during the Camp Jackson incident. The townsfolk were none the wiser to this action, and Karl would not be the one to tell them.

After a dozen such testimonies, Mayor Krum called Karl to answer the concerns of the public since as a member of the community and legal counsel for the Union Army, it was his pre-arranged duty to calm the growing hysteria of the town. Karl stood and cleared his throat.

"Thank you, Mayor Krum. Ladies and gentlemen, I understand your concern about the prison. You, like I, want to live in a safe and secure place to raise our families. You must recall this same facility was used by the state of Illinois only a few years back. I don't remember you voicing your concerns about your safety then. In fact, Alton has been a fast-growing Mississippi port city for many years, and this should only increase the town's potential. Think of all the advantages it will afford our community. More money will pour into Alton because of the Union activity here. This will create more job opportunities in trade; they will need supplies to keep the prison operational, and more commerce will be transacted both on and off the river. Having the Alton Penitentiary here provides us with more protection than many of our surrounding towns. We will have extra troops around to keep us safe. Do you think pro-slavers are going to raid an area full of blue coats? We have been deemed an important interest for Mr. Lincoln. This facility is a temporary necessity to help end the war."

The room listened in rapt attention. Thoughtful murmurs bounced about the room. Not wanting to risk the wrath of Krum's gavel, the listeners spoke in undertones but loudly enough that Karl absorbed the support for his words. Karl nodded to the crowd at the conclusion of his remarks and sat down.

"Thank you, Mr. Muller. Are there any questions for Mr. Muller?"

A hand flew up. After Krum called on him, the man asked, "So how many prisoners do you think will be held here?"

"Well, I think Mr. Hanson's number may be a bit inflated, but it may be determined by the length of the war," Karl answered. "I doubt if more than twelve hundred can be housed here." The hum of disgruntled reactions circled the floor.

Mayor Krum called for order again. "Like Mr. Muller has indicated, the decision to have a military prison in Alton is out of our hands. The government has already made its decision, and it is up to the citizens of Alton to welcome them the best we can and accommodate the operation of the Union Army as long as they are here. If there is any problem, we will need to address them to the Federal government, since it is not under civilian jurisdiction. So go home and rest easy. I think you will find you are better protected here than anywhere else in the country because of the extra soldiers Mr. Muller indicated will be stationed here." Grabbing his gavel, he rapped it thrice and declared, "Meeting adjourned." He rose and departed out the same side door he entered.

Karl gathered his papers and headed home to Lena and the family. Lena's pregnancy was becoming more evident by the day, and her energy level often waned when chasing after the girls and keeping up with the household chores; but he knew she would be waiting for him to get a report about the evening's events.

Sure enough, Lena sat by the fireside hand-stitching some winter clothes for the babies when he walked in. If the doctor was right and she was having twins, she wanted to be prepared with extra baby things. Besides, many of the clothes the girls wore were rather tattered after the two older children had their way with them. The girls were never gentle. They might as well have been boys the way they romped. Unfortunately, some of the clothing tucked away in boxes had become home for a nest of mice in the attic. Karl had brought them down days ago, and Lena had only now started digging through them to find the mess and salvage items. If it was not one thing, it was another.

Lena grimaced, her hand instinctively covering her rounded middle as the babies kicked again.

"Are you okay, dearest?" Karl furrowed his brow and knelt at her side.

Looking up to see Karl's concern, Lena smiled. "I'm fine. Every time I am ready to take a break, the babies think it is time to play." She patted her middle again. "How did the meeting go?"

"Not too bad. Hanson and others are concerned about the prisoner population getting out of hand and some may escape and put everyone in danger. I think explaining to them about how much protection we will have here with the extra troops helped appease most of them. I think some may be worried about unruly Union troops though, too. No one said it, but soldiers are not always well-behaved."

"But the troops stationed here will be under strict orders, right? If the town has a favorable relationship with the soldiers, we shouldn't have any trouble." She tilted her head to wait for a reassuring answer.

"I think so. It's always hard to tell how people will behave in new situations. From what I've seen, most of the soldiers are hardly more than scared kids."

"Well. I'm meeting with the ladies tomorrow for tea. Maybe we can come up with an idea to build better ties with the Union occupation of our town. It might help ease tensions on both sides when everyone sees they are only sons far from home."

"Good idea." Karl rose and offered his hands to help his wife to her feet. "Right now, I think you should head to bed, Frau Muller. You and those babies need your sleep." Putting her sewing aside, Lena followed her husband, and both turned in for the night.

*M*rs. Alma Knopf's maid finished filling the teacups of the eight women gathered in her drawing room. Lena's girls had raced upstairs to play with Alma's daughter, Susannah, and her collection of porcelain dolls. Dressed in their finer clothes, they looked less like tomboys today than usual. Lena had stilled them each long enough to braid Johanna's hair and comb out Dora's tangles. The unruly curls had escaped the attempted ribbon since Dora had no patience with it on her head.

"No, Mama!" Dora had proclaimed as she ran out of arm's reach. Defeated, Lena had let it go. No sense in insisting on a bow when it would be it would be yanked off the moment she was not looking, anyway.

Eyeing the sweet cakes on the proffered tray, Lena's hand touched her burgeoning middle. "I'm already getting as big as a house," she told herself. "I'd better sample only one." She selected a tea cake decorated with fine pink frosting.

Rebecca addressed Lena mid-bite. "My, my, aren't you coming right along? It looks like you will be adding to your family any time."

"No. Not yet. I still have a couple months, I think. The doctor thinks I'm having twins. That's why I look like I've been swallowing watermelons all summer. It wasn't at all like that with the girls."

The group twittered their congratulations over the news. Others chimed in with their family news and a bit of gossip about the women who were not in attendance before Alma finally asked, "Did anyone hear about what was said at the town meetings last night?"

This was Lena's opening to share her ideas about welcoming the soldiers stationed in Alton. "I did. As you probably know, Karl is legal counsel for the Alton Penitentiary. He told me about the concerns over bringing so many prisoners here."

Sally gasped, and her hand flew to her mouth. "Why, of course. Wouldn't you be? Our families could be murdered in our beds by some escaped prisoner."

"But Karl explained that Alton will be more protected than most any place in the Union because we will have more troops stationed here. No Rebels would dare attack a town with an entire regiment protecting it."

"I hadn't thought of that," said Rebecca. "Do you believe it will be safe, Lena?"

"War is never safe, but I think we can help build a working relationship between the soldiers and the townspeople. People won't be so fearful of these boys marching around here with their rifles if we reach out to them, and they will become more comfortable with us. Remember, as my husband put it to me, they are simply boys far from home. What can we do to help make their time here better?"

"Well, the holidays are coming," Nell's trembling voice broke through. "Maybe we could do something for them then. My boy joined up with the first wave of volunteers, and we miss him around our table every day." Her eyes returned to her lap, holding back tears as she rung the embroidered kerchief mercilessly.

"How about a Thanksgiving dinner? We could get the whole town involved and treat these lads to a feast to take their minds off the war," Rebecca volunteered. "It's still weeks away, which should give us time to advertise and to organize it."

"I like that idea," Alma agreed. "With an undertaking this momentous, we should have a name for our group." The ladies looked at one another in search of a decent name.

Nell perked up, gaining more volume. "How about the 'Loyal Ladies of Alton'?"

"That's a great name!" Alma gushed. Everyone agreed with nods of approval.

The women set to work dividing responsibilities. Alma would purchase an advertisement in the *Alton Telegraph*. Lena would ask Karl to contact Colonel Kincaid, the commander at the prison, to arrange feeding the Thirty-seventh Regiment who would be stationed in town as guards soon. Rebecca volunteered to contact the church for a place to feed everyone. Sally put her mind to designing patriotic decorations of red, white, and blue; and no one told her that was more suitable for Independence Day than Thanksgiving. Nell began to create a menu and a sign-up sheet for women to declare items they would bring to serve. Sarah planned to visit the butcher and grocer to see about donations to the cause.

The room was abuzz with plans; and Lena sat back, hand on stomach, pleased. The Lord looking down on His six days of creation could not have been more delighted when He saw it was good. Lena arched her back to allow more room for the babes and smiled.

CHAPTER 5

Let the wise hear and increase in learning,
and the one who understands obtain guidance.

Proverbs 1:5

PERRY COUNTY, MISSOURI

The Krueger family rattled each other's nerves as winter descended with no private space in the house and seven bodies bumping into each other at every turn. With the first flurries, Mama swept the twins outside to make snowmen, snow forts, or anything to make them burn off that boyhood energy. With a snowman made, a snow fort destroyed, and the boys shivering, they returned to hog the heat from the fire and slurp a cup of soup. At six years old, they created mischief at every turn.

Older sister Stella searched high and low for her sewing needle because the boys hid it in candle wax above the mantle. They relocated Tobias' boots under his bed, causing the livestock distress over the tardiness of their feed. They pulled out the bookmarks in Thomas' books, leaving him to leaf through them again and again to find where he quit reading because he refused to damage the pages of his precious books by turning down their pages. No discipline or distraction seemed to work for the twins. Their heads together, they whispered as they concocted one plan after another, much to the distress of their family.

This afternoon, as he shoved one arm into his well-worn winter jacket, Thomas announced, "I'm going to visit Frau Beltz to ask if she has any more books I can borrow."

"Wait!" Mama stopped him mid arm hole. "Take the twins. They need some exercise."

Thomas began to protest, but his mother's stare made it clear she needed a break from Henry and Herman, too. One cross word to his mother, and Papa would use the switch he kept for such disciplinary behavior. Thomas slumped the rest of the way into his sleeves and called to his brothers. "Come on, you two. Grab your coats. We're going for a walk."

Scrambling for an adventurous opportunity with their eldest brother, they were at the door before Thomas finished buttoning his own coat. Looking back into the room, Thomas caught Tobias and Stella with unabashed smug smiles at Thomas' lot. He shook his head at them and then smiled to himself. "Might as well make the best of it."

The white fluff blanketed the ground by only a few inches, and Thomas was able to keep the boys' throwing snowballs at each other most of the walk. "I'll bury you two in a snowbank if you use me for target practice," he threatened.

The two imps tilted their heads at one another in a knowing grin and let their missiles fly at their older brother. The snow struck the neck of his jacket and filtered down inside his coat. Shaking it off, Thomas pummeled his young brothers with some well-aimed missiles of his own. This started a snowball war of darts and dashes all the way to the Beltz farm.

Frau Beltz had been a teacher before quitting to start a family in Perry County but still had a delightful supply of interesting novels. Thomas had already read her Homerian classics about Odysseus. He had returned James Fenimore Cooper's *The Last of the Mohicans* a few weeks ago. He wondered if she had more adventure books. She had mentioned something about *Robinson Crusoe* or *Gulliver's Travels*. Both sounded like great reads. Thomas needed something to sustain him through the winter months cooped up with his family.

Opening the door to Thomas' knock, Frau Beltz was greeted by three snow covered waifs. "My, my, you three had better come in before you catch your death of cold." She ushered them to the blazing fireplace.

Stomping the drifts off their boots and shaking off their hats and coats, the boys warmed their hands over the welcoming fire. Noticing the ensuing puddle, Thomas tried desperately to mop up the melting snow with his scarf. "Oh, ma'am, I'm sorry. We're making a mess. I should have left the twins at home."

"Nonsense. It's a blessing to see you boys. With my girls married off, I miss having children around." She grabbed a mop and wiped away the excess moisture on the floor. "Can I offer you a sugar cookie? I was baking some for the church ladies, but I have a few to spare."

The children lit up at the mention of cookies but were polite enough not to attack the woman offering the sweet treat. Instead, they offered pleading eyes to Thomas for permission to accept the sweets. "I guess that would be okay," Thomas answered. "Be sure to say thank you," he admonished the eager eaters as they inhaled each morsel.

"Thank you," they mumbled with full mouths.

"You are certainly welcome. Here, Thomas, I will wrap a couple up for Tobias and Stella. You can take them home." Frau Beltz neatly wrapped a couple of cookies in butcher paper, and Thomas tucked them in his pocket. "Now, I guess you didn't walk all the way over here for a cookie, right?"

Thomas nodded. "I was hoping you'd have another book I could borrow, Frau Beltz. You have the best selection of anyone I know."

"I'm glad you love reading as much as I do, Thomas. You need to talk to your father about going to university. You have a fine mind, and they will have many more books than I."

Thomas knew his family had no money to send him away to school, but the idea nudged his brain into a hopeful yearning that squeezed his heart.

"Here you go. I think you will enjoy this one—*Gulliver's Travels*. It will take your mind far and wide, this one will. I bet it may spark an idea of traveling for yourself one day."

"I doubt I will ever be able to travel far from here unless I join the army or something. But I know Papa will never let me do that."

"War is not all fame and glory, Thomas. You will be better off cultivating your mind." Frau Beltz handed him a beautiful book bound in marbled calf leather. Opening it, he read, *By Jonathan Swift, DD, Dean of St. Patrick's, Dublin. 1815.*

"Wow. I don't know, Frau Beltz. This looks like a special book." Thomas brushed his fingers reverently over the gilded pages, noticing the enclosed artwork of a huge man roped to a beach and tiny men guarding him.

"Oh, it is, Thomas. When Swift wrote it, he told people he wrote it to 'vex the world rather than divert it.' He teaches many lessons about society. When you read it, think deeper than just the adventures." She glanced over at his two charges, who were now poking at the fire embers. "But I'd keep it out of the twins' hands for now. They haven't learned how to appreciate precious things yet."

"Oh, I will, Frau Beltz. I will. Thank you for lending me such a precious book." Thomas tucked it inside his coat to keep it out of the weather and away from any errant snowballs. "Come on, boys. We better head home now. It gets dark early these days, and we don't want Mama to worry." They were at the door again before Thomas could turn around. "Thank you again, Frau Beltz. I'll take good care of it."

Bundled against the wind that gusted more insistently since arriving at the Beltz farm, the Krueger boys decided they would race each other home. The youngsters had more energy; but Thomas had longer legs, so it was nearly a three-way tie as they rushed upon their front porch. A supper of simmering stew assaulted their senses as they swung the door open.

The twins tumbled in first with a shout of "We won!"

Thomas argued, "I don't think so." Winded, he added in gasps, "I got here . . . at the same time . . . you did."

Not in the mood to argue when dinner was so near, they dropped the discussion, their coats, their hats, and their gloves at the door.

"Now stop right there, you two," Mama scolded. "You hang up all this before you even think about one bite of dinner."

To a chorus of "Ah, Mama," they retraced their steps and did as they were told. Thomas had already completed hanging up all his items and moved out of their way.

Papa was seated near the fireplace, puffing on his pipe and repairing a bent gate hinge in his lap. "Look, Papa, Frau Beltz loaned me *Gulliver's Travels*. It is one of her treasures."

Papa examined the item in Thomas' hand. "That book is bound with fancy writing on it. You better take excellent care of it, so you return it in the same condition you borrowed it."

"Oh, I will." He paused a moment before continuing. "And, Papa?"

Papa took another puff and looked up again.

"Frau Beltz says I should consider going to university."

"Who would pay for you to go?" Papa raised one eyebrow. "I wish I could agree, Thomas. You are a smart boy, but what we raise is only enough to support the family. I do not have enough savings to send you to university."

Downcast, Thomas did not meet his father's gaze. "I thought you'd say that, but I will find a way."

"If you can find a way to finance an education, I would send you with my blessing, son." He reached out to pat Thomas on the back.

Thomas forced a smile. He knew Papa had to consider the future of more than one child; and although the family was not starving, funds for extra requests were difficult to justify. "Thank you. I will put my mind to it and figure out a way to go. Since they moved the Concordia School from Perry County to St. Louis, maybe I could find work in the city and pay my way through school? If it is okay with you, I will write to them and ask about arrangements for next term. It doesn't hurt to ask."

"Let me talk to your mother about it. You are moving a bit fast here. Next term is only a few months away. No one will let you enroll for free, boy." Papa pointed his pipe at Thomas, and he blew a couple smoke rings before he added, "Go ahead and write your letter to investigate the possibility. If something can be worked out, we will be happy to have you attend more school. A scholar in the family would make us very proud. The Lord always provides when there is a true need."

Thomas lit up and gave his father a quick hug. "That would be wonderful. It will help give you a little more room here, too, if I go away to school," Thomas said with a wink.

"Don't get too worked up about it yet, young man. Many things need to fall into place before you are moving out of here, I think."

Mama walked up just then. "What are you two talking about over here?" She tilted her head and gave each a quizzical nod. "Who's moving?"

"Oh, nothing, Mama. I was just showing Papa the book Frau Beltz loaned me." Thomas held it up. "Isn't it beautiful?"

"Goodness, yes. You had better find a secret hiding place to keep it away from the twins. Right now, wash up for dinner."

Thomas stayed up late crafting a letter to the school in St. Louis. He could not imagine he was the only young man who wanted to work his way through school, but how did he draft an intelligent request? He would need lodging and food, as well as a job that left time to study. One semester was already ending. Did they take students in midyear? The more he considered all the arrangements, the more overwhelming the prospect became. Never having organized anything for himself before, how did he start?

The biggest decision Thomas had ever made was which book to read next. When he had mentioned he wanted to join the Union Army to fight, Papa had shot that idea down flat. But for him to be so quickly agreeable to Thomas' idea of attending university surprised Thomas. He knew his father was likely confident the war would be over by the time he was old enough to enlist. Still, Papa would be proud of him as a scholar, wouldn't he? Frau Beltz was right to tell him to cultivate his mind. The Lord could always use an intelligent thinker wherever He sent him.

CHAPTER 6

For your obedience is known to all, so that I rejoice over you,
but I want you to be wise as to what is good and innocent as to what is evil.

Romans 16:19

FROHN, GERMANY

"Mama, Papa, can you please hurry? We are supposed to be at the church early tonight!" Maria hopped up and down like a preschooler rather than a young lady in her teens.

"Maria, the Christmas Eve service is always at midnight to welcome the Savior. What is your hurry? You don't sing first, anyway," Papa scolded.

"Oh, you don't understand. I can't sing cold. I will need to warm up after traveling into town. Why can't I live in town like civilized people?" She frowned back at her parents. "You can slip into church whenever you want. I need to look and sound perfect."

Standing at the door with her matching rabbit muff and hat on, Maria shifted on her feet while she waited for her lumbering parents. Maria began to overheat in her fur finery, angering her even further. "Please hurry. Heidi, Eva, and the boys have probably been there for hours already."

46

"If you wanted to arrive so early, why didn't you go with your sisters and brothers?"

"I was still getting ready. My hair would not lay right. I will be up front and can't look like just anybody. Besides, Martin is visiting with his old school chums now that he is on break from university, and he'll be talking boy stuff with Thomas. Heidi and Eva don't include me and treat me like a baby. They always think I am too young. I am fifteen years old, and I'm not a baby anymore!" Maria stamped her foot again, hoping her impatient display would influence her slothful parents.

Coats in hand, Papa helped Mama wrap up for the cold evening. Maria felt like scolding them further but thought that would impede their progress more. Once outside, the frigid weather kept them all silent. Maria did not speak, more to protect her precious voice than to keep peace in the family.

The church was already filling up as Maria had predicted. Since she had a prearranged place to sit toward the front as part of the Christmas program, she deserted her parents for her more prominent seat.

Untying her rabbit-trimmed hat with care, Maria arranged her blonde curls to frame her creamy face and weather-kissed cheeks. Shrugging out of her frock, she smoothed her skirt and straightened her deep blue collar edged in tatted lace. The darkened candle-lit church illuminated the blue of the dress and her steel blue eyes. An inch or two shorter than her older sisters, she feared she had stopped growing and would always be a bit dwarfed by them, so she straightened her shoulders and sat statue-straight on the hard wood pew. If only mother would agree to buy her a proper lady's corset like all the sophisticated ladies of the world wore, she would never slouch.

Finally, after the traditional reading from Luke chapter two about the Savior being born, it was time for Maria's moment. All those hours of practice would not go to waste tonight. God willing, no one would ever forget Maria Neubauer and her God-given voice.

Standing straight even without a coveted corset, Maria inhaled and began a melodious "Cantique de Noel." The "O Holy Night" carol, written two decades before in France, was the perfect song for Maria and her range. The clear notes enraptured the congregation. Her steady gaze swept the families she hypnotized with her voice alone. The sweet, strong tones built to a crescendo of the high C sharp *Noels* that vibrated the glass candlesticks perched on the altar. Her arms spread wide as she completed the final measure of the carol, rattling the dust from the rafters.

Spent and exhilarated, Maria returned her hands to their side. A clap came from the back of the church. A few others joined, but the elders scowled in disapproval—not because they did not enjoy the performance but because no one would dare hint at such a disapproving response to her angelic voice. This was a house of God, not a concert hall. All gifts shared in the house of the Lord are to His glory and His alone. No one expected applause here. All honor went straight to God for His good and gracious gifts.

The awkwardness of the meager clapping and the uncomfortable silence was not lost on Maria. She gave a brief curtsy and returned to her seat. However, she imagined herself performing in a grand concert hall or a beautiful palace. She knew she was touching people with her music, and she wanted to sing where she could absorb the thunderous applause of appreciative patrons. She had no argument about giving God the glory for her gift of song, but surely it wasn't wrong to receive some of her own recognition when sharing this gift with the world. Didn't God get enough glory? Weren't there churches in every town glorifying God? He should be able to share some of this adoration with her.

After the service, Maria was surrounded by congregants telling her how they enjoyed her music. "Thank you. Thank you," she repeated. What else could she say? Did God want her to say, "It was all God's doing?" That was not fair. He did not stand in front of all those people singing His heart out. That was all her.

As the crowd thinned out, Maria edged nearer to the double doors to the church. A tall slender man of about forty stepped up to her. She had not seen him at services here before but recognized him as the man who had started clapping after her performance.

Extending his hand, he offered his introduction. "Good evening. My name is Herr Bernard Schroeder. You have the most amazing voice, young lady. I would like to talk to you further about sharing that voice with the world."

Maria's mouth dropped open. Had God been listening to her earlier thoughts? Was He willing to have her seek her own glory in the world? Who was this man sent by God to church tonight?

Papa appeared beside Maria to interrupt before Maria uttered a word. Where had he come from? Papa would never let her see the world on her own. It did not matter that he sent his oldest daughter to America unchaperoned when she was not much older than Maria. *That may be helpful information to toss at him if he refuses to let me go,* Maria thought.

"Hello, sir. I am Herr Charles Neubauer, Maria's father. Any discussion about her performing outside the church will have to go through me. And we have not met, sir. What is your business?" Father used his most formal address as he spoke to his stranger. This man wore a topcoat and hat not accustomed to men in the village. His accent betrayed his foreign origin as well. Although his German was impeccable, he sounded like a city-bred man.

"Pardon me. I neglected to say I promote performers. I arrange concerts and tours for talented performers like your daughter here." Father raised an eyebrow, and the stranger continued, "I am here for the holiday to visit my sister and her family, the Beshoffs. They live a little west of town here."

"I have heard of them." Papa answered the unasked question. Their daughter was in Heidi and Eva's class at school. "But my daughter has no need for a promoter, Herr Schroeder. She is too young to leave her family. She certainly cannot travel unchaperoned in the presence of a grown man."

The promoter's smile grew tight. "You are very right about that, Herr Neubauer." He let out an awkward chuckle. "I would never want to put your daughter's reputation at risk. I neglected to tell you that I am traveling with my wife. She was feeling a bit ill this evening, so I attended the service without her tonight. Your young Maria will be treated like our own daughter . . . " He paused, as if seeing Papa's disapproving expression for the first time. "I realize this is sudden. You need to go home and spend Christmas with your family, and I will contact you again in a few days. Please think it over." With a curt bow, the man slipped away through the Christmas crowd, leaving the Neubauers to stare after him.

The shock of the encounter behind them, Maria's tongue loosened. "Oh, Papa. You have to let me go. It is like God answered my prayers tonight and sent Herr Schroeder to me. This is everything I ever wanted."

"Maria, you don't know anything about the world, and we don't know anything about Herr Schroeder. I'm not sending you anywhere with a man we just met."

"I'm not a baby." She looked to her siblings, who had by now materialized next to Papa for assistance. "We can invite Herr Schroeder and his wife over for dinner, and we can get to know them." Maria bid tears to her eyes, a ploy that often worked with her parents. "Oh, Papa, I may never get a chance like this again. I don't sew like Heidi or bake like Eva. This is my gift from God. Don't you think He wants me to use it?"

"We can talk to them, but I still say you are too young. Maybe this Herr Schroeder can wait till you are grown." Papa reached over to give his daughter a hug, but she stiffened and did not return his embrace.

Maria overheard her sisters' complaints after Father walked away. "You think Papa would let you or me go off with a stranger like that? We'd be lucky to be given permission for a ride to the city to shop," Eva whispered to Heidi as she agreed.

A few days later, Herr and Frau Schroeder arrived at Neubauer's front door. The tall, thin man incongruently escorted a short, plump woman into the room. Whereas he featured light blond hair with streaks of gray, she had dark, raven hair pulled back in a tight bun, causing her eyes to water. His movements were purposeful; whereas, she bumped into the boot rack near the door as she entered. Removing her cloak revealed a prim brown frock of the day. A touch of lace graced her collar, simpler than her husband's flair of an unnecessary fashionable cane.

Herr Schroeder beamed. "This is my wife, Hilda. We are so pleased to be invited into your home like this."

Hilda looked less than pleased as she surveyed the meager home in which she found herself. Mama always kept a neat and comfortable house, but the furnishings were functional rather than ornate.

"Please come in. Dinner is almost ready," Mama offered.

"Ah. It smells delightful," Herr Schroeder said with an exaggerated inhale.

Mama's sauerbraten had simmered all afternoon in preparation for the dinner guests, leaving the family's mouths to water in anticipation of the meal. Roasted potatoes and stewed red cabbage rounded out the evening menu.

The table, set for nine, crowded everyone in attendance together. Not since Herman and Lena had moved to America had so many plates been on the table. The children had grown since their departure, making less room for the nine adults seated around the family table since Martin had returned home for the holiday as well.

"I guess we will be a bit cozy." Mama glanced around for another option. "Maybe I should have the boys take their plates in the other room."

At eighteen and twenty, Thomas and Martin were full-grown men; but they started to rise at their mother's suggestion that it was too crowded for everyone.

"Oh no, we'll be fine like this." Herr Schroeder halted their retreat. "Having the whole family around a fine table like this will be such a treat for Hilda and me. We have no children of our own, and this is a true blessing." Hilda flinched at the declaration of her barrenness to the group. The uncomfortable woman had not said a word, as of yet.

Papa said grace. Soon, dishes were passed around, and everyone filled their plates.

"Your husband says you are in town visiting family?" Mama ventured into a discussion with the mute Frau Schroeder.

"My husband's sister." She glanced up, and attentive faces turned her way. "I have no family." Hilda's voice trailed off, and she concentrated on her potatoes.

Not knowing how to continue this line of conversation with the pained woman, Mama searched Papa's face for help.

"Well, Schroeder, what line of work are you in? You mentioned something about concerts at church the other night. Is that your only trade?"

Maria wasn't shocked that Papa dove right in. If these strangers were going to eat at the Neubauer table, he needed this man's motives concerning his daughter.

"That's right, Herr Neubauer. I promote talent for entertainment. Since I spoke with you and your daughter"—he nodded at Maria sitting opposite him at the table—"Maria, I have been in contact with my people in Bremen. There is a concert next month featuring some local talent, and I'd like to take Maria to sing and see how it goes."

Maria sat up straighter, eyes darting from Herr Schroeder to father, holding her breath. *Oh, please, Papa,* she silently prayed.

"What do you mean, 'see how it goes'?" Papa almost growled. "That is a long way for a young lady to travel without her family."

"Well, sir, if the audience loves Maria's singing as well as everyone here does, she could be singing all over Europe—maybe farther."

Papa shifted in his seat. Maria groaned inwardly This was not the approach that would be successful with her father.

Schroeder took in the sight of Papa's face and rushed to continue. "Don't worry, Herr Neubauer. My wife and I will be with her every step of the way. As I mentioned, we have no children of our own; and we will be like parents to her."

Not able to contain herself any longer, Maria added, "Oh, Papa, this is what I've always dreamed of. I promise to write all the time. You can come visit me in a big concert hall, too. Wouldn't that be wonderful?" Her voice rose an octave as she pleaded for her release. Papa's growing scowl prompted her to add, "Lena wasn't much older than me when you sent her all the way to America with no chaperone at all. You must let me go."

"Lena went to be with your brother in America. No matter what Herr Schroeder thinks, he cannot be a parent to you in our absence. You only have one set of parents."

"I am sure God did not give me this voice to tuck it away from the world. If it does not work out in the city, I can always come home, Papa." Maria batted her eyes again and debated whether tears were necessary yet.

Herr Schroeder inserted, "Maria is precious to your family. I promise we will never let anything happen to her. Although I could never replace her actual father, I will see to her needs just like a father."

Momma and Papa exchanged concerned glances. "I have asked around about your family, Herr Schroeder, and your local folks are fine people," Papa conceded. He tossed a look at Maria. "You can go to Bremen next month for this concert Herr Schroeder told us about, as long as you inform us of everything that goes on." Maria jumped up to hug her father before he finished saying, "But we must be informed how you are doing all the time."

"Oh, Papa. Thank you, thank you!" Maria smothered him with kisses as he pretended not to like them.

"Now sit down and eat your dinner before it's cold. Herr Schroeder and I can discuss some of the details after we eat."

CHAPTER 7

By day the Lord commands his steadfast love, and at night his song
is with me, a prayer to the God of my life.

Psalm 42:8

ALTON, ILLINOIS

Karl pulled the latest *Alton Telegraph* from inside his warm coat as he breezed through the cold into the front room. Finding Lena sitting on the divan with her swollen feet propped up on the ottoman like rounded turrets, he handed her the paper with a peck on the top of her head. "Look, honey. Read the article about your women's group. The Union Army appreciated your ladies' Thanksgiving for the troops."

Lena took the newspaper and propped it up on her bulging belly to read for herself.

Her uncomfortable shifting prompted another kiss from Karl. "The babies wearing you out today?"

"I feel like I'm as large as a barn. I cannot turn around without bumping into something. I can't see our own children when I look down anymore. I think I've tripped over Dora three times today."

Karl chuckled but realized Lena was not in the mood to joke about her pregnancy. A meal always waited for him when he arrived home from work in the past, but a glance at the kitchen revealed no meal simmering. He did not have the heart to ask, "Where's dinner?" If Lena had the energy, he might be met with a frying pan to the head. As it were, he was safe from any such antics in her present condition, as she could not move off the couch now. No need to add to her distressful state.

"Oh, here it is." Lena had found the article. She read aloud:

> *"At a meeting of the officers of the Thirty-seventh Regiment, Iowa Infantry, convened by order of Colonel G. W. Kincaid, Commanding Post, Alton, Illinois, for the purpose of giving a testimonial of their appreciation of the superbly excellent Thanksgiving dinner, spread before the entire regiment by the Loyal Ladies of Alton. The following resolutions were unanimously adopted:*

> *Resolved, That on behalf of the officers and soldiers of the 37th Iowa, the Colonel tenders his most grateful thanks to the Loyal Ladies of Alton for their care, sympathy, and friendship, manifested in their full, free, and willing efforts to rejoice the hearts of the garrison Grey Beards, by a rich and most sumptuous feast given by them at the soldiers' barracks on Thursday last; rendered doubly valuable by their own presence, smiles, and good cheer."*

Her demeanor lightened, and she smiled at her husband. "Now that is a wonderful sentiment. We worked hard on that. Too bad the church did not have enough room for the whole regiment, but delivering the food to the barracks accomplished the task."

"Yes, I think you overworked yourself."

Lena smirked at Karl for implying again she should stay home. Karl had warned her before, but she had only argued that she could not sit and allow everyone else to do their part while she did nothing. He knew what her arguments would be. All these women had children of their own. Pregnancy was not a disease. She was not an invalid.

Dragging her feet to the floor from the ottoman, Lena began to position herself to launch off the cushions.

"Stay put, honey. I'll fix dinner tonight." Karl nudged Lena's shoulder back to remain seated. "The girls about did you in today."

The little girls emerged from the bedroom where they had been playing with dolls. Dora and Johanna both cradled their ragdolls in their arms as they practiced for the new arrivals in their own family.

"Papa!" They flung themselves at him, their dolls dropping to the floor with little care for their whereabouts, while Karl scooped them both up in unison.

"I have plenty of help right here, don't I, girls?" They squealed with delight, since Mama often shooed them away from the kitchen. These days, Lena was afraid of stepping on them every other minute.

※

*L*ena slumped back into her cushions while she listened to the kitchen commotion behind her. Although she wanted to witness the destruction she imagined taking place in the kitchen, she thought better of it. The girls giggled with each of Karl's silly exaggerated ministrations. He pretended to be a monster raiding the icebox to find meat. Was that "Fe-Fi-Fo-Fum"? Where did he learn that? Glasses of milk were poured with accompanying "moos," and the cheese was chased by famished mice by the sounds of it.

Before long, Johanna and Dora presented Lena with a full plate of cut apples, summer sausage slices, cheese, and bread while she rested on the couch. "Here, Mama. Papa said it's fine for you to eat in here today."

Knowing Lena was breaking a family rule, she grinned back at the beaming cooks. "Why thank you. This is most generous of you. Give my regards to the chef."

"We don't haf no chep," Dora answered.

"No, we only haf Papa," Johanna added.

Laughing, Lena gave them a hug and said, "Then tell Papa thank you." They scurried back to the table, where their own full plates were waiting for them.

That night, Lena's body refused to let her relax in any position she attempted. The babies seemed to wrestle against her swollen middle, punching and kicking at every repositioned angle. Lena's lower back ached with the added pressure of the pregnancy. She never felt so burdened with her other pregnancies. Maybe she should just climb out of bed for a while before she kept Karl from getting any sleep either.

Twisting her legs around to the floor, Lena pushed herself up onto an elbow to coax the rest of herself upright.

With eyes still shut, Karl inquired, "Are you all right? Do you want anything?"

"No, I just can't get comfortable, and I didn't want to wake you."

Karl's eyes were open now. "It's okay. I'm already awake." He blinked at Lena. "Sure you're all right?"

"I don't remember being so uncomfortable with the girls. My lower back is killing me . . . " She trailed off into a not-so-muffled moan.

"Here. Let me rub it for you." Karl rolled over to reach her better.

Almost doubled over, Lena twisted away from him. "No." She panted. "I think we are too late for that. You need to fetch the doctor. I think these babies want out."

Karl shot upright. "Now? I thought we had more time."

Lena doubled over, gasping for air again. "I don't think . . . they are going to . . . negotiate timing with you . . . Karl."

Noting her distress, Karl rushed into the night to find Doc Russell.

※

*K*arl soon returned with the doctor and found Lena in much distress. Karl was banished from the room, where Doc Russell and his wife tended to Lena.

The girls woke to their mother's commotion of moans and muffled screams. Worried, they scuffled to their father's lap. "Is Mama hurt?"

"Having babies is hard work, but Doc Russell will help her. I sent the neighbor for Aunt Dagmar, so she can keep you while Mama is busy."

Their eyes lit up. They always loved playing with Cousin Katie. But just as quickly, he saw their faces cloud with worry.

Reading their thoughts, Karl told them, "Don't worry. I'll stay here with Mommy; and when she is ready, I will send for you right away."

Appeased, Karl fed the girls a breakfast of Kaiser rolls with cheese; and by the time they were dressed, Dagmar was at the door.

※

"*I* came as soon as I got word." The girls ran to their aunt and nestled into her skirt. Speaking over their heads, she asked, "How is she?"

"Don't really know. They've been here for hours. No one comes out to tell me anything. I've been keeping busy with these two." Karl collected the girls' breakfast plates to clear the table. Another not-so-muffled cry came from the bedroom.

"I'll peek in to see if they need anything; then I'll take the girls for the day—or longer. Just tell me," Dagmar encouraged Karl. Then she instructed the clinging children, "Grab your things for a sleepover, okay? Johanna, help your sister gather what she needs. You can each bring your favorite doll so you and Katie can play. All right?"

Both nodded and scurried toward their room.

"I'm going to check on your mama," she called after them.

With them out of sight, Dagmar opened Lena's door. The room was in disarray. Neither the doctor nor his helper realized the door opened. "Do you need anything? Karl is worried," she ventured.

Glancing up, Mrs. Russell said, "More towels, please. She is losing a lot of blood here. These babies are causing her quite a bit of distress. I'm afraid they may be rather tiny, too." She turned back to her work.

Dagmar closed the door and turned to Karl.

"What?" he demanded.

"I'm afraid it isn't going easy for her. Do you have more towels?"

Karl grabbed a stack from a nearby cupboard and thrust them at Dagmar. "Is she going to be all right?"

"They think the babies will be small."

Karl dropped his head into his hands. Dagmar placed a hand on his shoulder. "You need to pray, Karl. Lena needs you to pray."

He lifted his head to God as Dagmar delivered the bundle of linens. Dagmar hugged Karl before ushering the girls out the door. "She is in God's hands, Karl. Talk to Him."

Karl paced the floor and prayed all day. "God, I need her. The girls need her. Don't take her away. And what about the babies, God? They haven't even had a chance yet. Surely, You don't want them to die. Make them strong. Please, make them all strong."

He neither ate nor drank all day. Every unpleasant noise he heard resulted in an involuntary tensing of his whole being. He wanted to be in the room with Lena. He wanted to comfort her, to hold her hand, to soothe her pain. He remained a helpless animal wearing out the front room carpet with his incessant pacing.

The room chilled as the day went on, so Karl stepped out to gather more wood for the fireplace—anything to keep his mind off the turmoil in his bedroom. If only the doctor would come out with some news for him.

Karl was deep in thought as he loaded his arms with logs. The woodpile shifted, and a piece rolled out onto his right boot. Jumping back, he cursed.

From the shadows came a voice. "I'm sorry, sir. I meant no harm."

Whipping his head around, startled, Karl dropped his armload onto his other foot and screeched even louder. "What in blazes are you doing back there? Come out this instant. You about crippled me. Come out here right now and identify yourself!"

Rising from her crouched position, a tall black woman rose to face Karl as she was commanded. In her hands was an oversized kerchief knotted at the top. She began wringing it in her hands, eyes downcast.

"Who are you, and why are you hiding in my woodpile?"

Before she could answer, another wail pierced the air from indoors. Karl winced but stood his ground, waiting for an answer from this strange woman.

Growing impatient, Karl barked at her, "Look at me! You a runaway?"

She nodded her response and slowly met his eyes with hers.

"What is your name?" Karl strained to size-up the woman standing in front of him in the failing light.

"Juana, sir." She returned her gaze to the ground where she took note of the scattered firewood at his feet. "I can fetch the wood for you, sir. You can get back to your woman." She stooped to gather the kindling at his feet without further instruction.

"Did someone send you here?" It was not uncommon for slaves to be directed to him; he often arranged safe houses for them on their way north. But since he now provided legal counsel to the Union Army at the prison, he spent less time on the free-slave documents than in the past.

"Yessir. Some-un' tol' me you helped my boy Jubal a while back. He's up north now. I was told he's a soldier now." At the mention of her son's name, she straightened with a mother's pride. Arms now full of the scattered logs, she stepped back and awaited further instructions from Karl.

"I'm Karl Muller, Juana. I don't remember your boy, but I can't help you right now. My wife—" Another anguished scream pierced the night air.

"I know, sir. Let me tend your fire, and I'll find somewhere else to scram."

Opening the door to let her pass, Karl said, "You don't have to go yet. Go ahead and warm yourself by the fire. I could use the company." He raked his hand through his hair and searched the door for any signs of life. He was rewarded when the doctor eased the door open and slipped through.

The exhausted physician offered, "Karl, you have a couple little sons."

"Sons?" He almost whispered as he headed to the already closed door.

"Hold on a minute." The kind medic placed a hand on Karl's shoulder. "Let my wife tidy up a bit before you go in."

The doctor's worried brow alarmed Karl, and he held his breath before asking, "Lena?"

"Lena had a rough time of it. Not like with the girls. She lost a lot of blood, and the next twenty-four hours will be critical for her."

The blood drained from Karl's face.

"She won't have the strength to tend those babies for a while. You will need some help to care for them until she is stronger."

He nodded as the news sunk in. "Can I be with her?"

"You can hold her hand and talk softly to her, but I don't know if she will hear you. I gave her something to help her sleep. I'm sure it will be comforting for her to have you at her side."

All the while, Juana stood by the fireplace listening to the conversation. "You go on and be wif yer wife. I can see to the babies fer ye fer a while if ye want. Ya go to be wif yer woman."

Karl blinked. He had already forgotten she was standing by the fire. Had God sent her as an answer to those prayers Dagmar had encouraged him to offer? He nodded his approval to Juana as she followed him into the bedroom to meet the tiny cherubs before Karl knelt beside the bed of his sleeping wife.

Oh, Lord, don't leave us now.

CHAPTER 8

Contribute to the needs of the saints and seek to show hospitality.

Romans 12:13

Missouri

Touching the acceptance letter in his pocket, Thomas leaned into the January wind, hoisted his travel bag more securely on his shoulder, and touched the envelope as motivation to strive against the gale.

Dear Mr. Thomas Krueger,

He remembered the formal address in the letter. No one had ever addressed him as "Mister" before. Papa had dug deep into the family funds to help pay for the St. Louis school, along with kerosene and other incidentals. Thomas should be safe at Concordia while the war risked the lives of other sons. Thankfully, the local church helped sponsor anyone preparing for full-time church work. The twins were growing fast, turning seven over the holiday, and would be helping Tobias with more farm chores soon. Although Thomas was not sure church work was his path yet, he was well suited to pour himself into university studies. If God was providing him a way to continue his education, he was open to see where the Lord wanted him. Right now, he had a two-day walk to arrive in St. Louis in time for the spring semester.

Papa had instructed him to spend the first night in Ste. Genevieve. Many German immigrants were settling in that area. Thomas could find lodging for the night before heading north along the Mississippi River. The eager morning trek slowed by afternoon, and Thomas switched his cumbersome pack from shoulder to shoulder as he trudged along. The school supply list included all his bedding, a lamp and oil jug, a slop pail, and writing materials—besides personal effects. The requested list included two trunks or chests, but Thomas was not able to carry such a load by himself on winter roads without a horse or wagon. The steamboats were useless to paddle the frozen river this time of year. Mama and Papa planned to send more things after the thaw.

A few snowflakes whirled around his head, and Thomas prayed the weather would not delay him from his goal to reach St. Louis before classes began. Not many travelers ventured on the road with freezing temperatures and snow on the ground. He was thankful his mother had knitted him new mittens and a scarf for Christmas as he pulled the blue-gray scarf tighter against his neck to prevent the small flakes from sneaking inside his well-worn jacket.

Thomas took a brief break at noon to sample the roast sandwich. However, the rations only satiated his appetite a few miles before he needed to stop for a handful of dried apples. Although the snow drifts were manageable at about six inches on the roadway, it took an extra effort to lift his feet to propel his frame forward. By the time the sun sunk into the horizon, he had not yet reached Ste. Genevieve.

As the darkness descended, the lights of Ste. Genevieve grew brighter in the distance. The houses in the town were weatherbeaten and much older than those in Perry County. Vertical planks, rather than the horizontal logs used for his home, reached to the roofs. The heavy oak timbers were cemented together by a mixture of mud and horsehair, which cast a dirty sheen on the buildings looming above the fresh snowfall. Each abode was surrounded by an unwelcoming stockade fence. Whether they were to keep people out or in, Thomas didn't know.

Unsure of where to turn for a night's lodging, Thomas found a limestone building that appeared to be a store, although he saw no clear sign in front. Slipping inside before the winter elements followed, Thomas stamped his feet and sighed as he took in the pleasant warmth of the room stocked with mercantile wares. A grandmotherly woman rounded the corner of her counter and ushered Thomas further into the store.

"Oh, my dear. You are half frozen! Come in here by the stove and thaw out." She pushed him closer to the potbelly furnace. Thomas obeyed the woman without a word, basking in the lifegiving heat.

"I was just closing up. What are you doing out in the cold, child?"

Standing a little taller so the woman would not think him a child, Thomas answered, "I'm going to St. Louis, ma'am. I need a place to stay for the night . . . cheap." He cast his eyes down when he added his final word. He had not seen any fancy hotels as he approached town, but the woman could infer by looking at him that he did not have two extra nickels to rub together.

She smiled at his hesitation. "I don't know why a young man would be traveling alone to St. Louie in this weather, but my daughter has a back room. She'll let ya sleep there." Shaking her head at him, she added, "When did ya eat last?"

"My mother packed me some things, but I must admit I finished them on the way."

"Let me lock up here, an' I'll take you to Celeste. Since her boys joined up, she's mighty lonesome for youngsters to feed." She paused. "You goin' to St. Louie to join up, too?"

"No, ma'am. I'm going to school there."

Her eyes brightened. "Well, good for you. Too much killin' goin' on as it is. Glad ya aren't joinin' 'em."

The older woman led him to an adjoining living area behind the store, where a younger version of her stood stirring a kettle with a wooden spoon. The younger woman turned to her mother, entering with the now-defrosted Thomas.

"Celeste. I brought a young'un in for a bowl and a bed. Cain't leave him outdoors to freeze on a night like this, now can we?"

Celeste studied her bedraggled visitor as Thomas stood there taking in the meager kitchen surroundings. She pointed to a nearby table for him to sit. "What's your name, boy? Where you headin'?" Celeste interrogated Thomas as she filled bowls for all three of them.

"Thomas, ma'am." Thomas twisted his hat in his hands and stayed standing. "I'm heading to St. Louis for school."

"Where are you from that you have to travel so far to go to school? Don't they have schools where you at?" Celeste shoved the steaming stew on the table in front of a chair she pulled out for him. "Sit."

This time, he accepted the chair.

"Yes, ma'am. We have schools but I have schooled out in Altenburg, and my folks are letting me go to university—the one called Concordia. I am starting next week."

The hot beef stew in front of him coerced a grumble from Thomas' stomach. Without more prompting, he emptied the meal in front of him too quickly for polite company. He ate as if he had not taken a bite in days.

The silent stares alerted Thomas to the women's attention. "Sorry. I didn't realize how hungry I was. This sure hit the spot." Thomas wiped his mouth with his sleeve, and the women giggled at him.

"I haven't seen a boy chow down like that since Jefferson and Zachary left for the war." Celeste's mirth didn't hide the shadow of pain Thomas saw flash across her face. "It is a pleasure to watch a young man eat my cookin'," she added as she cleared the table.

The bed was comfortable and cozy for the night. It refreshed Thomas for an energetic start in the morning. The women replenished his pack with lunch provisions of dried fruit and jerky for his journey. Thomas thanked them for their kindness and thanked the Lord for steering him to such pleasant people and accommodations.

The morning gave way to bright sunshine, almost blinding as it reflected off the fresh fallen white before him. The cold, clear day sparkled like gemstones and the barren trees stretched snowy branches overhead, waiting to unleash their mini blizzards on unsuspecting wayfarers if the notion tickled them.

Thomas' second destination was Haefnerville. Too cold to take a steam ship, visiting these upstart towns provided his only means of lodging on his journey. Few traveled in winter without cause for fear of frostbite or an unexpected storm, so he met few along the way. It made it easier to stay clear of other travelers as he had been warned of army deserters and other ne'er-do-wells. Traveling alone left him little protection against such people, so Thomas trusted the Lord to keep him safe and remained wary of strangers on the road. The few he encountered did not pay him much attention.

Thomas chuckled at the thought. "I am sure they are more leery of me than I am of them. After all, I don't look like much, and I don't appear to have anything of value to rob."

Making excellent time in the sun, Thomas approached Haefnerville as many men poured out of the nearby glass factory. The day shift had ended in the adjacent town of New Detroit. The eleven taverns in Haefnerville beckoned the workers to a thirsty reprieve from the hot glass furnaces they tended all day. No private businesses were allowed in the company town of New Detroit, creating the bustling outcropping of opportunities for shops and pubs a walking distance outside the neighboring township. Many men staggered back to their homes in New Detroit once satiated with the ever-ready libations in Haefnerville. Others had built homes for their families in Haefnerville around the thriving business center.

Cautiously blending into the melee of muddied, sweat-stained bodies, Thomas looked for a respectable place to inquire about a place to stay. Much of the crowd filtered into the awaiting taverns that Thomas wanted to avoid, so he sought out an open store since that had worked so well in Ste. Genevieve.

It was difficult to peer above the heads of the men vying for the limited space on the boardwalks. All were trying to avoid the trounced snowy streets made of slippery clay-based soil. Swinging his bag to his other shoulder for a better view up the street, Thomas whacked an unsuspecting worker in the face.

"Hey! Whaddaya think you're doin'?" the offended brute blurted as he pushed ,Thomas into the muddy road. Thomas splashed face first into the muddy gunk of churned mess as the throngs of onlookers enjoyed his misfortune from the safety of the boardwalk. Laughter erupted along with pointing and other guffaws at this unexpected entertainment. Rising to his hands and knees, Thomas tried to swipe the offending muck from his face only to smear it further from ear to ear.

"Look'n like dat will have da slave-catchers after ya," he heard from the crowd. Another raucous roar followed.

Slowly gathering his belongings, Thomas worked at steadying his feet under him on the clay that clung to his shoes.

"Welcome to Tanglefoot, young man!" An arm tucked itself under him and hoisted him and his belongings back to the security of the boardwalk. "Best stay out of the street. Not sure the wagons can see you blended in with the street the way you are."

Looking up, Thomas stared into the steel blue smiling eyes of a giant of a man. His grizzled beard framed them, and a gray stocking hat pushed curly brown locks down below his ears. He released Thomas with his one working hand as the other arm swung limp in his tattered coat.

"Peter Schmidt at your service." He tipped his hat to Thomas in a gentlemanly gesture.

"Th-th-thank you," Thomas stammered, dodging another eager tavern seeker as he passed. "I didn't think it would be so crowded."

"It's all in the timing, *mein freund*. Normally, the streets here are pretty empty; but the fellas just got off work, and they are hankering for a drink to wet their whistle." Giving Thomas a once-over, the man asked, "Why have you come to Tanglefoot?"

"I thought I was in Haefnerville."

An inviting laughter sprung from the man. "Oh, you are. Tanglefoot is our nickname for it, as you have discovered for yourself." He brushed a clump of the street from Thomas' coat. "You got a name, fella?"

"Oh, sorry. I am Thomas Krueger." He started to offer a handshake before realizing this new acquaintance did not have a functioning right hand. It hung limp by his side below his sleeve. Thomas withdrew his own hand quickly and continued, "I'm on my way to St. Louis and wanted a place to stay the night is all. I'm going to school this semester."

"Don't get much foot traffic for St. Louie folks. They usually ride the steamers around here."

"The river's frozen." Thomas shrugged.

"*Ja.* I guess it is." The stranger titled his head to examine the boy he pulled to safety.

Thomas started to shiver. The once wet clay now froze onto his scarf, mitten, coat, shoes, and trousers. What a pathetic mess. Who'd take him as a lodger looking like this?

Reading his mind, Schmidt offered, "Come with me. The flop houses here serve the seedy drunks, not young school-bound men trying to make their way to St. Louie." Turning Thomas down a side street, he said, "My wife will be happy for a new face to talk to. The young'uns wear her down some, I'm afraid."

"You are so kind. I don't want to be a bother."

"No bother. There's always room for one more, right?" Taking the lead, Peter showed Thomas the way to his home, away from the crowded streets.

Entering the small log shack, Thomas saw two small children stacking rocks into tiny towers near the fireplace. A full bed was against one wall, a cot for the children snuggled up to the opposite wall. A rough-hewn table with a bench and a couple of chairs sat between them. A small woman of about thirty busied herself, stirring whatever was cooking over the flaming fire.

The woman spoke without looking from the pot. "Goodness, Peter, I thought this was going to burn before you got here. What took you so long?"

"I rescued young Thomas here from being trampled in the street."

She whipped around to face the disheveled houseguest. "Oh!" She wiped her hands on her apron and straightened her skirt. "I must look a fright chasing these two all day."

Peter laughed. "I think young Thomas has you beat there." Once she focused on his mud-caked attire, a smile escaped her, too. "Thomas, this is my wife, Molly."

"Dear me. We need to get you out of those soaked and nasty things before you catch your death." She reached to help him off with his jacket, placed his bag next to the table, and told him, "Sit here and take off those shoes and trousers, too." Thomas recoiled from the suggestion to strip in front of these strangers. "Go on now. It ain't nothing I haven't seen before, and we need to get you cleaned up." She was already brushing cakes of debris off the discarded clothing. "Wash up for dinner, both of you." Molly eyed her husband. "We'll eat while the ham hocks are still edible. Then I'll see ta your clothes for ya."

"Molly, I thought he could spend the night. He is off to St. Louie in the morning to attend school. Didn't want him staying at the Dirty Shame."

Molly's eyes widened. "The Dirty Shame? Of course not. We don't have much room, but it will be warm. We'll throw a blanket down for you by the fire, if that's okay?"

"That'd be fine, ma'am. You don't need to go to all that trouble about my clothes. I can work on them myself."

"That's a woman's work." Molly shook her head as she took the trousers from Thomas' hand. "No problem, young man. We are glad to help. That's what the Good Book says we should do; 'do not neglect to show hospitality to strangers, for thereby some have entertained angels unawares'—Hebrews 13:2."

"I appreciate this. It's quite neighborly of you both." Thomas covered himself in an offered blanket and sat at the indicated place at the table.

Molly set bowls of ham and beans in front of her family and guest. She cut cornbread and served each. "I hope it's still steaming. I had to take it off before it burned, you being late and all. But it's a blessing you brought young Thomas here to share our meal. Peter?"

On cue, Peter and his family bowed their heads for prayer, and Thomas followed by adding his own prayer of thanks for the Lord sending him these faithful people to assist him on his journey.

CHAPTER 9

And lead us not into temptation but deliver us from evil.

Matthew 6:13

BREMEN, GERMANY

Bremen bustled with excitement. The women wore the latest fashions of hoop skirts that matched the dainty parasols twirling overhead. Constant comings and goings around the ships filled the retailer with wonders from the world over. Every trinket, spice, or material desire traveled from ships in port to be later displayed in nearby shops. Maria was drawn by their temptations. She wanted it all. Things she never imagined in the small town of Frohn beckoned her here. Once she became a famous singer, she imagined, she would fill her closets with all this finery.

Buildings with ornate gabled ends stretched into the sky, lining the cobblestone streets and standing sentinel like the statue of Roland before the Rathaus. The stone Roland held his shield embellished with a mighty two-headed eagle in one hand and his unsheathed sword in the other. The legendary war hero had stood thirty-three feet over this ancient city for four hundred years, keeping citizens safe from invasion. The imposing figure punctuated the Bremen cityscape with both warning and welcome.

The Schroeders had moved Maria into their small apartment near the cigar factory. The odious smoky stench blended with the coffee grinding shop to the right of them, the soap maker to the left, and the bakery below them. Her senses were so assaulted that at night, the fumes wafted through her slumber and intermingled with her dreams.

January blew too cold to throw the windows open for fresh air, but opening the window would only invite more onslaught of the senses. So each night, she suffered this invasion that the mighty Roland himself could not defend against in silent resignation. It was a small concession for the privilege of being in a magnificent city in pursuit of her musical aspirations.

As a diligent daughter, Maria wrote home, omitting any unpleasant observations in case Mama or Papa insisted on sending her back home. She described the statuesque renaissance gables overhead that emphasized her safety under the watchful eyes of Roland. She drew close to copy the verse on the plaque at the foot of the statue for her parents.

> *I manifest your freedom.*
> *As granted to the city*
> *By Charlemagne and many other rulers,*
> *For this be thankful to God, that is my counsel.*

Bremen's proclamation of freedom reassured Maria she was in the right place. She was set free from her parents for the first time. Sure, she had Herr and Frau Schroeder, but they were not her family.

They would be helpful to establish her in the music world, but she was not obligated to them as a daughter to a parent. Maria would soon flap her wings and fly as high as these towering structures that surrounded her. She only needed to wait for the right time.

Herr Schroeder ate his usual toast and egg while reading the morning paper. Frau Schroeder dawdled around the kitchen, placing her own plate of an identical breakfast in front of her. "Coffee is ready if you want some. When you're finished getting your own breakfast, be sure to clean up after yourself."

"Danke." Maria did not expect to be waited on like a guest in the Schroeder home, but Frau Schroeder left dirty dishes in the wake of serving her husband and herself. Why make such a mess fixing such a simple meal? Extra plates and cups filled the basin. The frying pan had splattered oil everywhere; the butter for the toast was melted onto the counter; and the toasted breadcrumbs were scattered on both the counter and the floor.

Maria poured herself the indicated coffee and started to clean up the mess Frau Schroeder had left behind. With the myriad of nasal assaults swirling in the neighborhood, nothing edible called to her stomach. Tossing her words over her shoulder as she worked, she asked, "Herr Schroeder? Do we visit the concert hall today where I will sing?"

Looking up above his paper, he folded it and set it on the table. "Not yet, Liebling. I need to arrange everything first. I have a meeting with the choral master today. It won't be long."

Keeping her back to him, Maria tried not to sound disappointed; but they had arrived in Bremen almost a week ago, and she remained cooped up in these walls with Frau Schroeder. The woman only spoke to her if she wanted something. Granted, Maria paid no rent, so she felt an obligation to help but not be an indentured servant. She never did enough housework at home to hone any housekeeping skills, nor was she interested in doing so now. Maria had become a master of escape at home, contriving some excuse or another to disappear when work waited, leaving much of the mundane chores to her sisters or mother. But no siblings were in Bremen covering unfinished chores, so Maria hurried through assigned tasks before retreating to her room.

This morning, certain Bremen held many fascinating places to explore while she waited for Herr Schroeder to connect her with her singing career, she tried to find a way to escape her confines with Frau Schroeder. "Herr Schroeder? I saw the statue of Roland, but Bremen is so different from where I am from. I'd like to see more, if that is all right."

Herr Schroeder's eyes shifted from Maria to his wife. Hilda sneered and returned to stroking her cat, answering the unspoken question of her chaperoning Miss Maria about the city. "I'm not sure Frau Schroeder is up to showing you around just yet. Besides, it is quite cold outside. It would not be good for your voice."

Conflicting emotions of relief because a reluctant Frau Schroeder would not be accompanying her and disappointment that she might be stranded with the same unwelcoming woman swirled through her. "How about I only explore some of the shops on the block? I need to stretch my legs. I'm not used to being indoors so much, even in winter. I think it would be fun to track down all the aromas drifting through this place." Maria took Herr Schroeder's hand and added an alluring, "Please?"

Hilda scowled at Maria's flirting ways but interjected, "Let her go. The girl paces the floor like a trapped cat when you are gone. I have no peace." If she had the energy, she likely would toss Maria's cloak at her and push her out the door at once. But as it were, she sat, staring holes into her husband, waiting for him to agree with her conclusion.

Maria stared, too, with pleading eyes. "I'll tell you what," Herr Schroeder said finally, turning to Maria. "You can go out and meet the neighbors here. Don't wander away from our street. You can become lost, since you do not know your way around. When the weather warms up, we will show you all the sights. For now, this block is as far as you go without us. Okay?"

Maria beamed at her victory, gave Herr Schroeder a peck on the cheek, and returned to scouring the kitchen so Frau Schroeder would have no room for complaints before she escaped from her.

Herr Schroeder touched his cheek at the spot of Maria's brief kiss. His wife watched in dissatisfaction at the exchange. Maria paid little attention to either as she finished her chores and prepared to leave.

Maria pulled her cloak tight as she exited the building. She braved the cold for a couple steps, then ducked into the business next door. The aromas had beckoned her to this door for days, but she had never had a chance to venture inside before this moment. The Bickle Bakery sign above the door had a painted pretzel woven around the lettering. Inside, the kuchen and strudels that woke her in the mornings now lay under a glass display case begging to be eaten. Now safely through the door, Maria imagined immersing herself in the joy of the fresh baked goodness that greeted her.

"Ah, it's like being with Eva in the kitchen," she said to herself. For the first time, she felt the twinge of home tugging at her heart.

"Did you say something, Miss?" A matronly woman in her forties wiped her floured hands on her floured apron that matched her floured baker's hat. A few strands of brown hair poked beyond the rim of the hat, and she blew a breath upward to scare them out of her face as she addressed Maria.

"Oh, I'm sorry. It's only these marvelous baked goods make me think of home." Maria inhaled another deep breath.

"Glad to hear it. What can I get for you?" The woman stood close to the counter to see Maria's choice of pastry.

"Um . . . " Maria's plan did not include buying anything. She had no funds of her own to spend on treats before her famous debut. She only floated in to absorb the wonderful breads, cookies, and cakes. It was not proper to stand there and soak up the pleasing environment without a purchase she supposed, and she tried to think of a reason to stay. "I'm sorry. I must have forgotten my head. I didn't bring any money. Is it okay if I enjoy your baking for a few minutes before I go?"

She thought she must sound like a country idiot. Maria began to back out of the door before the baker answered.

"Wait, Miss." Maria turned back to face the kind woman. "I was experimenting with some new tarts. Would you mind giving them a taste and report if they are good enough to sell?"

Maria's smile illuminated her face as she approached the woman, who presented her with a moist apple tart. Her stomach growled, reminding her she had eaten no breakfast. Maria took one sweet bite and held the precious flavor in her mouth as long as was respectable before swallowing. "This is the best thing I have ever eaten," she mumbled as she licked her lips and prepared for a second bite.

The baker chuckled. "Glad you think so. I haven't put them out for sale yet, but I think they might sell rather well. Don't you?"

"Rather well? People are going to love these." Maria gave into the indulgence of another bite.

"I'm Frau Bickle. I haven't seen you around here before." She leaned on the counter for a better view of Maria.

"I'm Maria Neubauer. I'm new in town. I'm going to be a singer here at the concert hall."

"A singer, you say? I haven't known too many singers who sing for a living. My husband sings plenty when you put a pint of beer in him. I'm sure that's different." She laughed at her own joke.

Her easy demeanor caused Maria to laugh, too, and she did not want to leave this new friend. "Well, I mustn't keep you from your work. Thank you so much for the tart. Anytime you need a taste-tester, I live upstairs with the Schroeders."

Frau Bickle lost her smile at the mention of the Schroeders. "With that sour lady? She comes in here without her husband sometimes . . . " She hesitated. "I don't mean to speak ill . . . I'm sorry."

"That's okay. Herr Schroeder is connecting me with an upcoming concert. I shouldn't need to stay their houseguest for too long. Thanks again."

Not really wanting to go back and face Frau Schroeder, Maria decided to walk around the block. No sense wandering into the other businesses without any funds to buy anything. Checking window displays would have to be enough distraction for now.

It was nearing noon already, and the sun beat off the drastic cold of the morning as the rays radiated off the tall cityscape. If Maria stayed on the sunny side of the street, her window-shopping strategy worked rather well. However, the back side of the building loomed in the shadows. The smoke-stained buildings cast an ominous foreboding that the sun-streaked towers did not. Hurrying back to the front of the building, Maria turned back into the apartment entrance, slowing her pace up the stairs, steeling herself for the dismal interior of the Schroeder's flat.

"Well, you are back." Herr Schroeder met her at the door and helped her unwrap from the warm cloak she wore. "I hope your adventures were successful. I have great news!" He turned her toward him and sat her in the nearest chair. "We—I mean, you—are scheduled to sing for the choral master next Monday. He has a spot in his choir; he thinks he may have the perfect place for you."

"Choir? I'm a soloist." Maria wrinkled her nose at the thought of sharing the spotlight with others.

"Oh, dear, I know. It's just that you have to prove yourself before you can be a headliner, after all. You understand, don't you?" He took her hand in his and patted it.

"I guess. I thought . . . " She shook the thoughts of instant stardom away.

"Oh, I understand. We've heard how well you sing; but they don't know that yet, do they? We need your name out there before you are the star. And don't you worry—you will be a star soon enough." Maria curled her lip. Herr Schroeder added, words tumbling over themselves, "Trust me. This is wonderful news, Maria. You are on your way."

"On my way . . . " Maria murmured, unconvinced.

CHAPTER 10

But whatever gain I had, I counted as loss for the sake of Christ.

Philippians 3:7

ALTON, ILLINOIS

Karl sent word to Dagmar, asking her to keep the girls a while longer while Lena languished in bed after the birth of her sons. Lena's lusterless hair framed her pale face on the pillow as she slept, drained of all energy. Karl feared for her life, although the doctor assured him that she would recover in time with rest. Dagmar replied with a message that the girls were enjoying their time at the farm with their cousins, so she enjoyed keeping them as long as Lena's recovery warranted.

Karl rubbed his sleep-deprived eyes after he read the note from Dagmar. In the sitting room, Juana rocked both tiny bundles in the soft blankets Lena had knitted before their birth. Juana was God's blessing to the Mullers. Karl knew nothing of tending newborns. Lena had nurtured their daughters in their early days, and now she had no strength to tend to any of her children's needs. Juana had stepped in seamlessly as if she had always been part of the family and not a runaway slave Karl found hiding in the woodshed only days ago.

Karl had named the twins James Abraham and John Adam after the Sons of Thunder in the Bible and strong American leaders he admired. The miniature boys required strong names to help them thrive in a world they had been rushed into too soon. Juana found a supply of milk for them and heated bottles for the infants, leaving Lena to regain her strength. Overseeing the health of Lena and the twins, Juana fell into a routine of preparing meals, cleaning their whole house, and ministering to the young family with gentleness. Karl returned to work at the penitentiary, confident his home was in Juana's capable hands, while the girls remained with their cousins for an extended stay. However, he hurried back every afternoon to check on his ailing wife and the newborns.

This afternoon, the doctor's buggy stood in front of his house. Alarmed, Karl rushed through the door. Juana sat in the parlor rocking the babies in the same position he had left her in the morning. His eyes then went to the closed bedroom door where Lena rested.

"It's okay. He stopped by to see how she doin'. She slept most da day, but I think she's awake now."

Karl relaxed and edged toward Juana to take a closer look at his boys. "They sleep peacefully in your arms, Juana. Now, don't you go spoiling them on me." He smiled and bent down to give each cherub a kiss on the forehead before turning to the bedroom.

Karl opened the door as Doc Russell dropped his stethoscope into his medical bag and snapped it shut. He nodded to Karl with a raised eyebrow as if he held an unspoken question. "Oh, there he is. Your husband is home just in time to hear me tell you that things are looking good. This extra rest is helping you regain your strength, and you will be up in no time chasing those boys around the house."

"Yes, I just looked in on them. They are sleeping like little angels in Juana's arms." Karl smiled down at Lena for reassurance.

"I examined each of them before waking your lovely wife here. They are still small. It is normal for them to take a little while to put on some weight to be the bouncing baby boys you are expecting. Your maid is doing a wonderful job tending them."

Karl started to correct him about Juana not being their maid, but what would he say? What was Juana? He couldn't say she was a runaway. The war had not stopped the slave hunters roaming the area collecting a bounty on runaways throughout the state. He only added, "Yes, she is a blessing."

"I'll leave you alone with your family now." The physician lifted his satchel to leave.

"I'll walk you out." No sooner had they left the bedroom than Karl whispered, "So everything *is* fine?"

"It sure is." Doc Russell patted Karl on the shoulder. "Don't worry so much. You need to take care of yourself, too, young man. You have a family who needs you. I thought you were a frazzled critter when you came through those doors. I don't think you are getting enough rest yourself."

"I'll rest when I can. I bet you're glad you aren't down at the prison with the smallpox outbreak."

The doctor froze with his hand on the front doorknob. "You mean, you were exposed to smallpox, and you came home to your fragile loved ones?" His furrowed eyes accused Karl of this most heinous crime.

"Don't worry. I didn't touch any of the sick," Karl defended. "I helped a few men write letters home and get some affairs in order before they shipped them off to Smallpox Island." The doctor turned pale before him, so Karl rushed on. "See, they aren't allowing them to stay at the compound because the town is afraid of exposure, and they don't want it to spread to other prisoners. They send the men to Smallpox Island in the middle of the Mississippi as soon as they exhibit any symptoms. Everyone is being very safe."

Shaking his head, Doc Russell said, "I hope you haven't already brought it here." Looking back into the room where Juana remained rocking her charges to sleep, he focused back on Karl. "Do you think your maid can tend to the babies and your wife for a couple weeks by herself?"

"By herself? Why?" Karl took a step back.

"Because you need to stay away from your family and *not* go down to that prison infestation for a time. The incubation period for smallpox is ten to fourteen days. If you carry the disease, we should know if Lena or the babies contracted it within that span."

Karl's eyes grew wide. "You think I made them sick?" He almost collapsed against the doorpost. "I never thought . . . "

"I'm surprised the army didn't make you remain with the soldiers after you were exposed. They should have better protocol. The whole place should be quarantined." The doctor's ire rose at the implications for his practice. "The whole town may be suffering from this disease soon if they aren't more careful."

"So what am I to do?"

"Take up a room in town and contact no one. Have them leave your meals at the door. Take some books or something to keep you busy for a couple weeks, but don't interact with anyone. We don't need this spreading across town, too. The prison is bad enough."

Karl nodded, his concern mounting.

"I'll look in on your family while you are gone," continued Doc Russell. "If they get sick, I'll let you know. You could become ill, too, you know."

Karl nodded again. "I'm sorry. I had no idea I was putting my family at risk like this . . . and I just kissed the babies." He recoiled at the remembrance, and the blood drained from his face.

"Say your prayers, Mr. Muller. I think that may be your best defense. It's possible you did not infect anyone, but we must take precautions." He tipped his hat and retreated to his buggy with heavy resignation.

"I will." Not wanting to reenter Lena's room, Karl asked Juana to grab him a few things for his time away before he disappeared. "Juana, you've been such a Godsend. I hate to do this to you. You have been so kind to stay in our time of need."

"That's okay. God musta know'd you'd need me, Mista Muller. I got no one waitin' on me. I can stay as long as da Lord says."

Juana turned back inside after handing Karl his belongings to leave. She addressed Lena. "Missus Muller?"

Lena's eyes fluttered open.

"I's here to tell ya dat Mista Muller'll be stayin' in town a few days. Dere is sickness at da prison, and he don't want you or da babes to ketch it."

Tears snuck into the corner of Lena's eyes. *Oh, Lord, now what? Thank You for sending Juana to nurse us back to health. Please continue to watch over us, and do not let anything happen to Karl. I need him.*

On day ten of Karl's quarantine, the infants became fussy and feverish. Juana sponged them down with cool cloths soaked in freshwater, but the little ones stayed warm to the touch. They bellowed in unison through their discomfort and refused to take the bottles offered to them. There was no medication to comfort or cure their aching bodies. Standing by her vow to tend to the boys, Juana stayed awake around the clock to minister to them.

Hearing the cries of her children, Lena tried to go to them; but Juana insisted she stay away in her still weakened condition to protect her from catching the dreadful disease. If Juana did not pull the boys through, the girls still needed their mother. Lena's heart ached to hold her sons again. They were not even two months old. How could Juana be so cruel to keep her away?

*K*arl never exhibited any symptoms while held up in the Mineral Springs Hotel. When he received word of the twins' distress, he hurried home to help Juana in her vigil. A rash spread across little James; then John grew a rash on his tiny frame. Their wailing weakened until they emitted only mewing sounds, not much more than whimpers. Two days later, they made no sound at all.

Karl dragged himself out into the late February air and sobbed. "Lord, why? It was my fault. Punish me, not my innocent babies. I did it. I did." Speechless, he wept on the porch, away from Lena and alone in his grief.

*T*orn between blaming God or blaming Karl, Lena ached with the loss of her children. How could this happen? Didn't they pray enough, tithe enough, worship enough to suit God? And Karl? He spread that dreaded disease into their home. What was he thinking? In her numb state, she had no answers, only the weight of questions, accusations, and grief.

Dagmar and Herman returned the girls in time for the burial of their baby brothers, whom they never met. The house in mourning held an unknown black lady who gently took charge of the daily events. The subdued new figure floated among the grieving family, preparing meals, washing laundry, and operating a household in the mental absence of the adults who took up space but functioned in no other capacity but to supply tears.

At the gravesite, Lena held her daughters close, squeezing a bit too tightly as they squirmed in her grasp. Dagmar rescued them for a moment as Lena placed flowers on the tiny graves. Herman placed his arm around his sister's shoulders to guide her away from the grave. "Our family has seen its share of death, Lena. I promise there will be better days ahead."

Remembering the death of Herman's own daughter at a young age, Lena nodded. "I guess Hannah can meet her little cousins in heaven now, *ja?*"

"That's right, and we will see them all again. It will be a great reunion." Giving his sister another hug, Herman handed her back to her husband and daughters.

CHAPTER 11

For the Lord gives wisdom; from his mouth
come knowledge and understanding.

Proverbs 2:6

St. Louis, Missouri

Towering brick buildings greeted Thomas as he found the Concordia school on Jefferson Street. Additional wings housing classrooms and dorms had been added to the original structure. Nothing so large stood in Perry County or the villages he had traveled through to this point. This was the beginning of a new adventure, so he squared up his pack on his shoulders and marched into the front doors of what appeared to be a dormitory.

A woman in her forties dressed in a severe brown skirt and matching jacket stopped him before he took two steps inside the door. "Whoa, young man. First, stomp off those boots."

Thomas took a step back toward the door to comply with the demand of the plump gatekeeper of the doorway.

After Thomas tapped his boots a couple times, she continued. "You must be Master Krueger. We've been expecting you."

"Yes, ma'am." Frozen to his spot at the door, Thomas was not certain whether he should come further into the room or not.

"You can call me Frau Reincke. Herr Reincke and I run things here. You are just in time for dinner. It is served at six o'clock sharp each day."

Puzzled, Thomas did not know where to go. He had no idea where the dining hall was in this place, nor did he know where to place his belongings that remained on his shoulders. He did not desire to drag his heavy bundle any farther after his long journey.

"Friedrich!" Frau Reincke whacked the wall next to the stairs behind her with the palm of her hand.

A student bounded down the stairs and halted on the landing upon hearing his name. He peered through thick spectacles at Thomas and back at Frau Reincke, awaiting further instructions. "Take Master Krueger up to the sleeping quarters so he can put his things down and wash up for supper. You can show him around later."

"Yes, ma'am." Friedrich turned to Thomas. "Bring your stuff up here. I'll show you where to put everything." Not as tall as Thomas, Friedrich bounded upstairs with rabbit-like speed. Thomas had traveled far that day and was still burdened with his belongings, so he struggled to follow Friedrich's lead. Thomas hoisted his bag once more and ascended a few stairs before losing sight of his energetic guide altogether.

At the top of the stairs, he offered, "My name is Thomas," as he caught his breath. "I guess you are Friedrich?" He followed Friedrich to a dorm room full of tidy beds.

"Ja. The locals call me Freddy. I think I like it. So call me Freddy if you like."

"Freddy it is," Thomas said as he surveyed the room.

Freddy pointed to an empty cot midway into the room. "That one is for you. It's rather crowded right now, since the Fort Wayne boys arrived."

"Fort Wayne boys?"

"*Ja.* Since the war began, we have been receiving students from Fort Wayne, Indiana. There is no draft in Missouri like they have there. I guess we will have them until the war is over. That is why we are more crowded than usual."

Thomas set his bag next to the indicated bed and examined the row of identical beds. He'd need to memorize them all to find the proper one later.

"Hurry, Thomas. Don't make us late for dinner."

Freddy bounded down the stairway again ahead of Thomas and turned to the dining hall to the left of the staircase. Boys of all ages were seated at rows of long tables. Steaming bowls of hearty broth warmed them with each spoonful. A few boys with eyeglasses found it difficult to see through their fogged spectacles as they ate. A few acknowledged Thomas and Freddy's entrance with a welcoming smile after they retrieved their trays.

Two fellows made room for them at their table, and Freddy introduced his classmates to Thomas. "This is Stefan. He is one of those transfers I told you about." The pale-skinned red head nodded as he gulped another bite of his meal. "Next to him is Heinrich. His parents moved to Missouri last year—somewhere north of here, I think."

The smaller, mousy haired boy with thick round glasses stirred his meal rather than eating it. "*Ja.* I am close enough to walk home on weekends to help my family." He never looked up as he stirred. "I think there are too many carrots in my stew. Not fond of carrots."

The others shook their heads at him and gobbled up their own dishes with gratitude.

After the beef stew and dense bread were devoured, Freddy showed Thomas where the boys studied. "Every night, we have devotions with Herr Walther or one of the professors at 7:30. Then we have free time before lamps out at ten. You must be up at five. By six, you had better be dressed, have your bed made, and eaten breakfast. You are also expected to complete your own morning devotions before attending classes."

"I don't think I brought anything like that with me." Thomas searched the shelves in the study for an idea to complement a lack of devotional material.

"Don't worry. If you have something to read or study with you, that will do for now. You can look in the library later as well. They have all the books you'll need."

"I just feel like I should be taking notes or something." Freddy spoke so fast about rules and schedules, Thomas feared he would forget an important aspect of this new school.

"Follow the others. Most have been here for years, and you are the only one coming in this semester. The fellas are a good bunch; and if you are unsure about anything, they'll help you out."

"Thanks. I appreciate your help." Thomas memorized his surroundings to navigate the campus.

"Do you have a trunk for your things?" Freddy peeked around Thomas' meager backpack of clothing and personal items for more.

"Not yet. I walked two days to get here, and I couldn't carry it alone."

Freddy tilted his head and examined Thomas closer. "I don't know anyone who has walked two days alone to the school before. Most come by wagon or steamship."

Thomas hurried on, "My folks will send the rest of my stuff when the river thaws."

"I didn't think of that. Most of us moved in during the warmer months. I must say I am a bit impressed by your determination. I'm not sure I would have taken that on myself, and I am only from the Illinois side of the river."

"Well. I think my parents would rather I spend time marching to school than becoming a marching soldier."

"You want to be a soldier?" Freddy frowned, his expression puzzled. "Not many here are eager to be in the war."

"I think we should stand up for what is right, but my papa says I am too young to fight. So I am here." After a brief pause, Thomas went on. "Don't get me wrong. I love being a student, too. I've read almost everything available in Perry County, and I yearn to learn more. I think school is what God has in mind for me."

Later, excused from the evening devotion time to settle in for the night, Thomas collapsed into bed for much needed rest after his long journey.

As promised, all the boys rose at five. Taking care of his morning ablutions, Thomas returned to the dining hall for a hearty oatmeal breakfast. Reporting to the office, he received his list of courses for the semester and where to report for each. Classes began at nine, leaving him time to write home assuring his family of his safe arrival at Concordia and his warm reception everywhere on the journey. He detailed the attention of the Ste. Genevieve women and the kindness of Peter and Molly Schmidt, excluding the disgraceful business of being knocked into the mud. He knew the Lord was with him and now he was making new friends like Freddy.

Mama and Papa,

I will attend my first theology class in a few moments with Herr Walther. I met him last night before the school gathered for evening devotions. I had seen him a time or two when he was in Perry County, but he is more revered here. You would think he spoke straight from the mouth of God. I must say I am not used to being around so many rules or so many church activities. I am sure I will eventually become accustomed to their ways. They have been welcoming, and I am anxious to learn more. Can you imagine reading the Bible in the original languages? I look forward to this opportunity.

As for the war, no one is too concerned on campus much at all. This surprises me, since the Union arsenal is less than a mile from here and I read there was unrest in the city before now. I think they have their heads buried in their studies instead of the state of the country. I plan to remain aware of both my education and the war. Do not worry. My priority will be my courses. I know the sacrifice it is for me to attend school here. When the weather breaks, I will help with the landscaping and maintenance to help with tuition.

I must say farewell for now.

With all my love,

Thomas

As the semester proceeded, Thomas' notebook and pen kept busy with constant lectures. He soaked up the languages, learning to read

Homer in Greek and Virgil in Latin with little difficulty. The subjects of psychology and logic intrigued him. He was born for the humanities, and his scholarship was rewarded with excellent marks in all his classes. He wrote his next letter home to boast about his schooling.

Mama and Papa,

You will be very pleased that the Lord has given your oldest son a sponge for a brain. I absorb the teacher's lectures and the texts more readily than some of my colleagues. In the short time I have been here, I have been asked to help them grasp the finer points of lessons. The only subject they outpace me in is theology, since they have been immersed in it longer than I. However, even that is not beyond my grasp, and I am gaining more insight into the Word every day.

I am pleased to have discovered that there is a Literary Society here as well. We meet once a week and discuss literary ideals. My mind has never been so alive.

Newspapers are not allowed on campus, however. I suppose it is their way of sheltering us from the evils of the world. I think that is wrong. How can we be trained to work in God's kingdom if we are sent out like uniformed sheep to the slaughter? We must remember we are in the world, even if we are not of the world. So against the advice of my colleagues, I weekly trek to the local newsstand and read the headlines. We have Wednesday afternoons free from coursework, and it allows time for me to make my escape off campus. How else am I to keep abreast of what is happening?

For instance, after arriving here, I learned that President Lincoln signed the Emancipation Proclamation. According to the press, many in the North celebrated this act as a National Day of Prayer. At Concordia, no observance was held anywhere. Of the ten states named to implement the proclamation, the slave state of Missouri was not named; however, maybe they did not want to stir up any resentment.

It is a bit disappointing to be surrounded by those who do not see the need to be involved as citizens of our adopted country. Instead, there seems to be a deliberate effort to keep a separate little island of German Lutheranism here, so we do not lose our culture. Many here have come straight over from Germany to train as pastors for the missionary efforts in the German settlements out west. I don't understand why we cannot be both German and American. I am sure you understand. Or why did we leave Germany in the first place?

Sorry to become political. I am doing fine here. I am trying my best to make you proud.

Love to you all,

Thomas

"Stefan! Wait. I'll walk with you to class." Thomas folded his letter and caught up with his closest Concordia friend.

"Mailing another letter home?" Thomas' statuesque classmate shifted his textbooks under his arm as he spotted the letter resting atop a similar bundle.

"*Ja.* I must tell them about life here. They have not been to St. Louis since we first arrived here from the Fatherland almost ten years ago. So much has changed from what I remember as a boy." Keeping in step with Stefan required a longer stride for Thomas, but he kept pace without any effort.

"I am glad to be away from Indiana where the war is on their doorstep, but I do miss my family, too. I keep thinking I should have stayed to fight. Others I grew up with are already drafted if they did not volunteer. Being here can be seen as a coward's way out." Stefan shook his head at the thought.

"I was never in danger of being drafted. I am sure I was placed here, at least in part, so I would not join the Union Army. My father is hopeful that it will be over before I am legally old enough to be involved, but it is a consideration."

"You want to fight?" Stefan tilted his head to examine Thomas.

"I think it is our duty to stand behind our adopted country. Don't you?"

"I must admit that I think about it. Sometimes, it feels like being here is somehow cheating. Elsewhere, men are coping with battles and conflict while we go on as if nothing is happening. It is not right."

CHAPTER 12

The flowers appear on the earth, the time of singing has come,
and the voice of the turtledove is heard in our land.

Song of Solomon 2:12

BREMEN, GERMANY

"Herr Schroeder, everyone treats me like a baby at the concert hall. They are all so *old*. They won't let me shine like the star that I am. I don't know why you threw me into that group of has-beens." Hands on hips, Maria scowled. "I think they have sung the same songs over and over since the birth of Christ. Those rusty old goats!"

Maria shuffled her feet again to ward off the cold and to emphasize her displeasure with the state of her blossoming career. Since her acceptance after the audition, she remained ignored, like one in a flock of sheep being led around by a maniacal shepherd in the guise of a choir master. She would not be surprised to find him wielding a shepherd's staff at his singers rather than a baton. "It is drill, drill, drill. When do we ever sing real songs? Is there even a performance scheduled?"

"Now, now, Maria. You knew this would take time. They just haven't gotten to know you yet. You are much younger than they are, and I am sure some may be jealous of your unquestionable talent. Give it time." Herr Schroeder reached for Maria's arm to drape it on his as a proper chaperone, but Maria crossed her arms instead. "Goodness, girl. Did you expect to be famous overnight? These things take time. Don't be so impatient." Looking around for a diversion, he added, "Why don't we stop at that busy cafe we walk by all the time. It is time we stopped and see what the fuss is all about, don't you think?"

Maria glared at the attempt to divert her attention, but the thought of a treat still lifted her spirits, and she agreed. Anything was better than sitting home with Frau Schroeder glaring at her or being ordered to belt out more scales by Johann Wolfe. She chuckled to herself when she realized how she compared him to a maniacal shepherd moment before. "That's right, a wolf in crazy sheep's clothing; that's who he is," she muttered to herself.

"What?" Herr Schroeder held the door open to the diminutive café with pastry delicacies beckoning each passer-by from the window case. Marie sashayed inside like the diva she pretended to be.

"Oh, nothing. Just a little joke I made for myself," she answered as she flipped her hair. "I think Herr Wolfe is trying to disguise himself as a shepherd for his flock. The irony of a wolf watching over the sheep hit me funny."

"Oh. That is clever. You have a good wit, Maria. I would not be telling him that, however." Herr Schroeder closed the door behind them to keep out the winter.

"I'm not a fool, Herr Schroeder. I would not share that with the circle of old cronies you have lumped me with."

"How about we change the subject?" Herr Schroeder led Maria to an empty table near the window. "Do you like to watch people? You can learn a great deal about a place by observing its citizens."

"I don't mind watching, but I would rather be out in the world. You and Frau Schroeder keep me so cooped up. I haven't really been anywhere but the apartment and the rehearsal hall since I've been here."

Herr Schroeder looked up at the server who had approached. "A piece of apple kuchen each with our coffee please."

"Kuchen? You are trying to butter me up, aren't you?"

"Consider it part of my apology for not letting you explore and do more. Remember, I did tell your parents I would look after you, and I would not be keeping my promise if I let you run wild around the city unchaperoned, would I?" Before Maria could cut in, Herr Schroeder continued, "You mentioned a concert. Yes, one is scheduled for the Valentine's Gala. I will talk to Wolfe about an aria for you. He has already told me what a fine voice you have."

Maria sat up straighter. "An aria? Will you really? Did he say that?"

"Slow down. I can't guarantee anything. Those 'old goats,' as you call them, have seniority and probably some political clout for such favors. What you have is a fresh face and beautiful voice that may attract crowds that Wolfe has not been able to draw in a few years." More to himself than Maria, he continued, "Yes, I think that is the best angle. He might go for that." Looking back at Maria, he said, "You do your part and I'll do mine. Deal?"

Maria nodded her approval.

The aroma of the steaming cakes preceded the server as she placed them on the table. Maria dug her fork into hers with gusto, then sipped the steamy coffee to wash it down.

"Slow down, girl. Don't ruin that valuable instrument of yours by choking. That would ruin all our plans." Maria released her fork to the table and basked in the hovering steam of the coffee. "Besides, if you want to be treated as a true ingenue, you need to approach your food with more feminine designs. You cannot attack it like an animal about to escape your plate and inhale the poor thing. Didn't your mother teach you more manners?"

Another bite halfway to her mouth, Maria halted. Swallowing hard, she straightened in her chair. "Of course, my mother taught me manners. I promise to put them to good use from now on. I was not thinking." The next miniscule bite eased into her mouth, and she withdrew the fork with deliberate hesitation while savoring the morsel. "Better?" She batted her eyes at Herr Schroeder, which caused him to squirm in his seat and peer outside through the window.

Before Valentine's Day, true to his word, Schroeder convinced Wolfe to grant Maria a solo performance. Herr Wolfe forced Maria to practice range extensions and breathing support exercises for hours on end until he felt she was ready for her debut.

Maria practiced Franz Schubert's *Standchen* every waking hour. She would not miss the opportunity to impress Bremen. If she wanted to be appreciated, she would earn it. Her soprano crescendo of "thy dreaming heart" pierced the walls of the building nightly.

Frau Bickle knocked one morning, surprising her and the Schroeders with a delivery of warm scones for the household. "You fill the air with such life listening to your beautiful voice. I am sure I have more customers stopping by to hear your melodies drift into my shop. You have earned these."

Frau Schroeder stood holding the offered basket of pastries, dumbfounded. Stammering, she answered, "Why, that is kind of you.

I will add them to our dinner meal." She turned to Maria. "Say thank you to the kind lady, Maria. Don't be rude."

Maria brushed past Frau Schroeder and launched herself on Frau Bickle for a friendly embrace. "Thank you, Frau Bickle. You bake the most delicious treats. Thank you so much." Releasing the baker, Maria caught the scowl on Frau Schroeder's face. In the months since Maria had entered their home, she had never once hugged the mistress of the house. Did she care that Maria had an immediate affection for this new neighbor? Most likely, she wanted everyone to dislike Maria as much as she did. At any rate, Maria said her goodbyes and returned to practicing for her opening night.

The next evening, Herr Schroeder came home with a designer dress box from a sought-after dressmaker in the city. Setting it on the table, he motioned for Maria to come closer. "Come here. See what I brought you."

Frau Schroeder snorted. "You bought her a fancy gown, and we run around in these rags?"

"You, my dear, are not singing a solo for high society this month." Realizing this was not the best approach, he appeased, "Once we launch Maria into stardom, I will buy you the nicest frock in town. After all, we can't have her performing in her country *dirndl*, can we?"

"Can I open it?" Maria lingered over the ornate gift. With an approving nod from the giver, Maria tore into it with more fervor than on Christmas morning. She halted as she began to stroke the ivory silk gown nestled inside. The creamy fabric supported delicate lavender flowers embroidered on a tailored jacket. A silk corset hid boning strips, which fastened in the front to boost her girlish figure. Digging for more pieces, she found a white cotton chemise and a crinoline petticoat with ruffles. The ivory overskirt also was trimmed in matching lavender flowers at the hemline. A hoop like the ones she had seen high-class women wear in the city accompanied the box of finery. In awe, she touched the fine fabric as she lifted the dreamlike dress and held it to her frame.

"Well? Do you like it?"

"I love it. I have never owned anything so beautiful in my life." Maria wanted to twirl around the room, but the glare from Frau Schroeder kept her elation in check.

"All the high society ladies are wearing French styles these days. The hoop will accentuate that overskirt on stage. We want you to look the part of a star when you are up there, now don't we?"

Near tears, Maria turned to Herr Schroeder and lunged into his arms to offer a daughterly embrace. "Thank you so much. I will wear it forever. Can I try it on?"

"Humph." Frau Schroeder groaned from across the room. "I doubt you can keep it clean long enough to wear it on Valentine's Day. You had better put it away before you soil it. It is time for dinner."

Maria returned it to the fine box and replaced the lid. The thought of wearing the beautiful dress negated anything Frau Schroeder spouted. She was going to be a star.

Maria radiated youth and beauty for the Valentine's Gala. Her blond tendrils embraced the creamy silk bodice, encircling the floral accents. Maria's tiny waist melted into nothing inside the unnecessary corset. Ignoring jealous looks and whispers from the other choir members, Maria drew unbidden attention with her energetic presence.

Maria sang the choral arrangements alongside the others, harmonizing her soprano tones effortlessly as she waited for her time to shine alone. Heavy Helga Hoffmeier belted out her feature rendition of Wagner's "*Liebersverbot.*" Maria was next.

The orchestra paused as she moved into position. The light color of the garment was a Godsend. Even in dim lighting, the fabric reflected the glow of the stage. She took a deep breath to steady her nerves, a collective inhale rippling through the room as she stepped forward into the spotlight.

The instrumental beginnings set the mood as Maria's clear voice sliced through the broken-hearted story of Schubert's "Serenade." The vibrations of sorrow reverberated through the audience. By the time her yearning plea ended, the women were tearful; and the men hid damp eyes behind kerchiefs. How could someone so young feel that song so deeply? Her cheeks glowed crimson: she became the sole light of the stage as the admirers regained their composure and bounded to their feet for a resounding ovation. Amid the loud applause, Maria caught sight of a fresh snowfall through the high set windows of the hall.

Maria curtsied demurely and began to return to her place with the choir when Herr Wolfe touched her arm and turned her to the audience. "Ladies and gentlemen, this is the debut of our Snow Angel, Miss Maria Neubauer."

Herr Schroeder's difficult path to reach Maria was hampered by waves of admirers as the event ended. He pushed his way through the throngs of well-wishers to direct the novice singer in the crush. By the time he was at Maria's side, she was holding several bouquets. In February? These must cost a fortune!

"*Schnee Engel*! I like the sound of that." Herr Schroeder bent close to hug his promising young singer. "Sweden may have their

Swedish nightingale with Jenny Lind. Now Germany has their Snow Angel with you." He drew Maria in for another embrace. As Maria turned away from Schroeder's zealous attention, she found herself face to face with a distinguished gentleman sporting a curled mustache.

"Let me introduce myself," said the gentleman. "Samuel Talbot, at your service. I have something very lucrative that you must consider for your future, *Fraulein*." He took her hand to kiss it, and Maria noted his American accent.

"Consider for her future?" Schroeder stepped between Maria and the intruder. "I am Bernard Schroeder, Miss Neubauer's manager. She makes no decisions without me. As I am sure you know, she is a minor," Schroeder blurted out after emerging from the crowd.

"Happy to meet your acquaintance, Herr Schroeder. I am Samuel Talbot. I have connections with the music scene in New York. I would love to have you bring Miss Neubauer over to America. The audiences will love her in the States. Someone with such presence and an amazing voice will pack the halls wherever she goes."

"America?" Schroeder almost rubbed his hands in anticipation of the money this would bring.

Maria's heart leaped at the idea of singing in America, but she remembered Lena's letters. She interjected, "What about the war over there?"

"Oh, no worries, young lady. We are in the North. No Rebel will travel to New York and cause any trouble. Believe me. It is completely safe. I would not ask you to go if it were not." Talbot tapped his cane for emphasis.

Herr Schroeder interjected, "Isn't there a moratorium on immigration to America during the war, though? Will we be able to enter?"

"Of course, you will be able to enter. You will not be immigrating, will you? I can take care of all the arrangements for passage—first-class all the way."

The men shook hands and agreed to meet for further planning the following week.

Maria's mind raced. What would Mama and Papa think? Her sprinting thoughts kept her awake long into the night, tossing and turning on the pillow. Maybe, just maybe, she would see Lena and Herman. America cannot be so big.

CHAPTER 13

I will forget my complaint, I will put off my sad face,
and be of good cheer.

Job 9:27

ALTON, ILLINOIS

Karl stayed clear of the penitentiary in the wake of the smallpox outbreak and the death of his infant sons. A dispatch currier kept legal paperwork moving from his desk to Colonel Mason and back again. A steady stream of edicts, briefs, and pardons crossed his desk daily for the Rebels who signed promises to not return to the war upon their departure. Releasing prisoners on their honor to go home and stop fighting kept the prison from overflowing.

Many of the Confederate soldiers were sent into battle in the place of wealthy landowners with no wish to fight on their own behalf. The illiterate poor had no trouble switching allegiances to escape imprisonment and the dreaded disease spreading through the yard. These Rebels easily agreed to sign promises not to fight against the Union. The majority of them could not read the documents where they placed their mark, anyway.

No effort to keep the prisoner population down was more effective than the threat of death and deportments to Smallpox Island. Those destined to die were floated to the small uninhabited Sunflower Island in the Mississippi now renamed for the plague infecting them. Once shipped away, they had no hope of returning. Union soldiers suffered from the disease as well as the prisoners they guarded; and when they died, they were buried side by side, blue and gray, as victims of an invisible war. The virus lived in the air for hours, contaminating everything the men frequented. Hundreds died of disease on both sides without ever firing a shot. Since Doc Russell claimed the incubation period was two weeks, Karl knew he could not risk more of his family's health by going out to the prison again until the epidemic was over.

Juana stepped in at home as if she had grown up with the family. The girls returned from Uncle Herman's farm, but Lena had no energy to chase the youngsters and keep them out of mischief. Juana kept them in line with a loving touch by shepherding them to their room "so Mama can rest" and other such excuses to keep the girls at bay. Juana cooked, cleaned, and kept the household running for the Mullers. No specific arrangement was ever made between them. Somehow, there was an unspoken consensus that it should be this way until Lena could manage things on her own again.

The source of Lena's lack of energy was uncertain. Doc Russell thought the strain of having premature babies might have damaged her heart, leaving her listless and lethargic. More likely, her broken heart resulted from the empty arms of a mother who had buried her two infant sons. Considering that more likely, Doc Russell had encouraged Karl, "She needs some time to grieve. She will recover and care for her other children again before long."

If Juana chased, cooked, and cleaned in Lena's place, there was no hurry for her to feel better. The household was running fine in Lena's absence. If she stayed in bed, Juana brought her meals to her. If she needed anything, Juana obliged. Having Juana at her beck and call was a Godsend to someone who wanted to be left alone and wallow in her grief.

Karl came home night after night to his wife lounging about the divan or lying in bed. "Lena, you must get up. What will the children think? They need their mother."

"They have Juana. They can do without me." She spoke barely above a whisper as if it took her full strength to carry on the briefest of conversations.

"Juana is not their mother. The girls need *you*." Karl tried not to sound so stern. He grieved for his sons, too. The burden of guilt he felt for bringing death into their home almost broke him, but he could not further damage his family by not providing for them through his work. He had an obligation to the sovereignty of the Union, too.

Lena ignored him. She continued to stare unblinking at a blank wall. In exasperation, Karl raked his hand through his hair and let her be.

The next day, Karl bounded into the house with more gusto than usual. "Lena! I have something for you. In fact, I am sure it is just the thing to bring you out of this slump!"

Lena puzzled a glare at Karl. "What's all the fuss is about? Why are you yelling?"

Holding out a post to her, Lena gingerly took it and held it close before opening it. Reading the envelope, she said, "It is from my mother! I'd recognize her hand anywhere." A tentative smile brought much needed color to her face.

"Open it! Open it!" The girls scampered in from their rooms at the sound of Papa's excited homecoming.

"Girls, Mama has a very important letter. I am sure she will tell you all about it after she has a chance to read it. So why don't you scoot off a few minutes and give her time to read?" Karl lifted a girl in each arm, and they squealed in delight as he turned to take them from the room.

"Let them stay," said Lena "Why don't you read it aloud for all of us? I'm not sure I have the energy for it." She handed the letter back to Karl as he released the girls, and they climbed up on the bed next to their mother.

"*Dearest Lena,*

I have the most troubling news. Another of our darling children has flown off to America. First Herman, then you, and now Maria."

"Maria? Why on earth would Maria be in America?" Lena wondered aloud. Karl shook his head to indicate he didn't know and continued reading.

"*Your little sister Maria has always fancied herself a singing star. She has sung almost from the moment of her birth. Now that she is in her teens, she sings for every occasion that presents itself. A man named Herr Schroeder heard her aria at Christmas and asked to take her to Bremen to sing in the city concert. He promised to chaperone her, along with his wife, a rather taciturn woman. He and Maria begged long enough until your papa agreed that she should go.*

Now, only a few months later, we are informed that a promoter heard about her, too, and wants her to tour America. I think she was already on her way before we got a letter from Maria about her 'great opportunity.' Your papa was livid. He did not want to send Maria away. At least, you were going to see your brother when you crossed the ocean. Who will watch after Maria? We do not trust Herr Schroeder, who took our daughter away without our permission.

From what we understand, she will be performing in New York. Can you find her and look after her? We hear that your country is full of unrest. That is no place for a girl to be on her own. Of course, we are certain Herman will want to help, too. We are so glad we have you two there to help.

Love,

Mama and Papa"

"Maria, here in America! Karl, can you go to New York and find her?" Lena's doe-eyes searched Karl for an answer.

"Darling. I cannot go to New York right now. Do your parents have any idea how far New York City is from Alton, Illinois?"

"I doubt it. After Herman moved over here, we had Martin show us where his farm was on a map. Martin teaches at university now, so I doubt Mama has any idea that she is not down the road from us."

"I cannot leave my post and go cross country right now. You understand? You and the girls need me right now. I can't go away on this wild goose chase to find your sister in a city as crowded as New York."

"I know. It does sound a bit crazy . . . How about Herman? He is not tied to a job like yours."

"Lena." Karl shook his head. "You lived with your brother. With the spring thaw, he will have more work than ever while getting the crops planted." Not wanting the spark to disappear that the news from home ignited in her, Karl continued, "Maybe later, when things settle down, we can bring Maria here."

"I'd like that. The girls will love her. Johanna is the spitting image of her, you know." Lena's eyes furrowed. "Will she be safe where she is, Karl?"

"She should be fine in the North. All the fighting has been in the South to this point; and no matter what your mother thinks of this Herr Schroeder, I am sure he will do everything he can to keep her safe. If she does not sing, he does not make any money. She will not be able to perform near battlefronts. I am sure he will take care of her until we see her." He bent to give Lena a kiss. She accepted Karl's lips for the first time in months.

"Thank you. You put my mind at ease." Lena started to rise to her feet. "I think I should help Juana with dinner. I have lain around here long enough."

Karl offered his hand to help her up, then gathered her into his arms. "I have been waiting for you to say that," he whispered into her hair and kissed her again as the girls scampered off the bed to join the fanfare.

"Eww!" they squealed. Karl and Lena laughed as they broke apart and made room for the two darlings in their embrace.

CHAPTER 14

"And at the time for the banquet, he sent his servant to say to those
who had been invited, 'Come, for everything is now ready.'"

Luke 14:17

St. Louis, Missouri

"Thomas?" Stefan stood in the doorway waiting for a response while tossing a cork ball into the air and letting it bounce repeatedly in the palm of his hand. He stood with his other arm akimbo as he stared at Thomas, who ignored his summons and continued to read the letter in his hand. "Got some news from home?" Stefan edged closer and tried to peer over Thomas' shoulder as he snatched the ball from the air again.

Glued to the page, Thomas neglected to acknowledge Stefan's inquiry.

Thomas folded the page and returned the missive to the envelope. "Mama says they don't have the funds for me to take a steamer home for Easter. We don't have enough time for me to walk there over break either. She has been writing letters with some old friends in Alton across the river from here, and she says they have invited me to join them for the holiday since I am so close." Thomas clasped his hands and dropped them in his lap with a sigh.

114

"Is that a problem? Do you not want to go?" Stefan reclined upon Thomas' bed and extended his long legs out before him as he leaned back to stretch his six-foot-plus frame. He refocused his tossing to the ceiling overhead.

"I don't know. I haven't seen these people since I was learning to read. I'm sure they are nice, but I don't know if I'd recognize them after all this time." Thomas kicked Stefan's foot away from his covers. "I could stay here on campus, although a home-cooked meal sounds tempting."

"I can't go home either. Indiana is too far, and with the war raging . . . Think they'd let you bring a friend?" Stefan sat upright again and rubbed his stomach with his empty hand. "It takes a bit to fill up a growing fellow like me."

Thomas laughed and knocked the ball from midair onto the floor, where Stefan lunged to retrieve it. "I guess it wouldn't hurt to ask. I'd love to have company. I've not been to Alton before."

"Ask them. Right now, let's grab a bat and hit this around to get some exercise. You've been cooped up in here for too long." Stefan tossed the ball into the air and caught it again.

"Fine, but I want to pick up the *Anzeiger des Westens* to study up on the latest battle news." Thomas hopped off the bed to lead the way.

"Why do you want to stay aware of all the battle skirmishes? I only want news that the whole thing is over so I can go home again."

"One way to hurry it along is to enlist in the Union Army and do our part once we are old enough." Thomas glanced at Stefan sideways as he studied the ball in his hand.

"I admit I feel guilty leaving friends and family back in Indiana to fight when I am safely out in Missouri going to school. You don't need to remind me that I am not sacrificing like they are. Do you think I am a coward?"

"Stefan, I didn't mean to call you a coward. You are where your family wants you to be. However, I think you'd want to keep informed how the fighting is going, since you do have friends involved. I do not have anyone close to me in the battle, but I'd join up in a minute if I could."

Stefan flipped the ball over his shoulder to catch it behind his back as the two strode down the street to the newsstand. Thomas collected a paper off the vendor's stack while dropping change in the man's hand. "Look at this," he said, unfolding the paper. "Grant is trying to march on Vicksburg, but he is failing. The Union needs more of Ead's Ironclads down the Mississippi. With Vicksburg held by the Rebels, our supplies will be hurting in St. Louis, too. I've noticed the docks are emptier these days."

Stephan nodded. "Some of the guys said they made a trip down to Carondelet, south of town. They build those Ead's Ironclad ships in the iron yard down there. I can't imagine anything penetrating one of those monsters, but I am surprised something that heavy can float. The guns on those things are impressive. Did you hear the City of Alton steamer is going to be one of Grant's flagships? It isn't built like an Ead's fighting ship. If they keep enough steamers up here for us to navigate the waterways, I'm fine."

Thomas folded the paper to the center. "Don't worry. Have you seen the port lately? Plenty of steamers are lined up that are afraid to venture too far into Confederate territory." Thomas continued to read beyond the fold. "It says Lincoln is calling Vicksburg the 'Gibraltar of the Confederacy.' I am glad he has plans to end their stronghold. It also says they will cut the Rebels off from all their supplies of Texas beef and Louisiana sugar. With soldiers clambering everywhere, I understand why my mama doesn't want me to head down there to see them for Easter. Too much danger."

"*Ja*. Why don't you accept the Easter invitation across the river, and we can holiday with your family friends? Don't forget to ask about me. I can bring a little cheese with me for their hospitality." Stefan sent the ball sailing across the yard.

Laughing, Thomas pursued it.

"Stefan! I got a letter back from the Mullers in Alton." Thomas placed the message in front of Stefan, who was hunched over his Latin book in the library. "Not only do they say it is fine for you and me to come, but it also says Karl, the father, works with the Alton Penitentiary; and if there is not too much sickness happening during our visit, he may show us around."

"Sickness?"

"*Ja*. Smallpox has been running its course. They lost twin babies from the disease last winter; but with fairer weather, I think it has run its course for now."

"Smallpox?" Stefan's brow furrowed in worry. "Are you sure we should go?"

"They wouldn't invite us over if it were dangerous, Stefan. They have two little girls themselves, and they would not risk their health, I'm sure."

"All right, if you say so. I will purchase our tickets to cross the river."

CHAPTER 15

I am acting with great boldness toward you; I have great pride in you;
I am filled with comfort. In all our affliction, I am overflowing with joy.

2 Corinthians 7:4

NEW YORK

The shopping spree to dress Maria in gorgeous gowns for the American debut had soured Frau Schroeder's attitude toward Maria even more, if that were possible. Maria's male chaperones, in contrast, fawned over their debutante as if they were to present her to the Queen of England herself. Wary of Frau Schroeder's jealousy, Maria packed each new treasure away in the steamer trunk out of her sight and saved them for her triumphant arrival. No need to flaunt them before the unappreciative woman before being introduced to polite society in New York.

Once aboard ship, Maria twirled a dainty blue parasol appliquéed with delicate wildflowers as she strutted on deck during her daily walks. She spun it this way and that to catch the attention of sailors and passengers alike, under the disapproving eyes of Schroeder and Talbot. Each protective man had an agreed-upon schedule to tend to her bidding. They insisted that unscrupulous captains on other ships mistreated young women as they sailed the high seas, and they vowed no such treatment would befall Maria. They tried to convey this sense of danger to Maria; those in high or respectable positions did not guarantee decent scruples among men. Maria carelessly left the men to worry while she enjoyed the adventure.

The trip abroad held an air of excitement and mystery for Maria. Treated like a princess, she settled into a comfortable stateroom where Herr Schroeder and Mister Talbot resided next door and escorted her at every turn about the ship. The steerage of rough Irishmen spelled trouble for an unchaperoned *fraulein*, and her overseers were bent on keeping their charge away from the rogues on board.

Her chaperones' smothering ways chafed Maria's newfound freedom. Her overattentive overseers regarded a smile at a passerby or a too-long glance at a sailor as an opportunity for a scolding, so Maria refrained from any overt flirting. However, she was thankful that the relentless Frau Schroeder had remained in Bremen after claiming that a turbulent voyage would overtax her delicate constitution.

The trio traded ships in London. At the second port, masses of poor Irishmen engulfed the new ship. Strapping Irishmen in their napless hats, worn coats, and corduroy trousers hoisted knapsacks over their shoulders as they trudged up the gangplank.

"Don't gawk, girl. You will only encourage them to engage with you." Talbot turned Maria's young elbow away from the sight of the embarking men. "Why don't you settle in your cabin while the captain prepares to sail?"

With rolled eyes and a flip of her hair, Maria relented to his request but not before complaining, "Why does everyone want to treat me like a child?"

They were fortunate to have fair winds, and the voyage lasted only six weeks. Leaning over the rail, Maria sought the first glimpses of the Castle Garden Immigration Center as they approached New York Harbor. Since Samuel Talbot was a U.S. citizen, he avoided the inspection lines the noncitizens endured. However, he stayed with Maria and Herr Schroeder to assist them in their processing. Talbot whispered to a few uniformed customs agents while greasing their palms with cash. No one subjected the Germans to physical exams, and they were easily waved through the line.

The palatial Castle Garden reinforced Maria's images of America as a haven of prosperity and good fortune. The grandeur of columns and open spaces screamed "America," and she itched to see beyond the welcoming facade. Guiding the newcomers through the doors toward the bridge to the city, an array of unsettling images replaced the grand ones. Noisy vendors shouted from all sides to advertise rooms, transportation, train tickets, and promises of work. A din of languages tossed together fighting to be louder than the next.

Two men in military uniforms stood at either side of the gate, grabbing some of the young Irishmen as they ventured outside the protective confines of the Center. "You. You want to be Americans? You are hereby conscripted to fight for your new country." They were then whisked away to a holding area.

"Wha . . ." The weakened, near-starving lads put up little resistance as the officials led a dozen of them away.

"Mr. Talbot? Can they take them like that? Those boys did not come here to go to war." Maria tugged on Talbot's sleeve to direct his attention to the scene before them.

Talbot opened the *Harper's Weekly* he acquired from a hawking newsy, scanned the printed page, and sighed as he confirmed, "Says here Lincoln needs more troops for the war and has conscripted New York to supply them. 'All male citizens between twenty and thirty-five and all unmarried men between thirty-five and forty-five years of age are subject to military duty.'" He turned to Schroeder. "Good thing you are a married man, Bernard. They might conscript you for the army."

Schroeder cinched his hat lower over his face to appear less of a target, and the three brushed past the officers plucking random men as they exited the building.

"Having the little miss here will help, too. You can say you are her father if they try to stop us," Talbot said to Schroeder. "Stay close. I'll take you two to a safe place near the Brooklyn Concert Hall. I'll hail a hack, and we'll be there within the hour."

A black porter rolled the trunks out on a hand cart to the curb. Once he noticed the Irish families gathered at the port waiting for loved ones, he ducked back into the protection of the immigration guards as soon as Schroeder had tipped him for his service.

"My, my, he's a skittish one. Talbot, you didn't tell us that American black men liked to hide in the corners like that." Schroeder repocketed his excess coins.

"He acts scared. I thought they were free here in the North. Why would he hide?" Maria peered after the porter.

Talbot shook his head wearily. "The driver told me there have been near-riots between the immigrants and the blacks since I have been gone. They are fighting for the same jobs, and the black men are not compelled to fight in the war like the whites. It is building a wall of hatred between the racial groups. The recently freed or escaped slaves from the South are moving north for a better life, but they are hated because they are seen as stealing jobs that could be held by the immigrant newcomers. No one wins."

With their bags and trunks loaded onto the carriage, Talbot instructed the driver to take them to the Brooklyn Concert Hall. "We are going straight there?" Maria marveled. This was the place she would become famous.

"Yes. The lodgings above the hall have been secured for you and Herr Schroeder. It is most convenient for our purposes. Once we get you settled, I will introduce you to the director. I think it is important that we do not delay your introduction to New York."

Maria straightened her posture as if her new status required proper decorum. Leaning forward, she absorbed the unremarkable scene unfolding before her. The filthy streets accumulated mounds of horse manure. Dead cats, dogs, rats, and other decomposing vermin lined the same. Vegetable and household refuse grew to a few feet or more, and garbage boxes remained unemptied everywhere. Pools of stagnant water collected over clogged sewer drains, and the stench attacked their senses in the carriage.

"Close that curtain," Herr Schroeder chided. "That stink could choke a rhino." Maria retreated into the confines of the carriage. "Talbot, the slums of London were not as rank as all this."

"Pardon us." Talbot covered his unease from the same putrid assault with a handkerchief over his face. "When the heat rises, it does get a bit ripe. Don't worry. After we trot across the East River, it is only a few miles to our destination."

True to his word, once loading and unloading the goods to and from a Fulton steamship, Brooklyn opened to a less congested area. The music hall, although newer than the one in Bremen, attempted to be as grand. The brick Roman arches graced the facade and added grandeur to the five-story building. Entering through an alley doorway, the foyer welcomed a stairway to upper-level apartments.

Talbot handed Maria and Schroeder identical keys. "You're in 312. Schroeder, you are in 314. We won't be far for any of your needs, my dear." Talbot turned to a black lad rounding the corner from a side door behind the stairs. "Lewis!"

Stopping in his tracks, Lewis stood at attention while awaiting Talbot's order. "Young man, don't go running through the building."

"But, Mista Talbot, I just heard that Mista Douglass is goin' ta speak here next month. I's goin' to tell my ma."

"Fredrick Douglass? Speaking here?" Talbot shook his head. "Are you sure?"

"That's fo' sure. I heard it wit my own ears. Can I go now?"

"Since you have all this energy, why don't you help Miss Neubauer upstairs with her luggage? She'll be in 312. Then you can find your ma."

"Yessir." With a nod to Maria, he grabbed the nearest couple of bags and bounded up the steps with them.

"Goodness. What is all the excitement about?" Maria's eyes followed her belongings upstairs as they disappeared beyond the first floor.

"Fredrick Douglass is a freed slave who has become a champion for the abolitionist cause," explained Talbot. "It is an honor to have him speak here. I am sure he will draw a crowd."

The weariness of ocean travel crowded out all thoughts of abolitionist speakers or overzealous child porters. Climbing three flights of stairs to reach her room, Maria found the soft bed draped in a clean but worn comforter. It welcomed her before she even disrobed for slumber. As she drifted away, she thought she must write Lena a letter telling her she was in America, and she would visit her soon. After all, she couldn't be that far away now.

CHAPTER 16

Jesus said to her, "I am the resurrection and the life.
Whoever believes in me, though he die, yet shall he live."

John 11:25

ALTON, ILLINOIS

Karl laid the daily post on the table, keeping one letter in his hand to wave in front of Lena. "We have a message from young Thomas Krueger. Did you realize he has been going to school right across the river in St. Louis these past few months?"

Lena dried her hands at the kitchen basin. "Yes, his mother wrote to me soon after he decided to go to the German Concordia school. He always was a smart boy. I am not surprised he continued his education." She faced her husband. "Since he is so close by, I told her we would be happy to have him here for Easter. We are much closer than his home in southern Missouri." Lena slipped the note from Karl's hand. "Does he say anything about it?"

"Read for yourself." Karl relinquished the letter to Lena, but his oversized smile gave the answer away.

"This is wonderful," said Lena as she skimmed the letter. "And it says he is bringing a friend, too. It will be nice to have some company.

I have shut myself up in the house for so long, I must practice being a proper hostess again."

"College boys will be happy with anything that fills their stomachs, Lena." Karl wrapped his arm around her and drew her in for a friendly kiss on the cheek. "I'm sure you haven't lost your touch, and you have Juana to help now, too."

At the mention of her name, Juana walked in through the back door with a basket of clean laundry braced on her hip. "Some'm want me?"

"Oh, Juana. We have the best news. A college boy we haven't seen since he was the girls' size will be joining us for Easter. He is bringing a friend, too. We will need to cook a sensational feast." Lena's mind drifted off to listing menu possibilities for the occasion.

Juana glanced from Lena to Karl, then to the floor. Setting the laundry down, she shuffled her feet and stammered ahead. "Ma'am, I-I was thinking . . . you not needing me here no more . . . and I should be goin' to find my boy now . . . 'Member that's why I was lookin' for Mista Muller when I came here that night . . . " Juana trailed off without mentioning the twins' birth.

"Oh, Juana, I have grown to count on you so much. I have been selfish." Lena stepped closer to Juana as if she might hug her but stopped before giving into the impulsive gesture. "Of course, you have your own life. I don't mean to keep you from finding your son." Lena turned to face Karl. "Do you even have any idea where to start looking for Juana's boy?" She turned back to Juana. "What's his name again?"

"Jubal, ma'am. I think Mista Muller helped him before he joined up. Ya see, he's not as dark as me. His papa's white." Juana broke eye contact and studied her feet again. "Sometimes, he can pass for white if'n he tries. I hear tell of all the fightin', and I'm scared. Nobody'd know to tell me if'n he is hurt or dead. How will I find out about 'em?"

"I'm not sure if I can discover anything about Jubal or not, Juana; but you have paid our family a tremendous service these past months, and I will do all I can to locate him if it is possible. What last name would he be using?" Karl pulled out one of his legal notepads and jotted down the information Juana offered. "I've inquired about him a bit, and I think the judge sent him up north to join up; but it will be difficult to see where he landed."

"His papa's name was Foster, but I doubt he'd use that. He might try somethin' like Freeman. I don't rightly know."

"That will make it a bit tougher. Can he read or write?"

"No, sir. I think he did learn his initials, so that's why I think he may change Foster to Freeman. He learned the F sign. The chil'n on the farm taught him to make a J and F for his mark."

"Well, that's something to go on, I guess." Karl folded the paper and tucked it in his jacket pocket. "I'll investigate it, but don't get your hopes up right now. The army has its hands full with desertions. President Lincoln even pronounced a day of amnesty for all those who have been absent without leave, so the deserters who return to duty before April 1 would not be punished. Hildebrand is busy with his duties as commander besides falling ill himself in recent days. Thankfully, it's not the pox; but the man is not himself, that's for sure, and I won't be able to rely on any assistance from him."

"Is there something we can do for the colonel?" asked Lena. "Maybe we can send you with some of Juana's chicken broth tomorrow. The man has been so instrumental in the efficient running of the prison, we don't want him to succumb to sickness." She turned to Juana. "Let's start a pot simmering right away, so Karl can take it in the morning."

Juana retreated through the back door for the chicken coop.

"Being a soldier must be hard for these young men away from their families, Karl," said Lena with a sigh, watching her go. "And for their mothers. When will this all end?"

"The Union has been struggling to get a foothold on some of the Southern fronts, Lena. I won't lie. We just got word that Grant's attempts to take Vicksburg have failed so far. The Mississippi is too high to navigate ironclads right now. Without taking Vicksburg, the Rebels control all New Orleans shipments on the Mississippi. Regaining it is key for us."

"Don't worry." Lena slipped her arm around Karl as he visualized the battles around the nation. "The Lord will help us find a way to end this division in this country. I only pray that it will be soon."

Karl smiled down at his wife. "I did read some good news in the press this week. West Virginia voted to emancipate its slaves." Squeezing Lena tighter, he said, "All is not lost. You keep saying those prayers, and God will take care of the rest."

The soup did not help the colonel recover. Colonel Jesse Hildebrand died of pneumonia two weeks later, leaving Karl the daunting task of finding Jubal without his assistance.

CHAPTER 17

Do not neglect to show hospitality to strangers,
for thereby some have entertained angels unawares.

Hebrews 13:2

ALTON, ILLINOIS

Thomas and Stefan disembarked from the Alton steamer, hoisted their knapsacks on their shoulders, and strode the ascent up Christian Hill. The imposing federal penitentiary along the Mississippi slowed their progress as they studied the structure. The stone block walls fostered a curious draw for them, but they knew they were expected for a luscious meal at the Muller's at noon. They could not risk the detour that would delay dinner plans.

Standing in front of the tidy yard speckled with fresh sprouted tulips and daffodils, the pastel Muller home welcomed the perfect springtime setting for their gathering. The front porch stretched across the home with two rockers on one side and a hanging porch swing on the other. As the boys reached the door, it swung open to reveal a slight brown-haired woman wiping her hands of a soiled apron before reaching out to embrace them.

"Oh, Thomas, you are here! This must be your friend, Stefan." Her quick embrace released to study the young men in earnest. "My, you have grown into a handsome young man. I knew you would. How are your studies?"

Before Thomas could answer, Karl stepped into the doorway. "Gracious, Lena. Let the boys come in. You can catch up inside."

"Oh, dear, I have forgotten my manners. Of course, come in, come in." Stepping aside, Lena ushered the two students into her front room. Whereas Juana was keeping a watchful eye in the kitchen over the meal preparations, Johanna and Dora sat in their Sunday best of pink ruffled pinafores and starched white bloomers on the couch as they had been told. Dora squirmed and pulled at the high neck blouse where the stiff lace rubbed her baby skin while Johanna swatted her sister's hand down to force her to be more ladylike.

"Well, aren't you two a picture." Thomas swept his hat off and bowed to the girls sitting uncharacteristically still. "I didn't know there were princesses in the house. You must be Johanna." Thomas took her hand and kissed the back of it before returning it to her lap. Expecting the same treatment, Dora hid her hands behind her back; so Thomas could not do the same to her. He laughed along with the others. "I don't blame you. Some strange fellow comes into your house and thinks he can be friendly with you. You are a smart girl, Miss Dora."

"They are not used to many visitors, Thomas. With the smallpox outbreak, most folks have been staying to themselves; and I haven't been much for company of late." Lena trailed off, not wanting the loss of the babies to cloud the greetings. Wringing her hands, she pointed to her finest dishes ready for her guests. "We are about to serve dinner. Please be seated."

Thomas and Stefan nodded at each other. "After you," they said in unison and chuckled again. They chose seats opposite the girls, and Lena and Karl sat at each end of the table. Juana delivered dishes of hot potato salad, pickled beets, warm wheat rolls, and a platter of sliced honey ham.

"Goodness, ma'am. I haven't eaten like this since before leaving home in Indiana." Stefan drooled as each item found a place in front of him. "This is making my stomach rumble."

"I am thankful to have Juana here to help. She has been a Godsend. Karl, will you please say grace before this feast grows cold?"

"Fold your hands, girls," said Karl.

They bowed their heads and waited for Papa's word of prayer. "Lord, we are so grateful to have these scholarly young men join us today as we celebrate the resurrection of our Savior. Lord, we are thankful for all the bounty and blessings You bestow on us daily while You have us remain in our earthly coil. Please be with the soldiers and the slaves as we pray for an end to this war soon. In Jesus' name, amen."

Dora was already reaching for the breadbasket of rolls before her papa's amen.

"Dora. You sneaky little thing, you." Lena handed her a roll and plopped helpings of other items on her plate before she filled up on bread.

"Well, boys, tell us about Concordia," Karl said.

"Stefan has been at the school since '61. He relocated from Fort Wayne when Indiana started drafting the boys out of the school," Thomas offered.

"That's right. I have in mind to become a minister. My papa pastors a church near Chicago. So many new immigrant groups are coming over without trained pastors that I could be called to minister almost anywhere once I graduate. I think God has led me to Concordia for this purpose." Stefan shoved another bite of potato salad into his cheeks and savored it in his chipmunk face a moment before swallowing.

"And you, Thomas?" Lena had finished supplying the girls' plates and began eating her own fare. "What are you studying?"

"I am not sure yet. I love literature. Reading has been a passion since you started reading *Grimms' Fairy Tales* to us on our ocean voyage to America."

"I am surprised you remember. That was so long ago. I was intrigued that you could already read at such a young age."

"Between your stories from books and Karl's stories about monsters on the steamer, I think I was hooked from boyhood to search for more tales as a reader. I have read about everything available back home."

"I remember that. Your mother was so afraid I'd traumatize you and your siblings by scaring you with that story of the Piasa bird. I left out some of the best parts." Karl shook his head at the memory.

"How is your family? Your mother's letters sound upbeat. Was Perry County everything you wished it to be?" Lena continued.

"We have a good life in Missouri. Tobias will be a great farmer. He takes after our father and loves to be outdoors in the fields and working with the animals. Stella is a little mama to the twins. They were born after we immigrated, so you never met them. They are rough-and-tumble boys. They wear our mother out, and she is happy to have Stella's help with them."

"Herr Muller, what is it that you do? Thomas was not sure," Stefan inquired.

"I work with the army down at the penitentiary. I handle legal work and documents. It turns out that very few of the Rebel prisoners can read or write, but we inform them that they can petition to be released on their oath and bond not to return to the fight. We are eager to have them do so because our facility is not designed to hold as many as we receive."

"What does that mean? You just let prisoners go when they sign a piece of paper?" Thomas placed his fork on the table and stared at Karl.

"It may sound too simple, but many of these boys never wanted to fight in the first place and were sent as a substitute for someone like a plantation owner who had enough money to pay someone else to go in their stead. Many have seen the ugly business of death up close by the time they are sent here. Such men are happy to take an oath saying they will not take up arms against the Union again. The poor Southerners do not own slaves or have plantations affected by the slave trade. These Rebels are eager to declare seriously and truthfully that they were forced to take part in the war. Since they were coerced to take part in the conflict in the first place, they want to return home to their families or resettle out west."

"If enough of these boys swear to lay down their arms, the war has got to end soon." Stefan sighed in relief.

"I'm afraid we aren't going to convince the whole Confederacy to surrender, Stefan, but I like your thinking. Another issue both sides are facing is desertion, too. Some of the enlisted commitments of two years are coming due soon. Since no one expected this to last so long, the generals are scrambling for replacements." Karl savored another bite of ham.

When most plates were wiped clean, Thomas asked, "Can we see where you work? We saw the penitentiary on the bluff as we came ashore earlier. I'd love to see more, if that is possible." He folded his napkin as if to leave that very moment.

"You aren't going anywhere just yet, young man." Lena stopped him from rising. "We baked a vanilla pound cake for dessert." On cue, Juana arrived with the golden creation in the doorway.

"You boys go ahead and enjoy your dinner. I'll take you by the prison before you catch tomorrow's ferry." Karl sliced off a sizable piece of cake for himself. "We don't eat like this every day, and I plan on getting some of this delicious dessert before you two gobble it up."

Pleased with their full plates, Thomas and Stefan dug their forks deep into their own cake.

CHAPTER 18

Though an army encamp against me, my heart shall not fear;
though war arise against me, yet I will be confident.

Psalm 27:3

*T*he morning after the fine dinner and a chance to visit with the family for an evening, Karl ushered the two college students to the door for a guided tour. "The prison was decommissioned by the state of Illinois a few years before the war broke out because they built another facility upstate: Joliet. Lincoln reopened it for captured Rebels." Karl glanced over his shoulder at the young men in tow. Thomas and Stefan kept pace down the pathway above the waterfront, listening to every word.

"The army first commandeered it for drills and training; then Missouri was looking for a place to send over thirteen thousand captives after some of the first skirmishes over there. This facility has never had more than two thousand prisoners at any one time, though."

Thomas nodded breathlessly. "I read about those early battles when I still lived at home—both at Wilson Creek and Camp Jackson. The paper said many brave Germans fought for the North. Reading about those battles in my own state made me want to join up right away. My papa said I was too young and sent me to school as a distraction. He is hoping for it to end before I became old enough to go."

Thomas felt a twinge of disappointment at not being in uniform as he stepped aside for two soldiers heading into town with rifles on their shoulders. Other soldiers leisurely cleaned guns, wrote letters, or rested in the green fields near the forested slopes outside Alton. An occasional nod greeted them from a lad in blue as they hurried past their regiment.

Once they passed the peaceful view, Karl addressed the boys again. "War is no game, Thomas. Many of the troops that cycle through here to work at the prison arrive for a much-needed break from being in the thick of battle for a time. They camp outside town, cover shifts here for a couple months, then go back to the battles. The Seventy-seventh Ohio Regiment have been manning the post these past months. Colonel Mason took command after Hildebrandt died of pneumonia."

Stefan gave Thomas a side glance and added, "But all these fellows have been doing their duty, and I fear I am not doing my part. My family sent me to school in St. Louis, so I would not be conscripted to fight in Indiana; but when I see soldiers my age taking up arms, I am sure they look at me like I am a coward." Stefan's voice fell to a near whisper, hoping the young men they passed could not overhear his admission.

"Going to school to be a minister is not being a coward, Stefan. Maybe God has a different path for you than he does for those boys in uniform." Karl clapped him on the back. "We're almost to the gate." He pointed ahead to the guarded entrance.

"I think I should be wearing the Union blue, too." Thomas nudged Stefan. "They are no older than us." The faces of the young men guarding the gates were haggard and worn, aging them beyond their years.

"Here we are, fellas." Karl nodded up at the redheaded sentinel, who recognized him immediately.

"Afternoon, Mr. Muller. I didn't know you was coming in over Easter." The rifle-toting freckled teen shifted his gun to the other shoulder waiting for Karl to answer.

"These young men came over to spend time with my family, and they wanted to visit your fine operation here. Can you let us in, and I'll show them around a bit?" Karl craned his neck and shielded his eyes from the morning sun as he peered at the young warrior. He should recognize him; but they switched duties so often, he never knew any of them well.

"I'd stay clear of the north wing near the infirmary, sir. I hear tell the boys aren't feeling the best today, and we don't want you catchin' anything." His voice remained in a high register and not the deep pitch of a seasoned man. The soldier signaled for the gate to open.

The wood planks securing the door were lifted by two ground-level guards, and the door swung ajar for the three visitors to enter. They stepped inside, and the bar slipped back into place behind them as the entrance relocked.

"Could we catch something?" Stefan's eyes searched across the open area where many men milled about for an afternoon stretch. The interred wore threadbare, filthy, ill-fitting trousers. Their shirts missed buttons and hung on thin frames. Toes extended beyond their shoes, and portions of the soles were missing. Their eyelids hung heavy from lack of sleep, and their movements were slow and mechanical.

"We had a bad bout of disease." Karl purposely did not mention smallpox, so he wouldn't make the boys nervous. "It was the worst a few months ago; but now we vaccinate every prisoner, and the cases are almost gone. Don't worry. I refuse to take that deadly disease home again."

"I did not expect Union soldiers to be jailed here, too." Thomas' eyes tracked a surly man in federal blue trousers as he pushed others from his way to cross the exercise area.

"The Feds started sending deserters and other convicts from various forces in the West. I think there are about 160 here now at last report. We try to keep them separate from the Rebels, though."

"How many do they have here?" Stefan eyed the yard and almost lost his footing as the three of them walked to the office buildings located along the wall furthest from the Mississippi.

"Right now, less than a thousand Rebs here, I think. My job is to speak to each one about signing an oath of allegiance to the United States of America, so I meet most of them. There are about 160 civilians here, too, for various crimes against the nation. We even have two women."

"Women?" Thomas and Stefan erupted in unison.

"Some of them commit crimes, too, and they must go somewhere. They are kept separate from the men, of course. Former workshops at that side of the complex are now repurposed as cells. The worst offenders are held in them. They are on the other side nearer the river." Karl pointed to a row of buildings along the wall. Other dutiful sentries with their rifles on their shoulders marched near the entrances and switched places in preordained precision.

"It is heartening to watch the military discipline here." Thomas surveyed the wary eyes staring back at him from every corner. "I don't think the prisoners like us here very much."

"Well, they do receive a few guests from time to time, but I doubt you'd want to be on display like a monkey at the zoo if you were them either."

A man who had been resting on his haunches straightened to his full six-foot height and took a bold step toward Karl's guests. "Whatcha lookin' at, boy?"

Thomas and Stefan both flinched and hurried their walk beside Karl. A watching guard motioned with his rifle for the tall man to move away from the path to the offices and permitted the three to pass safely.

Karl turned the boys to the office building. "Do you want to meet Colonel Mason if he is around? He may be spending Easter with a family in town." With rapid nods, the college students arrived at the door marked *Commander*.

Karl's knocks were not rewarded. A nearby sentry offered, "The colonel got an Easter invite by one of the families in town. Won't be back in 'til tomorrow."

Karl tipped his hat in appreciation for the information. "Well, boys? Seen enough?" They surveyed their surroundings again and nodded in unison. "All right then, let's walk you two back on the riverboat before you miss it."

"Thank you, Herr Muller. It has been an eye-opening day." Thomas and Stefan shook Karl's hand and bid farewell.

Once the paddle wheeler pulled away from shore, Thomas turned to Stefan. "I can't wait any longer. Why should those fellows sacrifice everything for our country while we sit in comfort? I must do my part. I'm joining up. You coming with me?"

"Really? We have finals in four weeks." Stefan shifted his feet and refused to look at Thomas.

"After finals, then. We can be in the middle of the action by summer."

"My folks will kill me, but I admit I felt guilty seeing those fellows no older than us fighting for their country." Stefan raised his eyebrow at Thomas. "You and I would make a terrific team." He pulled his shoulders back and declared, "I'm in, but let's not tell our families."

"I agree. My papa'll tan my hide, too, if we let on."

Stefan frowned then. "But aren't we supposed to be eighteen?"

"You heard Karl. The army is scrambling for new recruits. You think a little thing like age will stop them from signing us? Besides, I discovered a little trick to enlist without lying. I'll let you in on it after we pass all our semester tests."

Thomas spit into the palm of his hand and held it out for Stefan. "Put 'er there." They shook on it before reaching the St. Louis shore.

CHAPTER 19

The mouth of the righteous utters wisdom,
and his tongue speaks justice.

Psalm 37:30

BROOKLYN, NEW YORK

Maria awoke to the sound of musical rehearsals in the building. The high-pitched trumpet startled her awake, and she bounded out of bed to unfamiliar surroundings. Recalling the tiring day before, she remembered being escorted to her new residence above the Brooklyn Concert Hall. She now took better stock of her surroundings. A sparsely furnished room held nothing but a worn brass bed and a functional pine nightstand holding a cracked washbasin and a clean but threadbare hand towel. In the corner, a door hung open to a tall wardrobe. Her attempt to close it proved fruitless, since the latch was broken.

"It might not be fancy; but at least, my career will be starting now that I am in America." Hugging herself against the morning chill, she turned to get dressed, the sound of tuning instruments luring downstairs.

An orchestra was in the second or third movement of a Beethoven piece Maria had heard during her stay in Bremen. Helmsmuller, the music director, chastised several musicians who were struggling with the upbeat climatic tempo. Maria peered around the doorpost and listened to their attempts.

"Hi-dee, Miss Maria!" The lad who had helped her with her luggage upon her arrival appeared behind her.

"Good morning." Maria braved the English words she had practiced during her travel time overseas. Mr. Talbot tutored her nightly so she could navigate America with more ease.

"You comin' to hear Mista Douglass talk? He's speakin' right here in our own building." The lad, who wore torn trousers held by one suspender, cast his eyes down at his oversized shoes in response to Maria's full attention to his appearance. He dug his unoccupied hand deep into his pockets. His other hand held advertisements of some sort.

"Who is Mr. Douglass? Why are you so excited . . . um, pardon, I don't remember your name."

"Lewis, ma'am. Lewis Meriwether Clark. My momma thinks I should grow up to be a great explorer. Just call me Lewis." Running his hand through his close shorn hair, he rambled on, "You never hear tell of Frederick Douglass? He's likely the most famous black man who ever lived. He's even talked with President Lincoln hisself."

Waving the flyers wadded in his hand at Maria, he continued, "I'm puttin' dese posters around all over so people will come. I better scram a'fore ma ketches me lollygaggin'."

Lewis turned and breezed out the door before Maria could blink twice. She wasn't entirely sure what was going on, but Lewis' excitement about the speaker was contagious.

On the other side of Lewis' escape route stood Herr Schroeder. "My, my. I almost got run over by the help." He straightened his jacket. "What are you doing this fine morning?"

"I was listening to the orchestra rehearse until Lewis stopped to invite me to Mr. Douglass' lecture. As you can tell, he is very excited about it."

"Douglass is not our concern. Once Talbot secures you a spot on one of the upcoming concerts here, these issues will be a minor distraction for us."

"You may be right. I think I'd like to attend this Douglass' talk, though. Lewis is sure worked up about him. He says he is the most famous black man who ever lived."

"If you are going, then I guess I will chaperone you. We can't have you appearing in public unescorted. Let's find some breakfast and take a stroll around so we can see where we have landed." Taking Maria's arm, the two of them found a nearby cafe across from city hall.

Once they ate their fare of cheese and meats, they wandered the bustling streets near the historical society and Montague Hall. A gathering of women fanning themselves from the welcome spring heat stood inside the doors as they opened for late comers to arrive. Another parasol-toting woman approached the steps, aiming for the entrance when Maria stopped her with a hand to her arm. When the woman turned to face her, Maria was amazed at her smooth, dark complexion beneath the fashionable bonnet. Maria dropped her hand as she asked, "Pardon me. What meeting is that?"

The delayed woman smiled with kind chocolate eyes at her interrupter, "It's the Brooklyn's female anti-slavery activists weekly gathering, my dear. Are you interested in our cause?" The tall woman stared down into Maria's face waiting for an answer as Herr Schroeder remained dumbfounded at Maria's bold interference.

Maria tilted her head up at the woman. "I am not sure what that all means. I am new in this country and don't know about these things."

"Come along, Maria. You are keeping the woman from her friends. I apologize, madam. She is young and . . . " Schroeder shrugged and tipped his hat in apology as he tried to tug Maria along the walkway.

"She is fine, sir. She has an inquiring mind. That is the best kind. If you want to learn more, come to our meeting next week as my guest. Better yet, our group is planning to attend a lecture by Frederick Douglass at the music hall this evening. You will learn much more from his talk. I must go now. My name is Sarah Tompkins, and it is a pleasure to meet you; but I must be on my way." She finished her short journey up the stairs to her Brooklyn friends.

Maria jerked her arm out of Schroeder's grasp. "Don't pull on me. I am not a child to be led around." Stomping her foot and straightening her skirt, she continued down the pavement ahead of him.

"Wait just a minute, little miss. You are still in my charge, and I will tell you what you can do." Schroeder caught her in two strides. "If they are a group of activists, I doubt your parents would appreciate you joining them."

"They were all refined city ladies. It's not like I found a nest of hoodlums. No one in my village was dressed as fine as any of them. My mother would be proud to have me associated with such women. You are not my father."

"There are no women of that sort anywhere near your home, so how would you know what your parents would say? Your parents put you in my care, and you will heed my instruction."

"Is that right? I'm sure my parents will have your hide for taking me across the ocean without their permission if they ever meet you again. I think I know better what my parents want for me than you do."

"Nevertheless, I am the only protection you have here, and I intend to keep my promise and keep you safe as best I can. Let's head back now before you get into any trouble." Herr Schroeder nudged her further down the walkway.

"Yes. Only because I want to rest before going to see this Frederick Douglass. I want to see what all the fuss is about." With another swish of her skirts, Maria sauntered toward her temporary home ahead of her protector.

After a simple dinner from the corner market, Maria peered out her third story window at the masses gathering on the street outside. "You'd think he was a renowned entertainer performing here tonight by the size of that crowd," she said to herself. "I'd better ready myself and arrive downstairs before there are no places to sit."

Schroeder found her on the stairway and escorted her down to the mezzanine, where Talbot waited for them. Many seats were already occupied. They wove their way around the lingerers and found his secured seats toward the front. Maria leaned into Schroeder. "I didn't expect this to be a packed house. Those flyers of Lewis' must have been given out all over."

"I think this man's fame extends beyond Lewis's efforts." Schroeder answered. "I doubt they all came because of his flyers." Maria recognized some of the women from that morning's meeting when they appeared across the auditorium in their finery and sat all together.

Talbot followed Maria's gaze. "Oh, so you met some of the anti-slavery activist women, did you? Many of those ladies are married to prominent black Brooklyn abolitionists. Many host travelers on the Underground Railroad, too. Ms. Mary J. Lyons runs a boarding house for black sailors." He discreetly pointed at each woman as he informed Maria of their status. "Ms. Christiana Freeman is the director of the Colored Orphans Asylum, and Sarah Tompkins is the principal of Grammar School Number Four. I suggest you make friends with as many of them as you can, young lady. They can advance your notoriety around here because they have influence."

"Sarah is the one I spoke with today. I should have guessed she was a teacher. She has kind eyes." As Maria said her name, Sarah saw Maria and tilted her fan her way.

The murmurs faded as an announcer emerged through the curtains to introduce the much-awaited speaker. As the plump emcee stepped away, the much taller Frederick Douglass walked onto the stage to thunderous applause.

"He hasn't said anything yet, and everyone loves him." Maria shook her head in awe.

"Someday that will be you, my dear. The world will be at your feet as soon as your career is launched," Schroeder added.

The audience din silenced as they listened for the charismatic Douglass to speak at the podium. His flowing wild hair and full beard cast an exotic aura about the man as his large hands grasped the lectern before him.

"He has such a commanding presence," Talbot marveled.

"Shush. I want to listen," Maria scolded. It was difficult enough to grasp all the English flung her way without interruptions.

Douglass' booming voice filled the auditorium.

"Up to now the black man has been regarded only as the means of putting money in the white man's pocket, like a bale of cotton, but hereafter he must be regarded as a man . . . with every exulting shout of victory raised by the slaveholding rebels, I have implored the imperiled nation to unchain against her foes, her powerful black hand. Slowly and reluctantly that appeal is beginning to be heeded. Stop not now to complain that it was not heeded sooner. It may or it may not have been best that it should not.

"Action! Action! not criticism, is the plain duty of this hour. Words are now useful only as they stimulate to blows . . . There is no time to delay. The tide is at its flood that leads on to fortune. From East to West, from North to South, the sky is written all over, 'Now or never. Liberty won by white men would lose half its luster. Who would be free themselves must strike the blow. Better even die free, than to live as slaves.' This is the sentiment of every brave colored man amongst us."

Maria whispered to Schroeder, "Is he trying to motivate the black men like we encountered at the docks to fight for America, too?"

"So it seems." He stroked his chin to ponder what that might mean for their future.

"There are weak and cowardly men in all nations. We have them amongst us. They tell you this is the 'white man's war'; that you will be 'no better off after than before the war'; that the getting of you into the army is to 'sacrifice you on the first opportunity.' Believe them not; cowards themselves, they do not wish to have their cowardice shamed by your brave example.

"In good earnest then, and after the best deliberation, I now for the first time during this war feel at liberty to call and counsel you to arms. By every consideration which binds you to your enslaved fellow-countrymen, and the peace and welfare of your country; by every aspiration which you cherish for the freedom and equality of yourselves and your children; by all the ties of blood and identity which make us one with the brave black men now fighting our battles in Louisiana and in South Carolina, I urge you to fly to arms, and smite with death the power that would bury the government and your liberty in the same hopeless grave."

As Douglass finished to another round of thunderous applause and a standing ovation, Maria and Talbot were swept up in the excitement. Over the clapping Talbot yelled, "If that doesn't incite black men to join the army, I don't know what will."

Standing off to the side of the stage was a woman in a German shift beaming with familial pride. "Who do you think that is?" Maria asked.

"Should we introduce ourselves as fellow countrymen?" Schroeder urged Maria toward the woman as others retreated to the exits, babbling away in excited analysis of the Douglass speech. Schroeder stretched out his hand to the unfamiliar woman. "*Guten Abend.* We have recently arrived from Germany, and you appear to be from our homeland as well. I am Bernard Schroeder."

Her eyes trailed the speaker as he retreated backstage. The woman turned to receive Schroeder's extended arm. "*Guten Tag.* I am Ottilie Assing. I translated Douglass' autobiography into German, and I translate his extensive articles for other publications in the Fatherland."

"So you are a writer. You may be able to help promote my young protege, Maria Neubauer. She is the *Schnee Engel*—Snow Angel—in Bremen, and we have brought her talented angelic voice here to share with the world."

Looking over at the blushing Maria, Ottilie shook her head. "Sorry, Herr Schroeder, I am not that kind of promoter. Mr. Douglass speaks for a cause that cannot be denied. He is not out for selfish gain." Douglass' retreat hastened her dismissal. "I must go now. *Veil gluck* in America, *Fraulein.* I hope you find success." She turned and followed Douglass through the back door.

CHAPTER 20

You make known to me the path of life; in your presence there is
fullness of joy; at your right hand are pleasures forevermore.

Psalm 16:11

ALTON, ILLINOIS

Refreshed from Easter, Thomas and Stefan's company, and the fresh
blossoms of spring, Lena brushed off her malaise of winter depression
and renewed her faith and hope for a better future. *I must get out of the*
house and rejoin the land of the living, she thought. *I've been wallowing in my*
sorrow for too long. It is time to bring some life back into this house.

"Juana, help me dress the girls to go out today. It is too gorgeous of
a day to stay indoors. Maybe we can pay my friend Alma a visit. Our
girls have not played together for ages."

Juana gathered the girls and slipped them into fresh pinafores
before brushing their hair and pulling the top back with a ribbon.
Dora squirmed during the entire procedure, while Johanna primped
and pranced around the room to view the finished result in the
bureau mirror. A twirl and a bow and she was ready to greet the world
beyond her home again.

"Better wrap them each in a light shawl, Juana. The mornings are
still a bit brisk."

Tossing a wrap around herself, Lena reached for a girl in each hand as they ventured beyond the front door. Holding Dora tight before she ran ahead, Lena scolded, "No, Dora, you must stay with me. I can't have you running in the street where you may be hit by a wagon or trampled by a horse. You are so small that I am afraid you will not be seen in the traffic. I can't let anything happen to Mama's girls now, can I?"

Dora reluctantly fell into step with her mother and sister. Johanna skipped along, swinging her mother's hand to and fro.

A few blocks over, Lena knocked on the door of a federal blue Victorian home. Alma's maid answered it. "Hello, madam. May I help you?" She peered down at Lena's miniature escorts on either side of her.

"Yes. I am Lena Muller, a friend of Alma's. Is she in? I hate to come unannounced; but it was too beautiful of a day to stay home. I thought our girls could play. It has been a while since they have had the chance."

"One moment, ma'am." Leaving the door ajar, the austere maid turned to seek out the mistress of the house.

A few minutes later, adjusting the fashionable hat that matched her light blue suit jacket and striped skirt, Alma appeared in the doorway. "Lena! It is so wonderful you are out and about. What brings you here this fine morning?"

"Oh, I'm sorry. It looks like you are about to go out. I don't want to keep you. The girls and I thought we would stop by for a while." She took the girls' hands again.

"Don't be silly. I am glad you stopped by. I am on the way to meet with the Loyal Ladies of Alton. You should come with me."

"I have the girls . . . "

"Hettie can keep an eye on the girls while we are gone. Susannah will be thrilled to have the company. She has some new dolls her father bought when he was in Chicago. The girls can have their own tea party. Right, Hettie?"

The maid nodded, stone-faced, at her mistress. "Take . . . " Alma hesitated, trying to recall the girls' names.

"Johanna and Dora," Lena assisted.

"Yes, Johanna and Dora, up to Susannah's room while we are gone."

The girls searched their mother for approval of this plan while Hettie motioned them inside and scooted them up the stairs. Dora clung to her sister as they obeyed the stern maid's directives.

"It is kind of you to take the girls for a while. They have had only each other to play with all winter. It will be a pleasant diversion for them."

"My carriage is ready for us." Alma turned Lena toward the stable area beside the house. "We are meeting at Rebecca's today. They will all be so happy to see you."

Alma's delay of finding Lena at her door meant the other women were already assembled in Rebecca's parlor upon their arrival. "Look who I brought with me!" Alma declared as she swept into the room. "Providence brought Lena to my door this morning just in time for me to bring her to our monthly Loyal Ladies of Alton meeting. So here we are!" Her flamboyant entrance shifted every eye to her and then, by extension, to Lena.

"Oh, Lena. It is so wonderful you could join us." Rebecca rose to offer a gentle hug.

"We were so sorry to hear about your babies." The others turned to scowl at Sally for mentioning Lena's tragedy.

"Never mind her." Nell stood to offer Lena a prime chair in the room. "We are happy you could come. We have many plans in the works that you can help us with."

"Yes. Let's call this meeting to order." Alma took charge. "This meeting of the Loyal Ladies of Alton is now in session. Nell, do you have a report on any old business?"

The soft-spoken woman rattled the notes in her hands and read. "We received a gracious thank you from the Seventy-seventh Ohio Volunteers for the extra bedrolls we supplied during that cold weather snap, as well as the few hygiene items the boys needed. It has also been reported that a few shylocks in the area have been raising the price of milk for the soldiers, charging them ten cents when the going price is only six cents a quart."

A flutter of disgusted headshakes peppered the room as Nell concluded her report.

"We must stop them from taking advantage of our boys," Sally interjected.

"I'm afraid we cannot do much about those who trade with the army. We can only do our best to help the soldiers in our own way," Alma answered.

"We might not be able to stop others from extorting our soldiers, but we can show our patriotism by providing a picnic for the entire regiment. That will give the volunteers a chance to meet the supportive citizens of Alton and demonstrate the true kindness found here in our town. We can show our esteem and respect for their sacrifice in saving the Union." Rebecca paused as the details of her idea evolved in her mind.

"I think that is a wonderful idea. Karl says the soldiers need more distractions when they are not on duty. I am sure they will love the idea." Lena happily joined the conversation of like-minded women.

"With the weather getting warmer, this is the perfect time for a thank you picnic," said Alma. The women began to make lists for supplies of food and workers. Lena volunteered to have Karl extend the invitation to the troops, and she offered to make a healthy supply of her potato dumplings for the event.

After the meeting, Lena gathered the children from Alma's, and they returned home singing a familiar song from the Easter service, "Christ the Lord is Risen Today." The girls joined in with every "Alleluia," and they laughed all the way home.

Thank You, Lord, for the joy of this spring day and reconnecting with friends to help bring me back to life.

Karl pushed the door open to two energetic girls jumping into his arms. "Papa! Papa! Know what we did today?"

"Slow down. You almost knocked me over. What are you two all excited about?" He set both girls down as they dragged him to the settee.

Lena smiled in their direction from the stove.

"We got to stay at Susannah's house," Johanna informed him. "She has four new dolls, and we had a tea party. It was very grown up." She straightened herself, folded her hands in her lap and crossed her legs at the ankle.

"My, my, you are growing up to be a genteel lady indeed."

Dora climbed onto his knee with no regard to lady-like manners whatsoever. Karl squeezed her against him, then pulled Johanna up, too.

Lena relished the exchange between father and daughters and her heart melted at her good fortune to be blessed with a loving family. Karl met her eyes and smiled wider. "Sounds like you gals went visiting today."

"We did. I thought it was time to get out of the house, so we walked to Alma's. Turned out it was their monthly meeting day for the Loyal Ladies of Alton. She took me along while the girls played with her Savannah. We had a full day."

"Oh? What are they planning now? The regiment has been quite pleased with all their efforts. The colonel sings their praises often."

"We are planning a picnic for all of them. We want the whole town to be involved so they realize how much we appreciate them."

"The whole regiment? You don't do anything halfway, do you?"

"We can do it. I told them you would ask Colonel Mason about arranging it with him. Is that all right?"

"Absolutely. I am so happy you are getting involved again, dear." He scooted the girls off his lap and rose to embrace his wife. "I think this is just the activity you need. By the way, I almost forgot, I have a letter from your sister for you."

"Maria?" Lena snatched the precious paper from his hand as he pulled it from his jacket pocket, and she began to read.

"Dear Lena,

I am sure Mama already told you I have ventured to America. We landed in New York a couple weeks ago. I live above the Brooklyn Concert Hall, where I hope to be headlining soon. So far, the hall has hosted a famous black man, Frederick Douglass, and there has been a local orchestra performing. My benefactors, Herr Schroeder and Mr. Talbot, are making plans for my career here. The whole prospect is exciting, and I hope you will be able to come when I am famous.

I also met some women who are anti-slavery activists in Brooklyn. Mr. Talbot says I would be fortunate to be associated with their group, since it will open doors to more opportunities for me in

Brooklyn. I am fascinated with these black ladies in such high society finery. After listening to Mr. Douglass the other night, I feel they have a just cause to rally around. It is so different from back home in Germany, but I guess I do not need to tell you that.

Do not worry about me. I wish to be with you. However, I learned how vast this country is when I asked how long it would take to go to you. I was told it would take more than a week if all conditions were fair. I was also informed that the way to Illinois is not safe during the war right now. So I guess that means we will not be together for a while.

Give Herman a hug for me when you see him.

Your loving sister,

Maria"

"It makes me anxious that she is in a city all alone, but it sounds like she has reliable people looking after her. I wish we could bring her here soon." Lena laid the post on the table. "When do you think we will be able to see her, Karl?"

"Like she said, travel is not safe while the war is raging. We may not be able to meet her until it is all over."

"I've been praying for it to end every day."

"I know. Don't give up. Prayers are likely the most effective tool we have in this conflict, Lena. Keep praying."

"The Lord knows that He is my fortress and strength when things are beyond my control. I will put my trust in Him for Maria's safety, too."

CHAPTER 21

Fight the good fight of the faith. Take hold of the eternal life
to which you were called and about which you made the good
confession in the presence of many witnesses.

1 Timothy 6:12

St. Louis, Missouri

"I promise to spend some time with you and the fellows if you come with me to buy the weekly newspaper for the latest news."

Standing behind Thomas, Stefan sighed loudly at his remark. Thomas' weekly ritual of reading field reports held no appeal for Stefan. The newsstand journal's recounted numbers of deaths depressed him. He feared loved ones may be in harm's way while he stayed safely away at school. Reading the accounts only reinforced his guilt of cowardice for staying in St. Louis.

As the two rounded the street corner a block from the school, marching Union soldiers chanted a song unfamiliar to Thomas and Stefan. In their familiar dialect, the words took root as they strutted in formation, rifles on shoulders. The chorus resounded after each verse.

Yaw! Das is drue, I speak mit you, I'm going to fight mit Sigel.

I gets ein big rifle guns,

Un puts him to mine shoulder,

Den march so bold, like a big jack-horse,

Un may been someding bolder;

I goes off mit de volunteers,

To save de Yankee Eagle;

To give em Rebel vellers fits,

I'm going to fight with Sigel.

The syncopated *boom-chick-boom-chick* rhythm and masculine voices drew citizens from nearby shops and offices to view the impromptu parade on their street until there was no space left on the walkways. Children peeked around their mother's skirts, and men paused their business transactions to take in the scene. Like a magnet, the citizens were drawn to the commotion; and many fell into step behind them. No one wanted to miss whatever this spectacle preempted.

"Come on, Stefan. Let's follow them." Thomas dashed into the crowd before Stefan could protest and he was swallowed up in the sea of people making their way down the street.

Stefan joined Thomas as he hesitated in front of a platform where a general stood at attention as the masses gathered to hear him. "Is that Seigel? The one from the song?" Being taller than most, Stefan had the best view of the men organizing to welcome the people congregating at the park entrance.

"I think so. I've read about him in the papers. President Lincoln promoted him because of his fighting experience in Germany before coming here. He oversaw the St. Louis school system before the war. He is well known around here."

The general waited for everyone's attention. His coiffured mustache traced around his upper lip until it brushed the stately goatee below. His dark unruly hair tucked behind his ears could use a trim, but his hat kept it in place. He stood with one hand on his saber, poised from his belt to fresh polished boots, somehow untouched by the spring mud. His long coat, pressed and belted, relegated the same care as the unblemished boots. He peered out across the curious crowd while the soldiers assembled behind him.

"Ladies and gentlemen, it is not news to you that this great war for the preservation of the Union has gone on far longer than any expected or hoped. However, our fine young men have been courageous; and you should be proud of the bravery your sons, husband, and fathers have demonstrated for this glorious country.

"Many of you, like me, came to this country for the freedom to live your lives as you see fit. You have invested mightily in this new land, and we do not want it to be destroyed by Southerners who want to divide it. That is why I am here today: to ask for all the able-bodied men before me to pledge their oath of allegiance to the United States of America and join me in defending it like these dedicated young men behind me." Seigel's hand swept back toward the soldiers behind him on stage. "Are you with me?"

Cheers of "We are!" and "We're with you!" erupted from the street followed by another chorus of "Mit Sigel."

Yaw! Das is drue. I speak mit you. I'm going to fight mit Sigel.

Over the cheers, Seigel pointed to a table near the stage. "Colonel Williams will sign you boys up, and we will win this war!" The listener's eyes followed to the indicated table where a soldier of lesser rank sat flanked by sentinels. "Right over here, boys. Your country needs you!"

Several young men sidled over to the recruitment table. Colonel Williams handed the first barefoot teen a pen to make his mark at the bottom of his paper form. "Sign here, boy. If you can't write, make your mark and give us your name for our records." The first lad in line snatched the pen, dipped it in the inkwell, and scribbled indecipherable letters on the form.

"Come on, Stefan. This is our chance to finally be part of this glorious fight." Thomas tugged Stefan's sleeve.

"But, Thomas, we have finals to finish. We can't go yet." Stefan held Thomas back before he was out of his reach again. Instead, he was only pulled along in Thomas' fervor to reach the line for enlistment.

"I'm sure they won't ship you off this minute. We can enlist now and go in another week when our tests are out of the way." Thomas and Stefan now stood in front of the table. "We want to enlist, sir." Thomas stepped up to present himself to the attendant.

"You boys over eighteen?" A mustached sentry stepped forward to address the new recruits ahead of them.

Thomas caught Stefan's eye and turned away from the sergeant.

Bending to tear off a corner of his purchased newspaper, Thomas scribbled "18" on it and slipped it in his shoe. Writing the same number on a second scrap of paper, he held it out for Stefan to do the same. Under his breath, he told Stefan, "There. Now we're not lying." A bit puzzled but obedient, Stefan slipped his note in his shoe as instructed.

The waiting sergeant pretended not to observe their antics as he waited for them to return their attention to him. "Well, boys?"

"We are definitely over eighteen, sir." Thomas beamed.

Now understanding his ploy, Stefan nodded and added, "That's right, we are over eighteen." Happy he did not technically lie to the recruiter; he followed Thomas' lead. If he ever did become a pastor, this is one sin he did not want on his conscience.

"We need to finish our finals at the Concordia school, sir," Stefan interjected." We can report to duty in another week if that is okay."

*T*homas shook his head at Stefan's adherence to schooling before his patriotic duty to his country but knew he was right. He understood they could not throw a whole semester of study and cost away when only a week's delay would not make a difference in their commitment to Lincoln. "He is right, sir. Tell us where to report in a week, and we are all yours."

"All right, boys. We need to refill the German regiment after that run-in at Chancellorsville. See us at the barracks as soon as those exams are out of the way. We'll be glad to have you."

Thomas puffed out his chest and walked straighter as he strutted back to the dormitory. Stefan kept pace with less of an exuberant bounce. "I hope we're doing the right thing?"

"Are you kidding? Of course we are. You heard General Seigel. They need more loyal Germans fighting to keep this country together. I think we have waited long enough."

"My folks sent me here to keep me out of the war, and I just enlisted to fight. They are going to tan my hide when they find out," Stefan groaned.

"Don't worry, Stefan. By the time they discover you are a soldier, we will have won the war; and you can return home a hero."

"I was sent here to become a pastor, not a warrior, Thomas. How did I let you talk me into this?" Stefan shook his head.

"You don't think they will need your prayers out there on the battlefield? Many of God's people in the Bible were both godly and strong warriors. They sang about David slaying his thousands and tens of thousands, and he was a man after God's own heart."

Stefan tilted his head in consideration of Thomas' logic.

Thomas clapped his shoulder. "Cheer up. Your family will understand."

"Let's study for those exams, so I can leave school with a clear conscience then." Stefan punched Thomas in the arm and sprinted toward the school grounds.

"Hey. Hold up! Your legs are twice as long as mine."

Both students disappeared into their academic stronghold with no thought of seeking their friends for some fun.

"Name?" The terse sergeant at the writing desk, pen in hand, searched for the next enlistee's name. He didn't even make eye contact with Thomas, who hopped up and down with anticipation.

"Thomas Krueger, sir." He smiled brightly.

"Here you are. Present yourself to Colonel Hecker. You boys will join the Eighty-second Illinois brigade."

"But, sir, we joined to fight under General Seigel."

"Seigel was called back to Washington. You will be under General Howard now. All Seigel's men are now under his command."

"Howard?" Another enlistee in line scoffed. "You mean we are fighting for Old Prayer Book?"

"You mean, he is a man of God? Maybe this is God's way of putting me where He wants me." Stefan's relief was obvious as he listened to the boy in line with them.

"Oh, he's religious, all right. He is a Bible-thumping abolitionist who lost at Chancellorsville. He better not get us all killed; that's all I'm hoping," the recruit behind them protested.

"There will be no talk like that about your superior officers in this army, soldier. Your job is to obey orders. That's all." The sergeant lifted his eyes to stare the new recruit down. "You don't want to be court-martialed for treason, do you?"

The berated young man stepped back in line without another word.

Stefan turned to Thomas. "I am glad we are going to be fighting under a man of God. This must be a sign that we are doing the right thing for a just cause."

"I was so hoping to fight under Seigel like we were led to believe a week ago." Thomas shrugged. "Oh, well. I guess it doesn't matter. This is still a German regiment, and God should be with us wherever we go." He turned back to the sergeant. "Where are you sending us?"

"You guys are lucky. We are heading north to Pennsylvania. Not down south in the thick of things like Vicksburg." The sergeant pointed to a map lying on the desk. "I'm happy because I have family in Gettysburg."

CHAPTER 22

The prudent sees danger and hides himself,
but the simple go on and suffer for it.

Proverbs 22:3

New York

"Maria, so happy you joined us today." Sarah escorted Maria into the Montague Hall and introduced her to several of the others gathered for the anti-slavery league weekly meeting. "We are assembling a four-day fair to raise funds for the Manhattan Colored Orphan Asylum," Sarah continued. "My friend Christiana Freeman here is the director, and the home needs so many things for those poor children. Would you like to help?"

Maria shifted in her chair. "I don't really have any skills for that sort of thing; but if you need someone to sing a bit, I'd love to lend my voice if Herr Schroeder will allow me."

"That is a marvelous idea. Others can sell their wares and provide games while you can draw people in with your lovely voice. I don't see why your Mr. Schroeder would object to that. Now, ladies, let us get organized. Those children need our help."

Sarah returned to her group, where she began directing tasks for committees. The studious assembly applied themselves to every detail of a four-day undertaking with such precision, Maria was in awe.

"All they want me to do is sing." Maria clasped her hands in front of Herr Schroeder to emphasize her point. "Isn't that what you brought me here for?"

"Maria, we cannot make a living if you sing in the streets. Who is going to pay us?" Schroeder turned his empty hands up for emphasis.

"Remember, Mr. Talbot said it would be a great idea if I got to know these ladies better. What better way than to help them raise money for orphans? Not only that, but this will also be a chance for people to be introduced to me and my voice. Right now, no one will pay for someone they have never heard of. Call it free publicity."

"I'm not sure this is a good idea, but I'll run it by Talbot for his opinion." Schroeder sighed and caught the pout on Maria's face. "Let's find some dinner, I'm starving." He draped his arm over her shoulder with an overlong squeeze and pointed her toward the door. Schroeder bent close to her ear and whispered, "You know how to get your way with me, don't you, you little minx?"

An unwanted shiver raced across Maria's neck and down her spine. Herr Schroeder had never embraced her with such intimacy before, and she recoiled from the advance. Stepping away, she distanced herself and added with indifferent bravado, "I'm sure Talbot will think this is an excellent idea. I will go practice, so I am ready."

She stepped away from Schroeder and placed her hand on the doorknob of an unoccupied rehearsal room, flipping her hair over her shoulder in a final act of dismissal.

"You do that. I'm going down to the Turnerverien Hall to stretch my muscles and visit with a few countrymen I've met there." Schroeder looked back as he departed. "Stay out of trouble while I'm gone."

The colorful streamers decorated the street, bringing life to the dull stone buildings. At one end, an arcade of games beckoned those who strutted their prowess of skill over chance.

"Can you toss the ball into a peach basket? Can you ring the bell by hitting the plate with a mallet? Can you knock over the stacked pins with only one throw of the small ball?" The hawkers called to players to try their skill at each station. A small fee was charged at each booth, and lines began to form as each patron challenged another to surpass their attempts at greatness.

Booths of food dotted the street, as well. Sweet scents of sugary confections, baked goods, and preserves encouraged women to swap recipes while the men sampled the wares. As the adults visited, the children were swatted away from free sampling until someone relented and bought them a sought-after treat. Fresh fruit had been brought in from outlying farms; so there was also an abundance of watermelon, peaches, and cherries that smeared across the faces of ravenous youngsters in attendance.

Other vendors sold handcrafted items. Smooth sanded wooden utensils and cutting boards graced one tent. Another held crocheted shawls, blankets, and layette items. A third boasted scrap quilts of all sizes and colors. A fourth displayed metal works such as knives and spoons for the kitchen. Any handcrafted item was available—if not from one vendor, then from another. Each seller promised that a portion of all their sales would be given to the orphanage.

A few festive folks in elaborate costumes juggled fruit or rings as they wound their way through the crowds. The Brooklyn anti-slavery committee had thought of everything to make this an enjoyable event for everyone. Laughter abounded.

Led to a small stage in the center of all the excitement, Maria braced herself to sing over the neighborhood festivities. Without instrumental accompaniment, the merriment below proved an obstacle for a typical concert. With nods from Talbot and Schroeder and a deep breath, Maria began soft and slow, trying to crescendo to a song people would turn toward. However, no heads raised her way; and although she projected her voice to the milling throngs, they were too engaged in their own festival activities to acknowledge her meager attempts to entertain. By the end of her second aria, someone from the crowd yelled to her, "Miss, let's hear something a bit more rip-roarin'. Ya know any camp songs?"

Camp songs? What was a camp song? Maria zeroed in on Talbot and Schroeder to the side of the platform and shrugged. She mouthed, "What do they want?"

"Maybe a marching song or something with a little *oom-pa-pa-pa*," Talbot answered. "This isn't the setting for an aria."

Maria's limited experience with anything beyond church hymns or classical pieces left her at a loss for something that would fit the day. Then she remembered hearing a popular tune sung around the city, "The Battle Hymn of the Republic." With the opening lines, the audience turned and began to sing along. Soon, many took part in a robust singalong. More suggestions for tunes that were not sung in Germany baffled her. Requests for songs such as "Liberty and Lincoln" and "The Battle Cry of Freedom" were shouted out from the crowd.

When she shook her head, the festival-goers proceeded to teach her the new music as everyone joined in the songfest.

Sarah and the other members of the anti-slavery league beamed at Maria's contribution. They applauded with extra fervor as she led another encore of a fan favorite. When patrons ventured away from the songstress to pursue other distractions, they left humming or singing to themselves; and it kept the joyful spirit of the event alive. Maria, flushed from singing loud and long, exited the stage with a bound and a twirl that unintentionally spun her into Herr Schroeder's arms.

He held her close for a moment before releasing her as she backed away and asked, "I'd like to see more, please. That lemonade stand is calling my name."

Schroeder bought her the refreshing drink as he praised her Brooklyn debut. "You are a marvel, dear. Everyone will want to attend a concert of yours after that rousing sing-along. You had everyone here humming along."

Although delighted with the compliments, Maria felt uneasy at Schroeder's growing flattery. Is this what fame does? Bring unwanted advances from men? He was supposed to be her protector, but she wondered who would protect her from him if he imposed advances he never would consider if his wife were around?

Maria turned to Talbot for the answer to the uncomfortable attention Herr Schroeder exhibited, but Talbot was focused on some men who were not enjoying the revelry of the fair. Most attending the festivities enjoyed their time away from their labors to support the needs of the community. However, along the periphery of the activity stood Irish and Italian immigrants watching the festivities with hands on hips and disgruntled headshaking. Their faces leaned together in secret murmured plans that did not waft across to uninvited ears.

Talbot's gaze was not lost on a few happy fairgoers who also saw the menace gathering down the street. "I think it is time to go." He took Maria's elbow and guided her toward their secure lodgings.

"Why?" She tried to pull away from his grasp. "There is so much here I haven't seen." Oblivious to the danger, Maria took another sip of her refreshment and turned to another booth.

"I told you before about the animosity between some of the new arrivals and the blacks here in the city. We do not want to be in the midst of any trouble if it breaks out. There are some rough men watching who may have evil designs. I think it is best we leave."

Maria searched for the threatening Irishmen dressed similarly to those on the Atlantic voyage. They congregated on a street corner, and more of them were arriving. Recognizing them as the menace Talbot described, she allowed him to steer her away from the danger as he suggested. "Do you think they plan to hurt them?"

"Right now, I think the size of the crowd may be keeping them at bay; but I do think they mean to cause trouble, and I don't want us to be anywhere near it."

"I am glad you are here to help advise us in these matters, Talbot." Schroeder kept pace with the hurried retreat.

"I hope they don't hurt anyone." Maria said a little prayer as her benefactors escorted her back to safer lodgings.

CHAPTER 23

I, Paul, write this greeting with my own hand. This is the sign of genuineness in every letter of mine; it is the way I write.

2 Thessalonians 3:17

ALTON, ILLINOIS

Lena scooted Dora off her lap as she heard Karl enter the house. She handed the picture book to Johanna in case she wanted to continue the familiar story with her little sister. Although not old enough to read yet, the pictures prompted an accurate retelling of the Mother Goose tales. Tom Thumb was their favorite because the girls felt so huge compared to the miniature man.

"I'm sorry, time got away from me as I was reading to the girls." Lena straightened her skirt as she rose; but before she could step into the kitchen, Karl caught her around the waist and drew her close.

After a quick kiss, he withdrew two posts from his jacket pocket. "This is a banner day for letters, my dear. You have two addressed to you today." He placed them in her hand. Lena turned the letters over to find postscripts from both Thomas and Maria.

"Where do I begin?" She traced her fingers over the envelopes, turning them side to side.

"Thomas' is likely a thank you for Easter and how finals went. Why don't you see how your sister is faring in New York first and if she has figured out a way to come to us yet?"

"Good idea." Lena slipped her finger under the seal of her sister's letter to discover its contents. She unfolded the two sheets of stationery and read silently before Karl interrupted.

"Ahem. You might want to read it aloud. I'd like to learn what's in there." His mischievous smile warmed her as she glanced up from the page.

The girls remained occupied with their retelling of the storybook, so she nodded. "I suppose. If she reports grown-up things, I may need to summarize if the girls are listening."

"If it is grown-up information, they will not understand anyway, Lena." Karl shook his head. "Never mind, I'll read it when you are finished." Distracted by the aroma of bread from the kitchen, he added, "Ah, Juana has started dinner. I'll wash up the girls while you read in peace, and you can fill me in later." Scooping up a daughter in each arm to delighted squeals, he carried them to the wash basin and splashed each of them with some playful water.

"Papa!" They protested and attempted to splash him back, but he jumped away before a drop hit him.

"Don't make a mess! Juana just mopped that area." Lena scolded them without looking up from her letter.

Karl shushed the girls with a finger to his lips while they giggled back at him.

"It says that Maria sang at a neighborhood fair in New York. By the way she tells it, the families who attended had a wonderful time. It's nice they can have a celebration like that even in time of war. With so many soldiers around here, we are reminded that we are in the middle of a formidable turmoil all the time."

"Has she had a chance to perform at the concert hall yet?" Karl asked.

"She doesn't say. She does say she saw the famous former slave and abolitionist Fredrick Douglass speak. It sounds like she was taken by his message."

"Fredrick Douglass? I would like to hear him myself. I understand he has the ear of President Lincoln."

"She says he was rallying the black men to join the Union forces and fight against the Rebels. Many must have done so because black regiments are forming in New York and Massachusetts."

Karl moved in close behind Lena to read over her shoulder. "Your sister relays more newsworthy information than I get most weeks from the *Alton Telegraph*. To be back east where so much is happening must be quite exciting. I wonder if she realizes how fortunate she is."

"I think she'd be more fortunate to be around her family. With Herman and I out here, I think we should try to transport her to her family as soon as it is safe to do so." She laid the pages on the table. "I will need to tell Herman of her writing, too. He never was much for writing, and I doubt Maria wrote him with the same details."

"Are you going to open the letter from Thomas?" Karl slid the second envelope closer to Lena. "Our young scholar may have more news for us, too."

"I thought I might wait until we completed dinner; but you are anxious for me to open it, and Juana can keep things warm for us." Breaking the seal, Lena slid the letter from its concealment. After reading only the first few words, she gasped. "Oh my!"

"What?" Karl stepped behind her to read over her shoulder again.

"Thomas and Stefan joined up."

"Joined up? Don't they need to finish school?" Puzzled, Karl resisted the urge to take the pages from Lena so he could read it better for himself.

"It says they waited until they took their final exams and headed to the enlistment officer the next day." Lena glanced away from the page to Karl. "Thomas' parents are not going to be happy about this, and Stefan's parents sent him to St. Louis to keep him out of the war. What were they thinking?"

"Some of that may be my fault. They were impressed with the young soldiers guarding the prison when I took them for a visit. Of course, those fellows were not in the middle of combat. Strutting around with a rifle on your shoulder is not a true example of what they will encounter. I am sure they have no idea what war is really like, but they are sure going to find out now." Karl shook his head. "Does it say any more?"

"They are with a German regiment, but he is disappointed that the general they thought they would be serving under is no longer the commander of their troop." Lena sighed and looked back up at Karl. "I just want him to be safe."

Karl wrapped his arm around Lena's waist and hugged her while she tried to continue. "At least, it doesn't look like they are heading to Vicksburg," he commented as he read over her shoulder. "The boys have been taking a beating trying to open trade along the Mississippi to the gulf."

"I'll never forget my first trip up the Mississippi from New Orleans. God kept placing you as my rescuer whenever I needed you.

I was so naive. I had no idea what to expect when I arrived from Germany. I guess God knew to send you to me." Lena peered into Karl's blue-gray eyes adoringly searching for her own. "I am so glad He did." She leaned in for a warm kiss from her husband. "Things are sure different now."

"Mommy!" Johanna interrupted the moment as she tugged her mother's skirt. "I thought we were gonna eat. Papa already washed us."

Lena laughed. "He washed you, huh? Like Juana helps with the laundry? Should we hang you out to dry, too?"

Karl snatched her from the floor and acted as if she were a bundle of linen to be taken to the clothesline while Dora tried to snatch her sister from the clutches of their father.

"Papa! Papa! Stop!" she squealed, and he returned her to the floor and patted her bottom toward the kitchen table.

"You are right. It's time to eat. Sit down, girls, while Mama gets the dishes on the table so we can say grace."

The Muller family bowed their heads over the steaming bowls.

Karl prayed. "Lord, we commit all our loved ones to Your care. Watch over young Maria in New York, where she is so far away from family. Help those who are trusted to guide her and protect her. Place people in her path to assist her in God-pleasing ways. Lord, watch over Thomas and Stefan and all the soldiers in this War Between the States. So many have lost their lives already. Spare these young men, so they can serve You. You know they have a heart for You, Lord, and Stefan is training to be a minister of Your Word. Protect them and keep them safe. Lord, also be with Juana's boy, Jubal. Help her to find him and reunite them if it is Your will. Bless our family. Help us to grow more in Your grace every day. In Jesus' name. Amen."

Lena looked up from the prayer to see Juana listening at the doorway, a faint smile on her face at Karl's prayer. Karl had sent inquiries about her son weeks ago but had not received any word about his whereabouts. With all the chaos of war, it was unlikely to receive word back about Juana's son. Too many families searched for loved ones on battlefields when news of mass casualties reached home to no avail. Often, soldiers carried no identification, or disfigured bodies fell beyond recognition. Wartime scavengers scoured the slain and stole anything of value that held clues to their identity. Graves of unknown soldiers dotted the landscape.

CHAPTER 24

Share in suffering as a good soldier of Christ Jesus.

2 Timothy 2:3

GETTYSBURG, PENNSYLVANIA

At revelry, Stefan yawned and stretched from his bedroll to nudge Thomas awake. "I didn't know there'd be so much marching in the army. All we've been doing for days now is marching." He uncoiled his long legs in front of him and gathered his gear as Thomas and the other men imitated his actions.

"Yeah. Not quite what I thought either. We haven't seen a Reb since we left St. Louis. Not sure how we can win a war this way." Thomas threw his pack on his back and fell into formation for another day's march.

"Double time today, boys. We have orders to defend a small town up ahead, 'cause the Rebs are on their way." The sergeant repeated his message up and down the line. His commanders were not going to be blamed for his German boys not being ready. General Howard blamed them for losing Chancellorsville, and it was time to show the newspapers that these boys were not cowards or deserving of the title, "The Flying Dutchmen."

"Hear that, Stefan? Sounds like we may be in this, war after all." The Eleventh Corp stepped up the pace and swept Thomas and Stefan along with them.

By 11:30, the Union troops arrived at the small town where roads converged from every direction like spokes in a wheel. The outlying farms dotted the surrounding hills. A seminary with a church and tall brick buildings stood on the hillside to the west of town. The shops and residences of clapboard facades were tidy and well maintained, but the town stood as no more significant than any other they had seen.

The morning robins darted around the serene countryside after fat worms as the July heat of the day grew. No sign of war anywhere.

"I don't see any Rebs around here. Do you?" Stefan whispered as they were ordered to take up defensive positions north of the settlement.

"No, but look. Howard is scouting the area from that dry goods store yonder."

Stefan turned in the direction of Thomas' finger. The one-armed general peered through an upper tower window with a spyglass.

"If they are out there, he will find them."

At that moment, gunfire rang out from the west. The shooting escalated as they held their ground and listened to the battle raging outside their view. "Shouldn't we join in and help?" Stefan offered.

"We follow orders." Thomas gripped his gun tighter with eyes peeled for the enemy.

Whispers down the line reported, "General Reynolds is dead."

"They killed a general?" Stefan's blood drained from his face. "I didn't expect they'd kill a general."

"I'm sure we will be fine if we just do what we are told. Don't worry. We'll watch out for each other." Thomas' conviction soothed Stefan.

Stefan nodded as the day became eerily quiet. The afternoon heat built as they lay in wait for something to happen. Every twitch or repositioning caused men to jump in anticipation of an attack.

Gray coats finally charged the line with a Rebel yell, splitting the silence.

"Shoot, Stefan. Shoot!" Thomas ordered.

"It's so hot, I can't grip my gun." Stefan shot his rifle and reloaded his weapon as fast as his scorched hands would allow. Men from both sides were falling all around him.

"Stefan. We've got to go. Retreat!" Thomas yanked his friend's shirt to follow his lead.

※

The echo of retreat bounced throughout the regiment; and the Yanks fled into the town of Gettysburg, scattering hither and yon. Dashing through alleys, behind stores and residences, they tried to shelter from the onslaught of Rebel bullets pursuing them. All the while, Colonel Von Gilsa swore at them in German to rally and fight but to no avail. The bullets were as thick as hail, and men were falling by the scores. No one paid attention to the angry colonel's shouts.

"This way, Stefan. Over here!" Thomas yelled over the din of the melee. He spotted a woodpile next to a modest homestead and leaped behind it for cover. As he turned to be sure Stefan followed his lead, Stefan fell face down in the street, which was already scattered with wounded or dead soldiers. "Stefan! No!"

As Thomas jumped up from his hiding place, another blue coat grabbed his sleeve to yank him back out of sight. "Get down, man. Don't call them Rebs over here." Pointing up the hill, his comrade continued, "Head to the top of the hill. We have guns up there."

"But my friend—"

"Leave him. You can't do anything for him now." The two scrambled up the hill to a waiting cemetery, where disheveled fighters crouched between the tombstones. Thomas had fired his first shots only an hour before; and now Stefan was gone, and Thomas hid among the dead.

Is this an omen, Lord? Did I make this decision without Your blessing? Did I drag my friend into harm's way when he was reluctant to come all along? Oh, Lord, what have I done?

He buried his head in his hands and slumped against one of the stone sentinel markers dotting the hill. "I'm not much of a soldier, running back through the same streets we entered whipped and beaten. I think General Howard may have had every right to call us The Flying Dutchmen after all," he mumbled to himself.

"Buck up, man. The fight's not over." Thomas' running companion nudged him out of his stupor. "We can't let the Rebels rattle us. Howard's superiors must have a plan for us. We have a bunch of canons perched up here. Get some rest; you've got to be ready for the morrow."

The men wrapped their cloaks around themselves as they huddled among the gravestones. The eerie sound of breathing men and tramping horses hovered over the underground dead as night fell. Sleep was beyond Thomas, who stayed awake thinking of Stefan.

At daybreak, a Union band played "John Brown's Body" in the distance. The troops rallied to the inspiring sound of reinforcements marching in from the south. The rested men stirred to a quick breakfast and set their watchful eyes looking for more trouble to come as they were ordered to hold their ground and not let the Rebels take Cemetery Hill.

Gunshots from other regiments engaged in the fight rang out across the way. The Cemetery Hill vantage point revealed how the serene pastoral farmland from the day before now was littered with canons and mangled bodies.

By the afternoon, Cemetery Hill was in a full artillery crossfire. The boom of artillery roared with screeches and hisses of shells tearing through the air overhead only to burst into the upended grounds striking whomever else lay in their paths. The sharp crack of musket fire and the sulfurous haze of smoke cast an otherworldly tint to the battle. Dante's seventh level of violent hell painted a no more sinister picture. No wonder he lamented, "All hope abandon, ye who enter here."

The firing ceased once it was too dark to see. The townspeople cowered in their homes for fear of being shot by either side. Rebels looted the vacated houses and helped themselves to unwelcome hospitality. The sharpshooters on the hill tried to pick off the Southerners when they ventured into the street. One such volley hit the mounted Rebel General Ewell in his wooden leg; he promptly replaced it and continued to command.

The shaky regiment held their post guarding the moonlit hill marking the Gettysburg battleground. The silence was broken by an occasional crack of a picket's rifle or the moans and cries of the injured left in no man's land between the lines. Bobbing lanterns searched the fields for casualties by mutual unspoken agreement to collect the wounded and returned them to the field hospitals, where amputated piles of arms and legs grew.

The second morning commenced with more fighting near Culp's Hill, and those guarding Cemetery Hill would be next if the Rebels broke through those defenses. Listening to the terrific canon blasts and gunfire while huddling among the gravestones unnerved the tattered Eleventh. Scarcely a leaf or limb was left on any surrounding tree as they suffered as much as the men who fell beneath them.

When the haze cleared on the slopes in front of the Yankee lines, the ground was empty of any advancing regiments. Only the dead and wounded lay in the aftermath of the morning rout. By eleven o'clock, Culp's Hill fell silent until a Union brigade broke it with three rousing cheers. Lee had not reached Cemetery Hill, but a bloody horror replaced the previous days of peaceful summer.

As predicted, the heavens rent asunder again with shot and shell, fire and smoke. Thomas thought he was safe hovering near the security of the canons; but the Rebels had recalculated the range and elevation from earlier bombardments, sending guns, men, horses, and ammunition chests flying with their barrage. The remaining cannons fired back with similar accuracy to beat down the assault. Scrambling to reorganize on the hill, an ocean of men advanced across the battle-scarred field toward Thomas and his bluecoats. "They're coming, boys!" echoed down the line, as if anyone could be blind to the oncoming danger.

The crash of guns and the exploding shells deafened the men as the roar became its own language of destruction. Onward they came. The constant volley of mini balls did not hold them in check, and they kept coming.

Face to face with a young freckle-faced gray coat with a gun, Thomas thrust his bayonet into the lad before a searing pain ripped through him and all went dark.

CHAPTER 25

May he defend the cause of the poor of the people,
give deliverance to the children of the needy, and crush the oppressor!

Psalm 72:4

NEW YORK

Talbot shook open the paper he had bought from an aggressive newsboy waving them about in the street. "Look at these headlines. 'Great Victory in Pennsylvania. Lee's Army Cut Up and Skeddadled!' The North will have this war won faster than a minnow can slip a dipper." He turned the page, pleased with his announcement.

"Pennsylvania? Is that far from here?" Schroeder set down his morning coffee and shifted in his chair.

"It's over two hundred miles from here. No need to worry about the fighting coming this far north." Talbot retrieved his identical coffee cup and sipped the steaming brew.

"I hope so. We haven't gotten much traction on Maria's career yet. All anyone talks about is this blasted war. Not much appreciation for the arts."

"On the contrary, Herr Schroeder. Society is looking to the arts to take their minds off the horrors they read every day. Give them a reason to dress up and parade around the town so they do not need to think of those poor boys giving their lives for their country. You'd be doing them a terrific service." He nodded toward Maria as she entered the room. "Once we can promote our young snow angel to the masses, she will be the only thing people will be talking about, I am sure."

Talbot rose and took Maria's hand while he pulled out her chair with the other hand. "Good morning, my precious girl. Breakfast is on its way."

"Thank you." Maria straightened her skirt as she slid into her chair in her most lady-like fashion. "What news do you have today, gentleman?" She unfolded her napkin prim and proper as if she held court this way every day of her life.

"We were talking about how we want you to be the headline news here soon instead of this nasty war," Schroeder injected. "I don't see why we don't have a concert booked for you yet." His stare landed on Talbot. "That is what we came here for, after all."

"Patience, patience, my friend. We need to pair her with someone everyone recognizes first, so she gets more exposure. Right now, no one knows how wonderful she is. She is our little secret, and we must release her in an acceptable fashion. Give them a taste and they will want more, I am sure."

"Isn't that what we were doing at the fair? We can't keep giving the public free samples of Maria's voice. We need to make a living. My savings are almost gone."

"I don't mind doing that. The fair was fun, and the people loved it." Maria put down her fork, eager to add her thoughts. "Mr. Talbot, do you have somewhere else I can sing if the concert hall is not ready for me yet?"

Schroeder bristled at the suggestion. "We can't keep having you sing for free! That's not how this works. If you don't earn anything, you may as well marry and croon children's lullabies the rest of your life. What am I here for?"

"I am still working on promotional arrangements, Herr Schroeder. I am not suggesting that a profitable music career is not in Miss Maria's future. These things take time. Remember, I am not earning a penny while we are idle either. I promise to make this happen." He smiled at them and stroked his chin. "I do have an idea, though. Let's go over to the Manhattan Colored Orphan Asylum. They will love to have you after being a hit at the fair. You will be doing your part for charity, and it will provide more exposure beyond the borough of Brooklyn."

"Another charity?" Schroeder threw his napkin on the table and stood up. "You think I traveled all this way to give her talent away?"

"Calm down. Soon, patrons will be clambering for tickets to her concerts. You will see." Talbot reached out to grab Schroeder's wrist to guide him back to his seat, but he turned to walk away.

"This is the last time you take me for a fool, Talbot." Schroeder muttered as he strutted out of the room.

"Do you want to sing at the orphanage, Maria?" Talbot ignored Schroeder's tantrum.

"I'd like that. Do you think Herr Schroeder will agree?" Maria watched her manager disappear through the doors.

"Let me take care of him. I have all the connections here. I will introduce you around, and soon the world will be falling at your feet, my dear." He took her hand resting on her fork and raised it to his lips. "I promise, you will be the talk of the town before I am done."

⚜

*M*aria's mind went directly to a vision of adoring fans applauding her debut.

"Maria?" She snapped her attention back to whatever Talbot was telling her. "Are you still with me? I will pick you up tomorrow morning, so I can take you to the orphanage. Financial backers are invited, and they have deep pockets. This will be your introduction to some influential people. You are on your way."

Talbot offered to pull Maria's chair out for her as she glanced down at her unfinished meal of eggs and bacon.

"One moment, please. You go ahead. I'll sit here by myself a little bit. I'll be along after I eat."

"Sorry, I didn't mean to rush you. Don't be late for rehearsal, and we can go over some songs for tomorrow." Talbot gave a curt bow and excused himself.

Talbot's carriage arrived as scheduled. Talbot, Schroeder, and Maria boarded it; and the horses clopped through the bustling streets, avoiding pedestrians and shopkeepers preparing for their day. They approached a four-story brick building with two wings.

"I didn't think it would be quite so grand." Maria poked her head out for a better view. Children in the upper windows waved down at them.

Talbot and Schroeder's attention were diverted to the disturbance down the street where a crowd of agitated men gathered.

Schroeder whispered to Talbot, "We may not want to stay here too long."

Talbot gave a knowing nod in response.

The director, Ms. Christiana Freeman, met them at the front entrance. "Welcome, welcome. We are so glad to have you visit us. We are gathering the children in the garden for you, Miss Maria."

The matter-of-fact woman guided them through the foyer of the building to well-kept grounds in the back. Children darted around the yard to find a place suitable for them on the grass.

"There are so many." Maria's mouth dropped at the sight of so many children dressed in white shifts and trousers.

"We have about seven hundred students housed here now, Miss Maria. We provide them with schooling, chores, and a routine to help them grow up to be responsible adults." A couple of boys poked each other as they sat causing each other to squirm. Ms. Freeman added, "Of course, we allow time for them to run off some of their young energy, too. That is why we maintain this lovely space."

"It is a beautiful place."

The roses were trimmed to accentuate all the bright blooms, and the hedge formed a tidy border around the perimeter. Maria bent to say hello to a few of the children, but they only stared up at her with their button eyes. "I think my English is not so good." She turned to Ms. Freeman.

"They know their place, Miss. They are not to bother the white visitors that come to tour the orphanage. It is seldom that anyone addresses them directly—especially someone as young and pretty as you. They are dumbstruck."

Maria chuckled. "Oh, I am nobody special. It wasn't so long ago I was their age." She reached out to stroke the hand of a girl with chocolate smooth skin and deep brown eyes. At first the girl drew her hand back but then stretched it out for Maria to touch her again. "You are so adorable and small."

The compliment elicited a toothy smile coveted by nearby children.

Maria rose and sat in front of the children. Several high-fashioned white men stood near the doorway as well. She assumed they had come to see her; however, their heads were together in agitation as they spoke to one another while they kept glancing at the front of the building.

She began singing a children's folk song from home; and although the orphans would not understand the words, the quick tune caused them to bounce in their seats to the rhythm of the music. Before she started the second song, a crash of breaking glass resounded from the street through the front windows.

One of the white visitors ran toward Maria and shouted, "Get the children out of here!" Screaming and chaos erupted as staff and visitors herded the children down the back alleys toward the river.

Behind them, a crowd rushed into the building, looting and upending everything from donated baby clothes to food as they ignored pleas from administrators to stop. Some broke windows, and others clubbed anyone who stood in the rioters' way.

"Where are we going?" The wave of women and children forced Maria to run with them for their lives from the men with clubs.

"We have friends with boats at the dock. Help the children into the boats, and we'll take them to safety." Ms. Freeman held a toddler and directed older children to help the younger ones down to the water.

At the dock, children were being handed to the sailors on the boats like buckets of water on a fire drill. "Miss! You must board, too!" The tattooed sailor held out his hand for Maria.

Maria looked around and found no sign of Talbot or Schroeder. "Where are you taking them?" she asked the sailor.

"Across the river to Brooklyn. You will be safe with the children," he answered with his hand outstretched.

Maria accepted the offer to board; and a second later, her new best friend with the big chocolate eyes was on her lap. "Smoke!"

The upper floors of the asylum were on fire. Panicked, Maria surveyed the masses of children sitting in the vessel with her. "Do we have everyone?" She looked down at the girl she touched in the garden. She grabbed Maria's hand. "It's okay, you stay with me." Maria held on to her tightly.

The boat shoved off; and Maria asked the sailor, "Why are they rioting? Why would they hurt these children?"

"It's the draft that has 'em riled up. The Irish are mad 'cause they must fight in the war and the blacks are taking their jobs while they're gone. The freed slaves don't have to fight. So the Irish are taking out their anger on the blacks. It don't matter if they're kids or not."

"That's heartless," Maria said under her breath. She began to hum a soothing tune and rock her new charge to sleep.

When they arrived on the Brooklyn shore, the disembarking was solemn. The wide-eyed children searched for answers from the adults.

Maria asked for them, "Where do we go from here?"

"I'm not sure we have enough homes in Weeksville to house all these children." Ms. Freeman said more to herself than to anyone else.

"I know where we can take them."

Everyone turned to Maria.

"There is plenty of room at the Turnverein Hall."

The Germans had established the gymnasium for their fitness regimen. Herr Schroeder found it soon after arriving in New York and made some acquaintances from his homeland. He made it a habit to exercise daily, for a sound mind needs a sound body. The Turners were opposed to slavery; and although Maria did not frequent it, she knew it was expansive and that it would accommodate many children and keep them from danger.

"Come, I will show you where it is." Maria led the way.

That evening, Maria helped the orphanage workers settle the children in the gymnasium. Neighbors had brought in blankets and as many comfort items for the children as they could find for the night. A soft rain began to fall outside that lulled the children into a fitful slumber in their new surroundings.

Mrs. Mary J. Lyons, a leader in the Anti-Slavery League, stumbled in, sobbing. "They burned our boarding house. We have nothing left. We are going to move to Rhode Island. The city is too dangerous."

"Moving? Are you going to let them drive us away?" Ms. Freeman pulled her friend close.

"You can say that when they just burned your orphanage to the ground? I'm surprised you want to stay."

"Where would be a safer place to go?" Maria interrupted. "There is war in much of the country. Is anyplace safe?"

"No place is ever altogether safe, my dear. We must trust in the Lord for His refuge and strength, but we have nothing left here for us," said Mrs. Lyons. "And, young lady, I am afraid you will not find anyone in the mood for entertainment for some time. You and your managers may need to find another line of work for a while."

As if on cue, both Schroeder and Talbot burst through the gymnasium doors. "There you are! We have been looking everywhere for you." Schroeder scooped her into his arms as if she were a long-lost lover. "We thought you may have been hurt."

"I'm fine." Maria pried herself out of his tight embrace. "I helped the orphans to safety."

Talbot surveyed the masses of children huddled around the gymnasium. "Was bringing them here your idea?"

"I don't think I was the only one who thought of it, but it does have room for many children, doesn't it?"

"It does indeed. You are a resourceful one, I must say." Talbot shook his head at the pandemonium before him.

"Mrs. Lyons told us the rioters burned down her boarding house, and her family is moving away to Rhode Island. She doesn't think it is safe here, and we will not be able to hold a concert for some time in this atmosphere."

Talbot and Schroeder looked at each other. "I think she may be right," Talbot began. "We may need to wait until things die down before trying to promote Maria again."

"And what do you expect us to do? Go home?" Schroeder bristled at the thought of going home without making his fortune. He had promised his wife fancy dresses and jewels when he returned, not empty pockets.

Maria threw up her hands in disgust at the direction of the conversation. "What can we do to help? We may have come here for me to perform, but that is not a priority right now. I have family in

America. Let me write to my sister for advice. She does not live in a
big city, but maybe it is best to leave the city now."

With a shrug, the men scanned the room of children and shook
their heads.

CHAPTER 26

Little children, let no one deceive you. Whoever practices
righteousness is righteous, as he is righteous.

1 John 3:7

ALTON, ILLINOIS

Lena readied herself to take the girls for a walk. The late summer heat created a sauna-like atmosphere inside their home as the humidity bathed them in a constant soggy dampness. Opening the doors and windows only invited the mosquitos and flies to take up residency, so it was time to brave the elements and face nature straight on today. If the Lord was gracious, He might supply a sufficient breeze to revive them on their way.

Dora tried to squirm away from Lena's firm grip, but citizens and soldiers filled the walkways and streets. Relinquishing hold of a small child amid a bustling river port town was neither wise nor prudent. Dora would have to tolerate her mother's dominance until they arrived at a safer place to run.

Johanna pleaded, "Mommy, I am big enough to walk by myself."

"It would be too easy to lose you among so many people, Johanna. You are a growing girl, but you are still small enough that a horse or someone carrying packages may not see you. Stay with me until we find some open places to play. If you two are good, we can stop at the dry goods store and buy some penny candy."

Both girls jumped up and down at the prospect of a treat. Papa sometimes brought home hard candy for them as a surprise, but being able to choose their own pieces was better yet. Dora began swinging her mother's arm back and forth in an effort to hurry along with their expedition.

Veering away from the downtown bustle, Lena steered the children east to the summit of Christian Hill. Finding an open area in the park, Lena released her daughters to run and play. Lena herself sat down on a tuft of grass and enjoyed the paddle wheelers lapping past one another on the Mississippi. Each ship vied for its spot at the Alton docks below. Her two imps chased each other around until they were dizzy and out of Lena's reach, so she called them back over to her.

"Look, girls. See all the ships on the water?"

They scampered back to the mother and plopped down next to her, legs sprawled out in front of them. "Have you ever been on one of them boats, Mama?" Johanna asked.

"Oh, yes. I traveled on one all the way from New Orleans. That is where I met your father."

"Is N'orleens far way?" Dora asked.

"Yes, it is rather far. We were on the river for several days, but your mama came from much further away than that." She sat Dora on her lap.

"How far?" Johanna asked as she leaned on her mother.

"I had to cross a whole ocean, girls. Uncle Herman did, too. Remember when I read your letters from your grandmother? They come from far, far away." The sun was reaching its zenith, and the heat was draining the girls of their youthful energy. "I think we better go home and take a cool nap. What do you think?"

Pushing herself off the ground, Dora perked up and exclaimed, "We gets candy, 'member?"

"Oh, I remember. We will go by the General Store before heading home." Hand in hand again, the three walked into town.

Stepping past a couple gray-bearded men playing checkers on the boardwalk, Lena overheard them discussing the latest battle news.

"The Union has won some hard-fought battles, but they are losing many valuable men," one of the men was saying. "Most of them are not much older than boys. Did you hear how many fell at Gettysburg?"

"I don't think Vicksburg was much better," added his checker buddy while shaking his head.

"Yeah, and then there was that riot in New York."

Lena spun around. "Riot? What riot?" She nudged the girls through the door ahead of her. "Don't touch anything. I'll be inside in a minute." She lingered outside to learn what the men could tell her.

"There was a big to-do in New York. They burned an orphanage to the ground and killed a bunch of black folks. Seems the Irish got riled up about being drafted for the war and took it out on those who didn't have to go fight."

The color drained from Lena's face.

"You need to sit down, ma'am?" The man nearest her began to rise to offer her his seat.

She steadied herself against the door jamb and shook her head at the fellow getting up to offer his chair to her. "No, I'll be fine. My sister is in New York. I hope she's okay, that's all."

Lena straightened and took a deep breath before entering to assist her girls in their selections.

When Karl arrived home from work, it was everything Lena could do to keep from attacking him with her concerns about her sister. She was sure that he knew about the riots. His nose was in every bit of news that was printed, but he chose not to tell her everything. She held her resolve until after dinner and the girls were tucked into bed. Then her floodgates of emotion rumbled to the surface.

"Karl, I heard some disturbing news today when the girls and I stopped for a treat after our walk."

Karl relinquished the paper he was reading to the side table and leveled his eyes at his wife's furrowed brow. "What did you hear that is troubling you?"

With the country at war, it left the door open for just about anything.

"I was told about riots happening in New York. I suppose that is not news to you?" Her hands now placed on her hips challenged him for an answer.

"I heard about it." Karl's voice sounded too casual to Lena, as if he knew more and hoped she didn't ask about it.

"Why did you not think to share this with me? You know I have been so concerned about Maria being alone in the city, and now she is surrounded by rioting!"

"You don't know if she is anywhere near the riots, Lena. New York is a city. She has two grown male chaperones to keep her out of harm's way." Lena kept him under her steely glare, and Karl began to fidget. "Lena. I did not mention this to you because it would only make you worry more, just like you are doing right now."

"You should have told me, and I think you should go to New York right now and bring her here. If it were one of your girls, you would be there in a heartbeat; and you know it."

"But she's not one of our girls. She is a young woman, and I am sure she is fine."

"You don't know she is fine! She could be hurt or frightened. She needs her family."

"Then send Herman." Karl hesitated.

"Herman cannot leave the farm in the middle of summer, and I can't believe you said that. Maria is my family, and that makes her your family, too. Where is your sense of honor?"

"I'll tell you what. Wait for Maria's next letter. Read what she says. If she asks to come here, I will do what I can to ensure she has safe passage to us. Is that fair?"

Lena searched the ceiling as if the answer was printed above her. "I suppose."

"While I am sharing troublesome news, I might as well share one more with you." Alarmed, Lena gave Karl her full attention. "I discovered that Thomas and Stefan were in Howard's unit at Gettysburg. They are both missing."

"Oh, no!" Lena buried her head in her hands and let the tears flow.

CHAPTER 27

But let all who take refuge in you rejoice; let them ever sing for joy,
and spread your protection over them, that those who love your
name may exult in you.

Psalm 5:11

GETTYSBURG, PENNSYLVANIA

The acrid smoke dissipated over the bloody fields as the groans of wounded begged for attention. The muffled cries sifted through a constant ringing in Thomas' ears as he tried to extricate himself from the mire of human suffering.

"Please stop those bells," he murmured into the ground. He did not have the strength to roll himself over. The dead weight of the freckle-faced enemy who moments before had stood staring straight into his own blue eyes now pinned him to the ground.

Thomas pushed himself inch by inch and worked at dislodging the slight gray-coat boy who had fallen to his death on top of him. The back of the intruder was blown away, and Thomas was not sure how much of the blood that covered him was from the other soldier or from himself.

The left shoulder of Thomas' jacket gaped open, revealing a wound of mangled flesh. The poor boy lying next to him had shielded him from the bulk of the blast, leaving Thomas with only a shoulder ripped to shreds. *Thank You, Lord, for sparing my life. Please welcome this boy into Your kingdom.* Thomas closed the boy's eyes over his fixed stare and did his best to scramble to his feet.

Holding his limp left arm to his side, Thomas got to his feet and stumbled through the rain-softened soil toward the field hospital. Light-headedness caused the ground to spin, and it was difficult to avoid the bodies of scattered dead and dying. Tripping over an appendage, he was suddenly steadied by a Union comrade.

"Careful there. You need the doc." The blue uniform steered him off the battlefield, where a tent of screams greeted him. The groans and cries of the injured hung in the air.

Wait. "Why don't I hear any canons or gunfire?" Thomas turned to ask his benevolent guide.

"We won. We got those Rebs on the run. The battle's over." He sat Thomas down on the muddy ground soaked in blood and rain. "You stay here. The doc will get to you when he can. They're plenty busy with fellas before you."

Won? So many dead and dying lay on the battle ground. Is this what victory looked like? The orderlies tried not to stack the amputated limbs too near the doorway, but the prominent growing pile was still visible from Thomas' waiting spot. He shuddered away from the sight.

Closing his eyes against the dismal scene, he drifted off. Awakened by a medical attendant with a roll of linen cloth, he sat up.

"We need to wrap you up and stop the bleeding before you bleed to death, soldier."

The medic helped Thomas remove what was left of his jacket, pulled back his shirt, and began winding the bandage around a wad of linen he placed in the hole in his shoulder. "Looks clean enough. Maybe you'll be able to keep the infection out."

Thomas winced and nodded at the attention.

"Let me help you to a cot over here where we can keep an eye on you for a while. The surgeon may need to pick out some grapeshot here, but I don't see any broken bones. You are a lucky one, aren't you?" The assistant led Thomas to a tent and deposited him in a cot.

Lucky? Landing at a field hospital did not feel that lucky—but many men around him had suffered far worse injuries. A soldier lay next to him, his bandaged head misshapen. A cavalry man nursed a bullet hole in his neck. Another lamented over a fractured knee, sure that it would be amputated before nightfall.

I don't believe in luck, Thomas thought. *The Lord has indeed blessed me in my time of need.*

Later that night, Thomas was carried to the surgeon. "Wait. Are they taking my arm?" He fought to sit up, but they held him down. Before he could protest further, he was given a drop of liquid in cotton over his face; and he drifted away into strange dreams of home, school, and Stefan rolled into one.

The sun was rising when he awoke, and he checked for his left arm. It was there but numb, and he was not able to lift it. His blood-soaked bandages had been replaced since last night. "Sir?" He attempted to call the orderly over to him, but his voice was weak. Again, a bit louder, "Sir?"

This time, a clean-shaven young man turned from the patient he was conversing with. "Yes? Do you need something?"

"I think they took me in for surgery last night. Or was I dreaming? I still have my arm."

The attendant smiled. "Yes, you still have your arm. Not all surgeries are amputations, soldier. They had to pull some of that grapeshot out of your shoulder before it festered. With any luck, you will heal up just fine now."

"My arm isn't working too well, though."

"It might heal all the way, and it might not. Hard to tell. Right now, just pray for everything to mend, so you can go home alive." He turned to the next bed where loud moaning drew his attention.

"Thank you." Thomas whispered after him. "I will." He said a prayer of thanksgiving and protection.

Within a few days, Thomas' shoulder healed enough to give up his cot to someone else and wander outside. He found an officer and asked, "What do I do now, sir?"

"You look fit enough to join the Invalid Corps, young man. A Class One regiment is forming for you fellows who are not recovered enough to join their regiments but can still serve the country."

"I can't lift my left arm too well now." Thomas let it drop in demonstration. "I don't know if I will be able to use it again, but I will go where you send me."

"That's the spirit, soldier. Report to Colonel Thompson, and he will add you to his new regiment." The mustached officer began to walk away before he turned to add, "You fought bravely, son. President Lincoln is proud of your service." He dismissed Thomas and departed.

Lincoln? The thought of fighting for the president had not really occurred to Thomas. He fought for honor and freedom and the preservation of the nation. To think he fought for the president himself was an honor.

Colonel Thompson camped beyond the workings of the hospital. Many patched-up men were deemed acceptable for the Invalid Corps and deposited in Thompson's camp with military efficiency. Those with mere scratches were sent back to their units to fight with the unscathed soldiers. His men still sported bandages on various appendages and winced in pain with every move. They helped each other to stand or march when ordered to do so.

After almost a week of gathering men for the Invalid Corp, orders came to move out and head to New York. There had been a riot in the city, and the governor requested the militia to quell the chaos. Not inclined to extract able-bodied soldiers from the front lines, the Invalid Corps was sent on this mission.

They headed to New York on a two-hundred-mile march. They made it in three days.

CHAPTER 28

Now there are varieties of gifts, but the same Spirit; and there are
varieties of service, but the same Lord; and there are varieties of
activities, but it is the same God who empowers them all in everyone.

1 Corinthians 12:4-6

NEW YORK

Schroeder rattled his morning newspaper over his breakfast of toast and eggs. Reaching for his coffee, he gasped. "Talbot? Have you seen these headlines? The military has taken over the streets of New York. Can you believe they brought cannons in to keep the peace against the rioters? The city is under martial law. I thought you said the war would not touch New York when you brought us here."

Maria hesitated, just in earshot of the table, before the men noticed her. Talbot and Schroeder were reluctant to speak openly about the events of the war in her presence, but she wanted to know what was going on.

"Just because the soldiers are here does not mean the war is in the city," reassured Talbot. "They are not fighting the Confederate Army of the South here. They are only keeping order from the angry mobs that burned down the orphanage and killed all those people. You should be thankful they are here trying to keep you safe."

"Oh, I understand that, but I thought this part of the country would be safe from this sort of violence. Maria's parents would never forgive me if I let something happen to her over here after promising to keep her safe." He sipped more of his steaming drink.

"Relax. No one should bother you. You are neither a member of the rich who paid their way out of fighting nor black, who are not forced to fight and who are a threat to take their jobs away." Pointing his breakfast roll at Schroeder, Talbot continued, "Stay away from certain areas of the city, and you will be fine."

"That's another thing." Schroeder laid his paper and coffee cup down. "How are we going to make any money if people are afraid to attend events?"

"The truth is, we can't. I have been thinking about this, and I think I must pursue some other endeavors until things die down. You can stay at the Brooklyn Concert Hall as long as you like. I have paid for your stay for the time being." Talbot looked away, not meeting Schroeder's scrutinizing eyes. "I'm sure this will blow over before long."

"Blow over? And what do Maria and I do in the meantime?"

Talbot stood to leave. "That is up to you. I will keep in touch." He tossed his napkin on the table and exited, leaving Schroeder staring after him.

Talbot passed Maria, sidestepping her and nodding before continuing on his way. She turned to Schroeder at the table and asked, "Where is he going in such a hurry?"

"To 'pursue other endeavors,'" Schroeder spewed through tight lips. "He is abandoning us here, Maria. With all his promises of making you a star, he is walking away."

"What? What do you mean, walking away?" Puzzled, Maria slid onto the adjacent chair at the table.

"With the mobs and the military presence in the streets, people are afraid to venture out to attend the theater or concerts right now. He cannot book any performances for you under these circumstances, so he is going away for a while." Schroeder smirked and continued, "He said he would keep in touch."

Maria stared at the plate the waiter delivered and pondered what Schroeder had told her. "Well, I may not be able to sing in concert halls, but I can still sing for the displaced children and others. Maybe I am not meant to be famous. Maybe God wants me to use my voice for comforting others." Her mind went to the orphan she had held in her lap during the evacuation.

Schroeder tilted his head as he listened to Maria's revelation. "In Bremen, all you wanted was to be a soloist and recognized as a star. What has changed?"

"I've been watching the orphans and how much they want love and attention. It made me rethink my motives. What honor is there in singing only for my own glory? God gave me this gift. Let me use it to serve Him and not me." She took a bite of her morning porridge. "Nothing happens that God did not already know about—the rioting, the burned orphanage, no fancy concerts for me here. God knew it all beforehand. Nothing happens by chance, and I think He wants me to fill my time helping others as much as I can. If He wants me to be famous, He will make that happen, not me."

Schroeder shook his head, but there was a hint of softness in his eyes. "When did you grow up?" He reached across the table to squeeze her hand.

Maria flinched and drew it back to her lap.

"I think we can still create some meaningful use of our time here." Schroeder's smile constricted in an alarming way Maria did not like. She shifted in her seat and stirred her bowl of breakfast round and round until her stomach settled.

Maria's mood lightened as she entered the Turner Verein. The makeshift accommodations for the orphans did not dampen their spirits. The facility, built by the Germans for physical activity and gymnastics, held places for the children to exercise and run. One of the boys was trying his prowess on the rings; another was climbing on a pommel horse. Girls were trying cartwheels on the mats and braiding hair in front of mirrors along the wall. Giggles and squeals of delight echoed across the soaring ceilings and reverberated off the oversized windows.

Although the warm July air stifled outside, the brick building insulated much of the summer heat away; and the upper window circulated a breeze through modern water-powered ceiling fans. The din of children playing almost overwhelmed the chamber, however, and the noise could be deafening.

A few of the girls ran to Maria at the door and took her hand. "C'mere. Let me show you what I can do."

Before she could reply, she was pulled over to the mats, where one girl was trying to do a backbend and another a summersault.

"My, my, how did you learn that?" Maria sat on a nearby bench to survey the cacophony of activity in the room.

"A helper here showed us," one of the girls volunteered. "Here, you try."

"Oh, no. I didn't come dressed for acrobatics." Maria shook off a slender arm trying to pull her off her perch. "I'll watch you. You are doing a great job."

Relenting, the girls went back to their tumbling and spotting one another.

Maria smiled in their direction. "When you are done, I'll teach you a song from my homeland."

"Homeland? What's a homeland?"

"Homeland is where you are from. Mine is across the ocean. A country called Germany." The girls still looked confused. "Yours is America—or even New York."

"No. My homeland was Georgia, but my mam and pap were killed comin' here," said the girl Maria recognized from the rescue boat. She leaned onto Maria's shoulder, and Maria put her arm around her and hugged her.

"I'm sorry to hear that." Knowing the others all likely had similar stories, she was not sure how to steer the conversation.

"Do you have a mam and pap?" another child asked.

"Yes, I do, and I have six older brothers and sisters. Our house was very crowded when I was little." They all giggled. "But I did not live with as many children as you do." She pointed at the activity around the hall.

"Why did you leave?" All their eyes turned to Maria.

"I came to America to sing. I also have a brother and sister who already moved here, and I hope to see them soon."

"Are they in New York?"

"No, a state called Illinois. I understand it is far from here, so I am not sure when I will see them with the war going on."

The children all nodded; they understood being far from loved ones.

"Are you ready for a new song?" The gathering around Maria grew, and a chorus of yesses erupted from them. "Everyone find a seat, and I will teach you a folk song called '*Die Gedanken Sind Frei*,' which means 'Thoughts are Free.'"

Before long, Maria had all the children singing and bouncing to the *oom-pah-pah* rhythm. "I think I will turn all of you into little Germans in no time."

Happy with her contribution to the high spirits in the Turner Hall, Maria sailed out the front door without checking for bystanders on the street. Bumping right into a young soldier in blue carrying a rifle, she sent his cap flying and almost fell herself. "Oh, I am so sorry. I did not see you."

The blue-eyed lad, no older than herself, held her up as best he could with his free hand. She stepped back to compose herself and saw a ruddy-faced youth staring back at her. "Thank you. I about took us both for a tumble."

Maria straightened her collar and smoothed her skirt.

The soldier paled and tried not to flinch as he lowered his arm.

"You don't say much, do you? Did I hurt you?" Maria returned a strand of hair behind her ear to better assess this handsome boy.

"It's not you, miss," he breathed in his reply. "I took some grapeshot in my shoulder at Gettysburg. I don't think it is all healed yet. It still smarts some." Trying to stand taller and stalwart, he gripped his gun tighter in his functional hand.

"Oh, I am so sorry. Did I reinjure it? Are you sure? You should have someone look at it." She pointed to the door from which she had emerged.

"No, it's no trouble. We have our own docs. I can have one of them tend to it later if I need." He straightened, rolling his shoulders back and raising his chin to punctuate his statement.

"I have caused you further pain. I can tell. It is the least I can do." Maria reached for his left arm, but it remained limp and did not respond to her touch. "Are you sure you don't need assistance?"

The solider stammered, "M-m-miss, I'll be fine, I promise. I'm just tired from being on guard duty for so long." He turned to walk away. "Forgive me, I must go." He stepped away from her.

"Wait," Maria called out. "I want to be sure you are okay. If you won't let me help you, please tell me your name so I can ask about you later."

The soldier turned back, a grin spreading across his face. Sweeping his hat from his head, he introduced himself. "Private Thomas Krueger, at your service."

Maria's smile grew to fill her face, and she dipped into her finest curtsy. "Maria Neubauer, kind sir."

They stood smiling back at each other a moment more than convention dictated before parting company, each of them smiling and humming a happy tune to themselves.

CHAPTER 29

I must speak, that I may find relief; I must open my lips and answer.

Job 32:20

ALTON, ILLINOIS

Karl caught his breath as he burst through the door of his house. "Lena! Lena! We have letters from both Maria and Thomas today. They are okay."

Lena wiped her hands on her apron. She and Juana had been canning peaches gleaned from a neighbor's orchard. A steamy strand of hair escaped the bandana around her head. She pushed it back with her forearm and faced her excited husband.

Checking if her hands were dry enough to take the letters, Lena waved them in the air as if she were shooing away the afternoon flies. Confident she would not damage the missives, she reached out to collect the precious messages. "I was afraid Thomas might be dead—I'll read his first." She slid the folded paper from its open envelope and began to read.

Dear Lena and Karl,

Being a soldier is not what I expected at all. First, it was only weeks of drills and marching. There was little target practice to conserve ammunition. Since most of us country boys grew up hunting, we needed no extra practice, I suppose.

Stefan and I found ourselves guarding a small town in Pennsylvania called Gettysburg. Not much of a town really. We wondered why it was so important, but it was at the junction of many road arteries of travel in the area. At any rate, many regiments from the North and South collided in Gettysburg, and we fought for three days in the July heat and some summer rain.

I am grieved to say I lost Stefan the first day of fighting. We were retreating through the town with the Rebs in hot pursuit. I turned to see him fall, and I had no chance to go back after him. I need to write to his folks and tell them how brave he was to fight for his country. I feel guilty for convincing him to come with me.

I must admit I did not escape unscathed myself. I suffered a shoulder wound the last day of fighting, but I will be fine. My left arm does not always cooperate with my wishes; but it is still attached, which is more than I can say for many of the others injured in battle. The Lord was with me. In fact, I have recovered enough to be reassigned to the Invalid Corps, and they have sent us to New York to help keep peace after their riots erupted.

Lena paused reading and caught Karl looking at her. "He went to New York. He is there with Maria." She paused thoughtfully. "If only they could connect."

"New York is not the size of St. Louis, Lena. I doubt they will meet. Thomas is a soldier, and I am sure Maria's chaperones will keep her away from any troops. Don't get your hopes up."

"With God, nothing is impossible."[2] Lena directed a defiant stare Karl's way, and he did not dare to argue. She returned to reading Thomas' letter.

Now that I am in New York, I have been assigned guard duty at the draft office. Most of the residents keep to themselves; and although they appreciate us maintaining the peace, enforcing martial law chafes them some.

I found a German presence at the Turner Verein Hall, and I have wandered into it a time or two when I am not on duty. They are using it to help some displaced orphans, but the Germans I have met are a welcome reminder of those back home.

I wanted you to know that I am fine and am out of harm's way for now. I know you worry like my parents, and I wanted to ease your mind.

I hope you and the girls are all doing well.

God bless,

Pvt. Thomas Krueger

"Well, that's a relief. That is sad news about his friend Stefan, though. That young man wanted to be a pastor, too. We will need to say a prayer for his family tonight and a prayer of thanks for protecting Thomas, too." Lena refolded it and slipped it back into the envelope for safe keeping.

Karl handed Lena the second letter covered in curly feminine script. She smiled as she recognized Maria's handwriting.

---

2   Luke 1:37

Dear Lena,

My career as a singer is not taking off like I was promised when I left home. I have had some opportunities to sing; but no pay is offered for them, and Herr Schroeder is quite disgruntled with Mr. Talbot not following through with all his promises.

I can't blame Mr. Talbot too much. When we arrived, the city was already in an uproar over recent immigrants being drafted to fight in the war almost as soon as they disembarked at the harbor. The tension between the Irish and the blacks was evident right away when we arrived here, but we were assured it would not affect our plans to entertain. That has not been the case.

With a curfew in the city, no one feels safe going out at night for concert events. Those with money are targeted by the poor because the rich can buy a substitute to go to war, and those without money pay the price of risking their lives. The classes here do not mix, much like the aristocracy at home.

Things have improved some since the soldiers arrived. Order has been restored, but much damage had already been done before their arrival. Many buildings were burned like the Colored Children's Asylum, and some lost their lives, too. I don't mean to worry you, but I was at the orphanage the day it burned and helped evacuate the children and take them to the Turner Verein Hall for safety.

"Karl! Did you read this? Maria has been at the same hall Thomas mentioned." Karl's smirk answered her question. "Why, you tease! You knew all along that the chances of them meeting were better than you told me a minute ago." She punched him in the arm, and he laughed.

"I wanted you to read it for yourself. I didn't want to spoil the revelation for you." He pulled her in for a quick hug. "God sure has a way of arranging things, doesn't He?"

"I never underestimate the power of God," Lena answered. "Now, let me finish."

> *I have told Herr Schroeder I am fine with not singing for crowds of people and becoming famous now. With some of these changes, I think God has different plans for me. I have been spending time with the orphans and teaching them the folk songs from home. They are wonderful students, and I enjoy teaching them.*
>
> *The Germans here have been gracious to protect the children and share what they have with them until other accommodations can be made. I even met a young German soldier who has started visiting the hall with offers to help. I think you may be proud of your little sister. Even Herr Schroeder said I was growing up.*
>
> *I hope to be with you soon.*
>
> *Much love,*
>
> *Maria*

"Oh, Karl, this is wonderful news, but they are still so far away. When will we be able to bring them home? If Maria is not earning anything for Schroeder and herself, he is bound to be frustrated with their situation. We need to bring her here."

"I had that thought, too. They cannot live indefinitely on Talbot's good graces." He sat in his favorite chair and stroked his chin. "I was thinking I may be able to travel to New York. If I can convince Schroeder to go back to Germany and leave Maria for her family to take care of her, then I could bring her home." Karl paused, considering. "Actually, it doesn't matter what he says. He doesn't own her. I am sure she will be better off with family than in a city under martial law."

Lena leaped into his lap and squealed. "Karl! You can go to New York?"

"All right. Slow down. I don't have it all approved to leave, but I think the firm will allow me some time to make the trip."

He was trying to hold her squirming body still enough to capture a kiss before the girls bounded from their room into the fray.

"Mommy, whatcha doin' sittin' on Papa?" Dora asked as she found room to climb up on the chair herself.

"Ya, Mama. What're you doin'?" Johanna added.

"Well, girls, I think your papa is going to take a trip to go find your aunt Maria and bring her to our house. Isn't that terrific?"

"It's not all arranged yet." Karl threw his hands up in surrender from all the attention. "I have to check with my boss; but if I go, can you help take care of your mama while I am gone?"

"We can be helpers, Papa," Johanna offered.

"Me helper, too," Dora volunteered.

The Muller family huddled together in a group hug until Karl started to tickle the girls and they fled back to their room. Lena gave her husband a last knowing squeeze before she stood, too. "I need to get back to these peaches with Juana. We will figure out the details later."

"That we will." Karl nodded as he smiled, letting her leave his lap.

"Juana? Did you hear the news? This is time for a celebration." Lena danced into the kitchen.

"I did. That's wonderful. If'n I only had news from my Jubal." Juana stared at the peach pit in her hands.

"Don't worry. Karl will keep looking for him; and if you stay with us, he will know where to find you once he's discovered his whereabouts."

Juana's worry did not leave her face. Lena reached out and hugged her. "I know it is selfish, but I don't know what I'd do without you here with us, anyway. You are like part of the family. I promise we will do everything we can to find your son."

Juana replied, "Yes, ma'am." But to Lena, she sounded unconvinced.

CHAPTER 30

Rise up; come to our help! Redeem us for the sake of your steadfast love!

Psalm 44:26

NEW YORK

Thomas frequented the Turner Hall after guard duty every available opportunity. His letter about the German patrons welcoming the other transplants from their homeland had been the truth. The conversations slipped from English to German and back again with ease among the participants. The orphans who roamed the facility began repeating a few phrases of German themselves. They stopped and were seated if someone ordered, "*Sitzen sie das!*" Many children began responding to the adults with "*Danke schoen*" when offered any assistance.

One young German drew Thomas to the gymnasium more than any feelings of heritage or camaraderie. The lovely Fraulein Maria drew the children to her like piglets to the dinner trough. The minute she walked into the room, little girls latched onto her skirts and led her to the wall, where she taught them songs of her homeland. Her lilting voice filled the cavernous interior, and the tunes transported Thomas back to his childhood when his mother or Frau Lena would sing to the children. The tunes wrapped him in warm waves like hugs from home.

Watching these black boys and girls singing German folk songs did not fit the image of an America anyone back in Europe would imagine. The joy of watching the incongruent mix created a fellowship those outside these brick walls could not fathom. In the streets, riots and violence lurked. In here, harmony and love grew. It was a haven in the middle of chaos.

Thomas was drawn there for all these reasons. Admittedly, he wished to spend time with Maria, but her guardian was always hovering. The gym attendant said he was her manager or something, but the way he lingered made Thomas think the man wanted to be more to her than a business arrangement. He reminded Thomas of a wolf stalking the sheep, waiting for the right time to spring into action. The young Maria ignored the lurking man as she flitted around interacting with the children.

Providing a sense of protection to this innocent maiden gave Thomas another purpose for strengthening his uncooperative left arm. The gym housed barbells that he tried to lift with his near-lifeless arm. Beginning with the smallest weight of five pounds, Thomas lifted the barbell with his strong right hand and placed it in the left before it would slip out and fall to the floor with a thud. The repeated resounding ring of rejection echoed across the gym, turning sympathetic glances his way.

Beads of perspiration bubbled up on his brow over the simple task. He did not exude the image of a stalwart soldier stationed in New York as he hoped he might. A strapping young man did not want the children or Fraulein Maria to be privy to his weakness, but the open gymnasium left nowhere to hide.

After multiple thunderous thuds, his fear of discovery materialized beside him. "Can I help you?" Maria escaped from the children's attention and appeared next to the young private. "Maybe I can help close your hand over the weight as you place it in the palm, then see if it can hold on to it a bit longer until it regains some strength."

Maria reached the incompetent left hand and manipulated the fingers into a loose fist as Thomas complied, dumbfounded. Her warm touch sent spider crawls of sensation up his arm. That electric jolt ignited the rest of him, and he craved more of her touch.

"How's that?" Maria smiled at him.

Thomas flushed and saw her expression turn to one of concern. "Are you okay? I'm not hurting you, am I?"

"No, no," he stammered. "It's so embarrassing that a little thing like closing my hand can take all my strength. I have never been so pathetic before."

The blood drained from his face, and he wondered where her bodyguard had gone as he slumped to the floor.

❀

"Help! Someone help me! He is not well." Maria felt Thomas' forehead and almost recoiled from the heat he emitted. "He has a fever. We need to find him a doctor."

Some of the male gymnasts hurried to their side and lifted Thomas to an unoccupied mat. Maria wetted a rag and placed it above his eyes while an attendant ran for a nearby doctor.

Thomas moaned as the soothing cloth dampened his face.

"Lie still. You are burning up." Maria loosened his uniform and peeled his shirt away from a soiled bandage covering his left shoulder. "When was this dressing last changed?" She further pulled back the bandage to find a festering hole in his mangled shoulder. "No wonder you fainted. We need to fix this before you succumb to this infection."

Turning to one of the gym attendants, Maria ordered, "Find some fresh bandages from him." She revealed the raw wound as she further lifted the bloodied cloths. Schroeder, who sat near the door searching the newspaper for business, strode across the room to investigate all the commotion. With one peek at the exposed injury, he turned white and excused himself to go outdoors for some fresh air. The others scrambled to fill Maria's requests.

"I found Doc Baker. His office is down the street." A gym attendant was leading a man through the crowd to the patient.

"Oh, Doctor, I'm glad you're here. This poor soldier needs attention." Maria stepped aside to allow him room to examine for himself.

Placing his black bag next to the bed, the white-haired man with a handlebar mustache unbuttoned his topcoat and peeked behind the soiled linens draped over Thomas' shoulder. "Who has been tending to this young man? This dressing has been on far too long, and an infection has set in."

"He has been coming in to rehabilitate his left arm, sir, but we do not know who has been responsible for his care. I imagine the army does those things," Maria volunteered.

The doctor scoffed. "The army has their hands full with men in their hospitals. The walking wounded are not their top priority. If these fellas don't see to their own needs, they often don't have any care at all."

He continued to poke around to examine the extent of the damage as Thomas briefly roused and recoiled from the pain. "Stay still, boy. Whoever took the grapeshot from your shoulder missed a few. Those fragments are causing you additional damage as you try to work your arm." He shook his head. "I can rummage around in there and retrieve more; but since he is a soldier, someone should take him to a Union surgeon to tend to him."

"But, doctor, you implied he would not necessarily receive the best treatment from them. Can't you take care of him?" Maria tugged on his sleeve as she pleaded for his assistance.

"I will do what I can for now, but he is the army's concern. Tell the officers in the barrack that we have . . . " He paused "Who is this?"

"He introduced himself to me as Thomas Krueger," Maria volunteered.

Schroeder overheard her answer from the doorway and furrowed his eyes at her.

The doctor continued, "Private Thomas Krueger here, and he passed out from an infection settling in his shoulder wound." Turning back to Thomas, he continued, "I'll patch him up here so he can be transported, but they need to send some boys to come after him and take him to their own hospital."

He twirled his mustache and surveyed the population in the gym. "Find somewhere else for the children to go for a bit. And, Miss"— he looked at Maria—"do you think you can administer a few drops of ether while I dig this grapeshot from his shoulder? It will make it more comfortable for him, and we don't want him screaming to frighten all these children."

Maria stepped forward. "I'm sure I can help. Just tell me what to do."

Thomas' face paled below the damp cloth. "Is he going to be all right?"

"We will do our best. Once infection sets in like this, the lad will have an uphill climb to fight it. Brace yourself. Many don't make it." He probed it again.

Maria gasped. She had never seen death up close before, and she did not want this handsome bluecoat to fade away before she had a chance to learn more about him. He had been a perfect gentleman to her and spoke kindly to the children as if he were a brother to them. Her heart said it was her duty to do everything in her power to help him recover.

Following the doctor's careful directions, Maria dripped medication over Thomas' nose while the doctor reopened the ugly shoulder and withdrew three more fragments of grapeshot. He placed all three onto a handkerchief Maria supplied from her pocket. "He can have these as a souvenir if he wishes." He folded the pellets into the kerchief and gave them to Maria. "When the soldiers come to take him away, he should be ready. Make sure they change those bandages daily and keep dredging it to clear it of infection. I cut away as much damaged flesh I could while I was in there."

Maria kept nodding at the doctor's instructions as if the patient were her responsibility. "Yes, sir, I promise that the other doctors will learn what you said."

Did that mean she would go to the Union hospital with him? She had given her word. She must go look after this young man. She searched the room for signs of where Schroeder may have stolen away during the doctor's surgery. He must have taken a walk before he succumbed to the gruesome sight. So be it. She could handle herself. She was not a child.

Soon thereafter, a couple of soldiers came in with a canvas cot supported by two poles to take Thomas with them. As they rolled him onto his right side to slip the apparatus under him, Thomas' groan echoed across the room.

"Careful. You'll hurt him. The doctor just operated on him." Maria steadied Thomas as the two puzzled soldiers gave each other a sideway glance at the young woman's orders. Rolling him back onto the cot, they each grabbed the ends of the poles to walk him back.

"Wait!" They halted at Maria's order. "I have his jacket and cap."

"Throw them on top of him, lady, and we'll be sure he gets them."

"No. I have instructions from the doctor, too. I'm coming along." Maria draped Thomas' jacket over her arm and snatched his cap from the ledge. Over her shoulder, she told the gym attendant, "Tell Schroeder where I went and that I'll be back later." She flipped her hair down her back and kept pace with the stretcher bearers, carrying her new responsibility out the door.

CHAPTER 31

For you have been my help, and in the shadow of your wings
I will sing for joy.

Psalm 63:7

New York

Schroeder finished his breakfast and tossed his napkin down on his emptied plate. "Where is she? Just because we don't have any concerts booked doesn't mean Maria should be able to sleep all morning. *Ach du liebe Zeit!* Where is she?"

The waiter reached in front of him to clear the dish of crumbs away. "Pardon, sir, but if you are referring to the young lady who usually joins you in the morning, she left some time ago." He straightened to take the plate away.

"She left? What do you mean, she left?" Schroeder slammed the table.

"Yes, sir. She was down here as soon as we opened. She ordered a pastry and a glass of milk and was on her way early." The waiter tried to back away before Schroeder could ply him with more questions.

"Wait a minute." Schroeder halted the waiter's escape. "Do you know where she went?"

"I try not to meddle in my customers affairs, sir. I did not ask her business." He turned to the next table and addressed another patron.

"Early, huh? She has never been early a day in her life. What's got into her?" Schroeder muttered to himself. Then he remembered that soldier boy Maria had taken a liking to at the gym. She had followed him to the Union hospital and hadn't returned to her apartment until late. Schroeder hadn't even had a chance to ask her about it, thinking he'd hear her story that morning. Who would have thought she'd be out of here before the crack of dawn?

Schroeder stroked his chin. "I should go after her and give her a piece of my mind but boy, do I hate hospitals. All those foul odors and grotesque sicknesses." He leaned back in his chair with a sigh. "Blast it, Maria. How can I keep an eye on you when you run off on your own like this?"

*M*aria sat on the stool beside Thomas' bed she had occupied the previous afternoon. He tossed and turned in a feverish stupor for hours while she wiped his brow and kept a fresh supply of cool cloths on his forehead. The sun had sunk below the horizon before she decided to go back to her room yesterday. She had returned without meeting Schroeder when she slipped in last night.

She had been surprised not to see Schroeder storm after her when she left Turner Hall with the army. It was fortunate that she was able to hurry away before their normal breakfast time in the morning. It saved any unpleasantness between them. The Lord knew she needed to be there to help Thomas recover. God had placed him in her path for a reason.

The orderly passing by on his rounds paused by Thomas' bed and asked, "Do you want a cup of coffee, miss? We made a fresh pot. I might be able to scrounge up a biscuit for you, too, if the boys haven't gulped them all down already. Mrs. Sanders takes good care of us."

"I'd enjoy some coffee, thank you," replied Maria, welcoming this bit of kindness.

So focused on Thomas's needs, she had not absorbed their surroundings with any detail. The antiseptic and putrid stench that had assaulted her yesterday welcomed her back today. The rows of other sick and injured soldiers lay half-dazed in morphine-induced repose. An occasional moan, muffled tears, or delirious mumbling created background noise to the wheeled cart of ministrations for the men and the scuffle of military boots seeing to each concern.

Some of the patients were missing limbs. Others faded away under the covers that would soon be pulled over their heads. A few appeared to be on the mend with hopes of leaving the facility under their own power someday.

The orderly reappeared with a steaming cup of coffee. Maria reached for it, careful not to spill in on herself, and thanked the young man. Nodding toward Thomas, she asked. "How is he doing?"

"He had a rough night, I think. His sleep is more peaceful now than when I came in. You were here when I came on duty last night. You his wife?" the orderly asked.

"Me? His wife? Oh, no. We don't . . . I mean, I was with him when he fell ill, and I wanted to see he that was all right." Maria fumbled with the coffee she held and realized how foolish she sounded. Why was she here? She did not know anything about this young man other than he frequented the gymnasium and conducted himself with kindness. However, this guiding force to be by his side until he recovered beckoned her to stay.

She turned back to the orderly. "It's all right that I stay here, isn't it? I can help be sure his bandages are changed and . . . " She looked at the other occupied beds. "If you need me, I can help with more, if that is useful."

"You don't need to volunteer to help on the floor in order to stay, miss, but we won't turn you down either. We are short-staffed around here most days. Battles like Gettysburg fill up the beds." He started to leave, then added, "You can stay as long as you'd like." He turned to the needs of a moaning patient nearby.

Maria turned her attention back to Thomas and whispered a prayer. "Lord, there are so many young men injured and dying in this war. Please ease their suffering and help restore them to health and to their families. Please bring Thomas back to us, Lord. I admit that I selfishly want to know him better. In Jesus' name, amen."

At the amen, Thomas' eyes fluttered open. He opened his mouth to speak, but his dry lips refused to cooperate.

"Here. Let me give you a drink." Maria reached for a nearby water pitcher and poured some into a drinking glass. Lifting his head, she held the cool water to his mouth and allowed it to dribble across his lips. He sipped the refreshing contents and sighed as Maria laid his head back on the pillow.

"I'm glad you are awake. I think it is about time to change the linen on your shoulder. Dr. Baker said to change it every day."

Thomas' eyes followed her as she began to unwrap his shoulder. Just then, a bearded man in a white blood-smeared coat stormed up behind her and demanded, "Madam, what do you think you are doing? Who are you? You can't just waltz in here and start doctoring my patients."

Startled, Maria straightened and faced a man who towered over her by at least a foot. His gray eyes narrowed, and his nostrils flared as he chastised her behavior. "I was only trying to help. I was told you may be short-handed, and I assisted the doctor who operated on him before he was brought in yesterday." She tried to bring herself up to full height, but there was no matching the dominance of the man before her.

"Young lady, you cannot treat patients in a hospital without doctor's orders. In this case, that would be me. I'm Dr. Harris. If you want to volunteer, you can read or write letters for the wounded. Visit with them and keep them company if you wish. But you are not trained to nurse these fellows, are you?"

Maria fixed her eyes to the floor for a moment before answering. "It is true. I am not trained to work here, but my mother taught me the importance of hygiene and clean air as a practice to fight contagion." She looked around the room. "It might serve you well to open the windows for a late summer cross breeze here, I'd think."

"You are only a girl, and you have the audacity to tell me how to run my hospital?" Although his beard hid much of his face, it was clear that Dr. Harris' anger was causing it to redden. "Get this . . . this girl out of here!"

The befriended orderly shook his head at Maria as if to warn her not to say another word, but Maria didn't heed the gesture. "I beg your pardon, Dr. Harris. You said I could volunteer to read or write for these men. I promise not to do any unauthorized doctoring if you allow me to stay. I promise to be helpful and only do what I'm instructed." She raised her head and met the doctor's eyes.

The room of the sick and injured reacted to the morning entertainment with interest. They decided to advocate for Maria against her formidable foe. "Let 'er stay"; "C'mon doc"; and "Don't send her away" echoed around the room.

Dr. Harris' eyes narrowed as he turned his attention back to Maria. "All right. Only stay out of the way of the medical staff, Miss . . . "

"Maria Neubauer, sir. I will follow your instructions to the letter." She smiled and winked at the helpful voices from the surrounding beds.

"Why do I predict this is a promise you cannot keep, Miss Neubauer." He shook his head and took a step back before continuing to make his morning rounds about the room.

Maria sat back down at Thomas' side. His cracked lips broke into a welcoming grin. "What are you smiling at, soldier?" She could not help but mirror his smile back at him.

In a hoarse voice, he answered, "I have never seen anyone stand up to a superior officer like that before. You are a marvel." His eyes clouded. "Did you say you came in with me yesterday? What happened? The last thing I remember was you helping me with my arm at the gym. You came over, and . . . then there's nothing."

"You passed out. Some infected fragments remained in your shoulder that were causing you trouble. The local doctor dug the rest of them out and had the soldiers bring you back to the army hospital." She pulled a kerchief from her pocket and opened it. "Here. He even saved you the pieces for a souvenir."

"You kept them for me?" He tilted his head. "You are an odd girl."

"Odd?" That was not the impression Maria had hoped to make. She folded her hands in her lap and drew back a little.

Reading her hurt expression, Thomas apologized. "I'm sorry. I didn't mean anything by it. You are the most fascinating girl I have ever met."

Maria raised her gaze with renewed interest. "Well, you heard the doctor. I can help as long as I don't play doctor myself. Do you have any letters to read?"

With his good arm, Thomas pointed toward his jacket draped across the side table. "You'll find a few in there if you'd like."

Fumbling through the stack of a dozen worn and wrinkled missives in Thomas' jacket pocket, Maria pulled one out, read the return address, and froze.

Seeing her expression, Thomas tensed. "What's the matter?"

"Why do you have a letter from my sister?"

CHAPTER 32

I said, "Let me remember my song in the night;
let me meditate in my heart." Then my spirit made a diligent search.

Psalm 77:6

ALTON, ILLINOIS

Karl shook his *Alton Telegraph* open as he sat in his comfortable chair after a filling dinner of roast and flour dumplings smothered in Lena's brown gravy. His daughters had already scampered off to bed with their favorite dolls, and the household settled into the quiet of the evening.

"I know you want me to make arrangements to bring Maria here, but I'm reading here that the Rebs just shot a Lutheran minister and his son in Indiana. I may not be a soldier, but I'm afraid the civilians aren't any safer." Karl shifted in his chair and glanced over the newspaper at Lena.

"I don't want anything to happen to you." Lena moved closer and draped an arm over the back of Karl's chair. "But I also worry about Maria. A rioting city is no place for a girl to be by herself either."

Karl nodded. "On the other hand, with Union victories at Vicksburg and Gettysburg, the Confederate Army should be on the run, according to the reports I've read. If I stay on the Ohio River steamers as far as Pittsburgh, I can take a train north from there. Getting to New York should be safe enough. The Rebs should be skedaddling south with their tails between their legs by now."

"Please be safe. Don't take any unnecessary risks." Lena kissed him on the forehead. "The girls and I need you back here."

"I'll be safe." He swept her into his lap and wrapped her in his embrace. "I'll take the first steamer out in the morning for an early start."

"As long as you hurry back." Lena fell back into his arms, and they sat in the dusk until darkness overcame it.

Karl arrived at the Alton pier early and hopped on the new steamship, the *Tarascon*. *How fortunate to board one of the newest ships in the fleet,* he thought. *I'll make good time on the river with her.* Karl beamed at his good fortune and took it as an omen that this trip must be ordained by God.

The ropes were released, whistles sounded, anchors weighed; and the slapping of the paddle wheel pushed the vessel down river. The ship slid into the deeper channels, for it was resting low in the water. The mooing below deck indicated the hauling of cattle for Union troops stationed along the river.

Wary Captain Stewart paced the deck and kept a steely eye out for any trouble. Karl approached the virile man in his fifties who twirled his mustache and nursed his pipe in the early morning mists. "Good morning, Captain. Looks like a fine day to be on the river."

"The river is the least of my problems during this infernal war. What do you think the odds of me getting paid for this shipment of cattle once they are delivered?" he grumbled. "The army is full of crackpot promises takin' over and givin' my crew orders as if they were enlisted men; and if they don't jump high enough, they are subject to military discipline. I should be the only one givin' orders on my ship. Blast those Union skags."

Karl took a step back from the fuming captain, unsure whether he should engage his wrath any further. The captain did not look at Karl as he spoke but kept his focus on the river currents and shorelines. Karl thought he may be talking more to himself than to anyone else, so he decided to retreat to another area on deck.

Before taking a step away, Captain Stewart turned to him. "And you, sir. What business do you have on my fine ship today? You aren't wearing a uniform, yet you are a man of fighting age." With a puff of disdain, he continued, "You too coward to fight?"

Surprised at the direct question, Karl sputtered, "Why, no. That's not it at all. I work in a civilian capacity at the Alton Penitentiary. I am employed to assist with their legal services. I assure you I am providing a service for the Union in my own way, sir."

"Is this a legal mission you are on then?" Seemingly unsatisfied with Karl's answer, the captain turned back to the river.

"No, it is a personal mission to retrieve my wife's sister from New York. She is young, and we would not want her traveling across the country on her own with the war on and all." Karl stopped. Why was he spilling this personal information to a complete stranger?

"If I or my crew were not providing transport for the army, we would be arrested for cowardice. It has happened to two captains already. General Wright took the *Florence Miller*, a tinclad packet, away from my friend and called him a coward. Yet you wander the country without someone drafting you into service?" Stewart's dark eyes stared into Karl's.

"I'm sorry about your friend, Captain."

"I'm lucky to have command of my own ship anymore. The army is weaponizing civilian transports up and down the river and using civilian crews as combat personnel. It doesn't matter if we have other contract obligations. I just delivered wounded troops back to their homes in St. Louis. I don't mind helping the poor boys home, mind you, but the government will not be paying for the service; and meanwhile, I am not available to haul paying customers—as if any want to travel these days."

"I'm sure the war will be over soon, and you can get back to your regular trade," Karl tried to reassure him.

"Regular trade? Do you know how much risk I take in this business? It is not unusual to be fired upon during these Union transports by the Rebs. The army will only pay for damages that are from 'direct enemy action.' You're a lawyer. You know that's only a euphemism to deny compensation." He turned to scowl at Karl. "I'll be lucky to have a ship afloat by the time this war is over. And don't tell me it's almost over. They've been telling us that for three years already."

Knowing this was true, Karl did not attempt to refute his comment. With the war the only subject on everyone's lips these days, there didn't seem to be any less contentious topics left for the two men to discuss. Karl retreated to an unoccupied area of the ship and dug out one of his books to read.

After a few days of incessant mooing of jostled cows below deck, the cattle were delivered to Union soldiers stationed in Louisville, Kentucky. Stewart loaded more military supplies for troops along the Ohio while in port. He grumbled through the entire process to anyone who would lend an ear—and even to those who did not.

Finally, after a week traveling with the cantankerous steamboat captain, Karl traveled on a second ship before he disembarked in Pittsburgh, where he booked passage on the Reading for points north. On the train, he could reach New Jersey in another day, then take the ferry to New York with the address he had for Maria.

Navigating the remaining trip was blessedly uneventful. The ferry was less treacherous than the days on the steamer. The constant transport for passengers back and forth to Manhattan or Brooklyn and the other boroughs provided more reliable transportation than catching a steamer to cross the Mississippi to St. Louis.

Once in New York, Karl only needed to find the Brooklyn Concert Hall where Maria was staying. Locating the tall brick building with Roman arches, he opened the unlocked front doors. Slipping inside, he listened to an orchestra practicing a symphony he did not recognize. No one was around to ask directions before a shirtless black boy bounced around the corner of the lobby. A rough-cut rope held his oversized trousers fast to his waist. Both Karl and the boy sized each other up a moment before either of them spoke.

"Excuse me, young man. I am looking for Miss Maria Neubauer. Do you know where I might find her? I was given this address for her. Does she live here?" Karl tried to speak in his softest dad-to-child voice so as not to frighten the lad away.

He was unfazed by the stranger before him, however, and answered. "Sure. I know Miz Maria. We's good friends. She's not here now, though. She's at the hospital."

Alarmed, Karl drew in a sharp breath. "What is she doing at the hospital? Is she hurt?"

"Oh no, sir. She goes every day to be with a soldier she is helping. He fainted at the gym where she helps the orphans."

Karl scratched his head. "Can you tell me where this hospital is, so I can find her?"

"I can, mister, but Mr. Schroeder might not like it." The boy looked around for any sign of Schroeder. "He tries to keep Miz Maria close, and he don't like her spending all her time there. He's asked me to help keep the fellas away from her for 'im."

Karl chuckled. "Don't worry. I'm not just some 'fella' after Miss Maria. I'm her brother-in-law here from Illinois. Her sister sent me here to find her."

The kid tilted his head in a skeptical pose. "I never hear'd her talk about no sister in Ill-noise a'fore. Maybe I should go find Mr. Schroeder for you." Before Karl could convince him that he was no threat to Maria, the lad disappeared around the corner and up the backstairs to the rented rooms.

Karl stood alone in the foyer, wondering if he should follow the boy or wait for him to return with Maria's manager. He knew from her letters that Schroeder was trying to promote Maria's music career, but they had not had much success with her launch since their arrival. He was anxious to meet this man who had been able to spirit Maria away from her family and country with promises of fame and fortune when he did not have a solid plan to achieve it—during a war, no less.

Within moments, the boy led a man in a rumpled suit down the stairs to Karl. Sure his own appearance could not exude much authority either after days of traveling across the country, Karl held out his hand. "Herr Schroeder, I presume."

"I am. And who might you be?" Schroeder grasped Karl's hand and held the firm handshake a little longer than necessary, as if vying for strength.

"I'm Karl Muller. My wife, Lena, is Maria's sister, and she sent me here to find her and bring her back to Illinois with me."

"What? You will do no such thing! I can't launch a singing career for her in the middle of nowhere. We must stay in New York, or she has no chance of making it as a singer."

Karl stood his ground. "By the sound of it in her letters, you haven't been able to launch her career here, anyway. I think the best thing for her now is to reunite with her family, who can take care of her."

"Her parents left her in my care, not yours. I do not give you permission to take her away from here." Schroeder's voice grew louder.

"We received word from Maria's parents that you had no permission to bring her to America in the first place. You have no right to keep her from her family, and we will take her wherever she needs to go to keep her safe. She will be with people who love her. My wife has been worried sick about her since she knew she came here alone."

"She was never alone. I have kept my word and have chaperoned the young Maria her entire trip here."

"I'm not sure an adult man without his wife should be chaperoning a young girl alone, Herr Schroeder. It does not look proper at all." Karl's stare forced an involuntary squirm from Schroeder.

"What are you implying? I have been the model of decorum with Maria. You can ask her yourself." Schroeder's crimson face fumed at the accusation.

"I'd love to ask her myself. Can you please tell me where I can find her?" Karl's patience was wearing thin atop his travel fatigue.

"I suppose she is at the Union Hospital. She has been . . . volunteering." He rolled his eyes at the word.

"The boy said there was a particular soldier she was helping. What's his story?"

"Some kid in uniform collapsed at the gym where Maria's been teaching the kids some songs. She thinks she should help him recover, I guess, and followed him to the hospital. She has been up there daily ever since." No longer red-faced, Schroeder spat out his story for Karl.

Karl tucked this information away for future reference. "Point me in the right direction, and I'll let her tell me the full story."

CHAPTER 33

"I say to you, rise, pick up your bed, and go home."

Mark 2:11

NEW YORK

"Other than Lena telling me Johanna is the spitting image of her sister Maria, I don't even know what she looks like," Karl mumbled as he pushed through the doors of the three-story hospital. Orderlies were pushing legless men in wheelchairs through the doorway of a gathering hall, where a few men were already playing checkers. None of the normal jocularity in the pursuit of a win accompanied the game, only intense concentration.

A clerk with thick, round spectacles fumbled with some papers on a desk and did not look up to address Karl as he spoke to him. "Whatcha need?"

"I'm looking for a girl who . . . "

The clerk cut him off. "We don't treat women at this facility. You'll have to check with the community hospital for any females." He now raised his head to the fool who thought he could find a woman at a Union Army hospital. He pushed his glasses back on his face and smirked.

"No, you don't understand. She wouldn't be a patient. I've been told she comes here to help. A volunteer who reads to the men and such." Karl shifted his hat in his hand and tried to stand taller to emphasize he was not the fool the clerk mistook him for. "She is my wife's sister, and I came to look after her."

The clerk sighed. "We have a few young ladies of charity who offer their assistance to the doctors when they can." He paused. "Your wife's sister have a name?"

"Oh, yes. Sorry." Karl shuffled his feet, which only made him appear more foolish at each turn. "Maria Neubauer. She is blonde . . . blue-eyed . . . and . . . likes to sing," he stammered, trying to think of what information about her may be helpful for the clerk to determine which young lady he wanted.

"Ah, the singing lass." The clerk's face lifted into a smile. "I know which one you mean. I think she has everyone on the second floor madly in love with her. She only has eyes for the private in bed 202, though." He now examined Karl with more purpose. "If you plan on taking her away, you may have a fight on your hands."

"Please just point me in the right direction." Karl sighed.

"She's up the stairs and to the right. She was singing a while ago, and I'm sure she's still there." The clerk pointed his pencil toward the staircase and returned to his paperwork.

Karl entered the room at the top of the stairs and surveyed the rows of cots filled with wounded men. Some moaned; some tossed in restless sleep; and some stared soullessly at the ceiling. About a third of the way across the room sat a blonde girl in a simple blue frock on a ladder-back chair facing away from the door. She was visiting with a soldier in the bed beyond her when a familiar giggle traveled across the rafters to Karl. It had to be Maria. Her melodious laugh echoed like her sister's.

In a few strides, Karl was behind the girl and placed his hand on her shoulder. "Pardon me, miss."

Maria jumped. "You shouldn't sneak up on a person." She stared up at him. "Do I know you?"

"Karl!" Thomas exclaimed from the bed. Until then, Karl had not focused on the soldier lying there. He was only one of the many lying in similar beds filling the room. Now, the familiar face beamed back at him.

"Thomas? I didn't expect you to be here. Last I read, you were guarding the draft house and keeping order after the riots."

"I'm afraid my wound in Gettysburg came back to bite me. Maria here has been taking care of me, and I should be able to be released soon." He nodded at Maria.

Maria nodded, too. "Karl? Are you my brother-in-law Karl? I have read so much about you in letters from my sister. Thomas and I made the connection a few weeks ago when we both had letters from the same people. He said he met you when he was little, arriving here from Germany. He says you tell wonderful stories, too."

"I've been known to spin a yarn or two. I save most of those for my girls now." Karl glowed from the praises.

"Wait until you meet their girls. They are adorable," Thomas interjected.

Karl shook his head. "I can't believe my good fortune finding the two of you together. Lena has been praying you would somehow meet; but I kept telling her New York is a city, not a township, and the chances were slim you would ever meet here. But then she read you were each spending time at Turner Hall, and she prayed that you two would somehow get acquainted."

"I'm sure it was a God thing," Thomas said as he and Maria exchanged knowing glances and smiled at each other.

"What about your singing, Maria? Have you given up on that?" Karl needed to assess the situation about heading home again. "I met Herr Schroeder back at the concert hall. He is not a happy sort, I must say."

"The riots and unrest have made it difficult to hold any concerts. He is frustrated because his vision of me achieving fame and fortune under his tutelage is not happening. The truth is, I'm not sure if singing in music halls is what the Lord wants me to do anymore. I can honor God while singing in orphanages and hospitals and churches, can't I?" Maria's gaze returned to Thomas. Karl was certain this was a subject they had already discussed between them.

"I think those are noble ways to use your gift. Will we have a problem getting you away from Herr Schroeder? Do you have some sort of contract with him?"

"I think he has already broken the contract he signed with Mama and Papa when he brought me to New York. They did not approve of this, judging from the letters I received from home. They never were comfortable with me being alone with him from the beginning."

"I don't like the way he lurks around her either," Thomas added, while gripping the edge of his blanket. "I don't think the man can be trusted."

"Your parents expressed their same misgivings about him in letters to us, too. In fact, Lena has been trying to send me after you since the day we found out you arrived in New York. It was not feasible to come until now." Karl stroked his chin. "I'll see what I can do to rid us of Schroeder. I'm sure he won't be happy going home empty-handed; but you are no slave, and you do not belong to him." Everyone nodded in agreement.

Karl then turned to Thomas. "And what about you? Once you heal, do you go back on active duty?"

"Well, I've already been assigned to the Invalid Corps once. I don't have much use in my left arm, which makes shooting a mite difficult. They may be willing to let me go home."

"I'll talk to your doctors and superiors about arranging it. I have a few connections with the army that may be useful." Karl paused and examined Thomas' condition again. "Have you thought about what you might do once you are back home?"

"I have given this considerable thought. Remember how Stefan wanted to be a pastor? Well, I lost him at Gettysburg, and I want to continue his dream. I can finish my studies at Concordia and be a minister to one of the new congregations forming out West. New German towns are springing up all over. They need pastors, and I think the Lord is calling me to help fill that need. I am sure he saved my life for a reason." Thomas glanced over at Maria. Her face remained placid.

Karl's gaze bounced from Thomas to Maria as if he were reading their thoughts. Could Maria shift from singing in city concert halls to being a rural church wife so easily? That was something the two of them would have to work out on their own. His job was to pave the way for a safe journey home.

Karl saw a doctor in the hall and approached him to learn about Thomas' condition. "Doctor? Private Thomas Krueger tells me he is to be released soon. Can you tell me if he will be eligible to return home? I am a family friend and am available to escort him there if he is released."

The doctor searched the row of filled beds and tried to remember which soldier was Krueger. Seeing Maria and Thomas staring back at him, he answered, "Oh yes, the soldier with the constant lovely companion." The two overheard the doctor's comment and ducked their heads when he acknowledged their connection. "His wounds are healing well, and he no longer has a fever from infection. His superiors may want him to rejoin his regiment, however."

"He tells me he has little use of his left arm. Wouldn't that qualify for a medical discharge? He would not be much use in a battle." Karl pushed his advantage.

"I write the medical report, but I do not create the orders for these young men." The doctor realized Karl was waiting for more of an answer. "I'll get his discharge papers ready, and you or Private Krueger can check if the colonel will sign off on sending him home. Since they started the Invalid Corps, not every wounded soldier goes home who once did in the past. That is not my call."

Karl shook the doctor's hand. "Thank you, Doctor. I appreciate your assistance."

The doctor went to the next patient on his list and Karl returned to Thomas and Maria, who had their heads together in whispers.

"What are you two whispering about?" Karl asked as he approached.

They broke apart with mirrored grins on their faces. "We were basking in our God's providence that He sent you here to fetch us home again," Maria answered.

"And that we will all go together." Thomas reached for Maria's hand with his right-hand grip. She turned crimson again and shifted in her chair.

"I don't have everything arranged yet, but the doctor is working on your medical discharge papers; and then we will approach a superior to also discharge you from the army. Don't get your cart before the horse now, Thomas, but I think we will be able to take you home soon."

CHAPTER 34

May he grant you your heart's desire and fulfill all your plans!

Psalm 20:4

NEW YORK

The next morning, Karl found Schroeder at his usual breakfast table nursing a cup of black coffee and searching the newspaper for any openings in New York's social calendar.

"Drat!" Schroeder tossed the paper down, missing the remainder of the uneaten eggs taunting him with their sunny disposition by a breath. Reaching again for his lukewarm coffee, he raised his head to Karl standing across the table, waiting for his attention.

"Well, I suppose you found her at the hospital like I told you." Schroeder grimaced at the temperature of his coffee and his uninvited guest.

"I did." After Schroeder did not invite him to sit, Karl ventured to invite himself by adding, "Mind if I join you?" He slipped into the unoccupied seat opposite the disgruntled manager without waiting for his bidding.

"Be my guest. As if I could stop you." Schroeder sneered as Karl hailed the waiter for coffee. "I need a warmup, too. This cup isn't hot enough to melt butter," Schroeder added when the waiter arrived, holding disapproving mug aloft.

"So? What do you want to talk about? I haven't been able to get Maria away from that den of germs long enough to advance her fame like we planned." Schroeder continued before Karl could answer. "Did you have any luck convincing her that squandering her days with all those sick and injured is a waste of her time and talent? A young girl should . . . well, I have no idea what a young girl should be doing, but I doubt it's spending all her free time at an army hospital." Exasperated, Schroeder shook his head and stirred his eggs to stop them from grinning at him.

Karl waited for Schroeder to look up. "I did talk to her and the young man she is devoting her time to."

"That boy from the gym? Is she spending all her time with just that one boy?" Schroeder's head jerked up, and he almost rose out of his seat. "That's all I need—a girl smitten with an injured soldier. What will her parents think?"

"I happen to know the young man. His name is Thomas Krueger. My wife and I have known him since he was still in breeches, and Maria could not find a finer person to spend her time with." Karl continued when Schroeder's expression did not change. "He is about to be released from the infirmary, and I intend to take both of them back to Alton with me."

This hot poker of information speared Schroeder to his feet. "What? You can't take Maria away from me. We have an agreement!"

Karl kept his composure and his seat. "You yourself said you cannot find venues for her to sing in this volatile climate. You cannot make the money you intended for either of you without her performances. Her sister wants me to bring her home, and that is what I am going to do." Karl sipped his coffee, unconcerned with Schroeder's reaction.

Schroeder's face reddened. "You can't! I have a contract with her family to promote her."

"My wife and I have letters from the family, and I know they did not give their permission for you to bring Maria to the States. In fact, they have been distressed about you taking her away from home from the beginning of your so-called 'agreement'; and if she is to be in America, they want her united with her family. Maria's sister and brother in Illinois are eager to look after her, whether she sings or not." Karl pushed his chair back from the table. "There is nothing you can do to stop me from reuniting Maria with her family. She is neither your slave nor your ward." He stood up. "I plan for us to leave as soon as I secure Thomas' discharge. You, however, can go wherever you want. I believe you have a wife waiting for you back in Germany?"

"I have no intention of returning home empty-handed to my wife, Herr Muller. Maria has been like a daughter to me." Schroeder gripped the back of the chair he now stood behind.

"But she isn't your daughter, and you have no claim on her. In fact, an unchaperoned young lady traveling with a middle-aged man will not help her reputation in the least. Her family will take care of her needs from now on. You are dismissed." Karl rose and walked away from the steaming Schroeder without another word.

"Colonel?" Karl allowed himself to be escorted through the wood paneled doorway that mimicked the same paneling of the colonel's office. A paper strewn claw-foot desk centered the room, and the officer remained hunched over the semblance of paperwork before him.

The officer only glanced at Karl's entrance; when he realized the man before him held no rank or uniform, he asked, "What can I do for you? I'm a busy man."

"Thank you for seeing me, sir. I am Karl Muller, and I have medical discharge papers for Private Thomas Krueger. I'd like to take him back to his family." Karl held the papers out for the colonel to take them from him. With a sigh, the overworked officer retrieved the offered bundle.

He scanned the documents. As he read, he commented, "So this private has already been in the Invalid Corps. Why shouldn't he go back to them? If he has recovered from his current ordeal, he should resume his duties." He now gave Karl a more discerning assessment.

Directing the colonel's attention back to the paperwork in his hands, Karl continued, "His left arm is of no use to him, Colonel. He cannot shoot a gun. As you can see, he suffered his initial wounds at Gettysburg in meritorious service. He came here to assist in keeping order after the Draft Riots and performed those duties until getting an infection from his earlier wound. I'd like to take him home to his family."

"Are you family?" The colonel shifted in his squeaky chair to consider Karl's request.

"No, sir. A family friend. I've known the Kreuger family since Thomas was a small boy. I had come to New York on other business when I learned of his condition."

"The army needs all our soldiers, Mr. Muller. Even the ones with disabilities can help by serving as cooks, clerks, orderlies, guards, or other assignments. If he cannot shoot a gun, we can issue him a sword for his good arm." He checked the papers again. "He does have a good arm, doesn't he?"

"He does, sir. There is always a danger that some shrapnel remains in his wounded shoulder and the infection may return, however. He may experience pain in that shoulder the rest of his life." Karl grasped for his best arguments to gain Thomas' release. "If you require him to complete his enlistment, I work as legal counsel at the Alton Federal Penitentiary; and I am sure Private Krueger can assist in operations in the West. He would also have family nearby if he relapsed."

The seated officer stroked his chin. "Tell you what. President Lincoln is going to attend the graveside memorial dedication of Gettysburg in a couple weeks. We have been asked to provide members of the Invalid Corps as guard escorts for him. You will be going that way to return home to Alton, will you not? I can dispatch him to the second battalion for the presidential guard regiment; and afterward, he can continue duties at the Alton Prison."

"That sounds like a perfect arrangement, sir. I appreciate your concession on this matter."

"I'll have the proper travel documents drawn up for you, and you can be on your way, Mr. Muller." He nodded at Karl. "I hope you arrive home in safety." He shook Karl's hand in earnest.

Karl beamed as he left the military offices. Not only would he be able to bring Maria and Thomas back home, but he would also be able to see President Lincoln in action. *The Lord is blessing this trip beyond measure,* he thought.

CHAPTER 35

I remember the days of old; I meditate on all that you have done;
I ponder the work of your hands.

Psalm 143:5

$\mathcal{T}$homas donned his sky-blue Invalid Corps uniform. The dark trim accented the long coat and matching hat that marked him as part of the prestigious Presidential Honor Guard. He basked in being selected for such a duty, although he wished he did not have to wear the conspicuous uniform that identified him as disabled. The stamped designation on all his official papers of "IC" reeked of the "Inspected-Condemned" notice that appeared on dilapidated properties to be demolished. He neither wanted to be seen as condemned or useless to others. His arm may not work, but he was certain the Lord had more for him to do with his life.

Many able-bodied soldiers sneered at those in the Invalid Corps as lazy or shirkers who hid behind minimal injuries to stay away from the front lines of real fighting. When Thomas patrolled the streets of New York, he experienced derisive comments from those on the street at times. Only men who had not seen combat mistook his sacrifice. Those who escaped without injury thanked God for their blessed fortune.

The sympathetic civilians would ask about the battle where he was wounded or what he had suffered during his service. However, conversations about the war were not topics for mixed company or timely matters for simple greetings on the street. Thomas had kept his answers polite and brief as possible while he kept to himself—until he met Maria.

Maria's enthusiasm drew others to her like butterflies to blooms. Whether it was the children at the orphanage who followed her like little lambs or the men in the hospital ward who anticipated her arrival every day as much as he did, Maria exuded cheerfulness. She exemplified James 5 of the Bible: "Is anyone among you suffering? Let him pray. Is anyone cheerful? Let him sing praise." She sang praises often and cheered many who suffered.

"Private Krueger? Are you ready?" The knock at the door startled Thomas as he slipped the button into his last jacket hole with his only obedient hand. He opened the door to another similarly dressed soldier, and they walked side by side down the stairs to meet the rest of their party.

They fell into formation and waited for the president's carriage to arrive at the train depot. After the horses halted, the tall president exited and returned his stovepipe hat to his head. A small group crowded to see him off, and he waved at them good-naturedly as his long stride stepped toward the steam-driven locomotive already huffing and puffing in anticipation of its journey.

A distraught farm woman broke through the throng, waving a daguerreotype photo in her hand of a young soldier. "Sir?" She reached for the tail of Lincoln's topcoat. "Can you tell me what happened to my boy? He's been missing since Vicksburg, and no one can tell me where he is." She dropped to her knees, pleading as tears escaped her eyes. "Please. Tell me where to find my boy, Jasper. I must find where he is." She released her grip on the president's coat as she dissolved into a puddle of tears.

Lincoln bent down to peer into the woman's face. "Madam, I am sorry you cannot find your boy. I'm afraid there are many missing young men in this war." He shook his head "I only pray that our Heavenly Father may assuage the anguish of your bereavement and leave you only the cherished memory of the loved and lost and be assured the solemn pride that must be yours at his service to the republic." He stood erect again. "My every prayer is that he is found safe and sound for you, dear mother." He turned and continued through the station with a slow, deliberate gait.

The tearful woman nodded and stepped away for Lincoln to pass. Although she still did not know where her son was, she calmed under the president's attention to her cause.

Thomas fell in line behind him with his detachment as he mounted the steps to the private car. To his right, Karl escorted Maria into another car reserved for dignitaries accompanying Lincoln to Gettysburg for the Soldier's National Cemetery dedication. It was reassuring to know they were nearby and that he would soon be traveling back to St. Louis with them.

The journey on the tracks was delayed in Baltimore when they were transferred to the Northern Central Railway by a team of horses. Once underway, the serene countryside belied the purpose of the sobering trip as rolling hills of fall farms whisked by the chilled windows.

The first sight of Gettysburg revealed stacks of coffins on the depot platform with names of the dead written on the ends to be sent to cemeteries elsewhere upon the family's request. The dismal scene did not dissuade the crowd from welcoming Lincoln and his entourage. Weary Lincoln only wished to retire to the Will's house for his arranged lodging. He had no speech for the waiting people and allowed the Honor Guard to escort him through the maze without a word to them. Instead, Secretary of State William Seward delivered a few words to appease them before retiring about midnight after they were serenaded by the Baltimore Glee Club.

The next morning, Lincoln was paler than the day before. Thomas thought how enormous a weight he bore for this nation. The tall man hesitated mid-stride, adjusted his jacket, and patted the notes tucked away in the breast pocket for reassurance before mounting the provided chestnut bay horse that he rode from his lodgings.

A military contingency under the command of General Mead was already assembled with the state marshal and others noted guests waiting for the speakers. People of all ranks and backgrounds swarmed around the prepared stage in anticipation of the ceremony. An able-bodied column of soldiers fell in to salute the president when he arrived. They had marched to Cemetery Hill and occupied space to the left of the stage. The procession advanced to the front, leaving room for the civic authorities to pass as well.

The honored ladies stood to the right of the stand with a fine view of all the activity. Maria was able to join them, since she accompanied them in the reserved Lincoln car from Washington, DC.

By noon, the military band played a rousing tune to gather everyone together. During the opening prayer to consecrate the moment, the sun broke through the clouds, enlightening the previously gloomy day. The esteemed orator chosen for the day stood before those congregated in Gettysburg.

If some thought Lincoln was the premier speaker for the day, they were mistaken. Former Secretary of State and Harvard professor of Greek literature, Edward Everett, was the most noted orator of the land, and he rose to address the masses milling around on the grounds.

His rich tones, precise and perfect utterance wafted across the meadow. Both mellow and beautiful, he painted word pictures with his vocal instrument. The masses leaned in while he spoke about the ancient battles of the world from memory: "Athen's pathways gleamed with the monuments of the illustrious dead . . . " He spoke of the American Revolution, then the current distress of the nation. He recounted every major movement of the battle of Gettysburg itself before pulling his focus back to European wars for comparison.

Thomas remained stationed with the Honor Guard during the two-hour oration on military history. He whispered to his colleague, "I have read every bit of news about the war that has been printed from the beginning, and Everett has shed more light on current events than I ever read on my own." It was difficult to concentrate on all his historic details while surrounded by the gruesome memories of hiding among the same tombstones they now occupied.

His friend rolled his eyes as if he had heard more than enough already. "I don't know about you, but I would love to sit down. My leg is killing me." He reached down to rub the offending appendage, and Thomas remembered it was the site of his injury.

"Hold on. He must be about done."

On cue, Everett concluded his remarks with, "Wheresoever throughout the civilized world the accounts of this great warfare are read, and down to the latest period of recorded time, in glorious annals of our common country there will be no brighter page than that which relates THE BATTLES OF GETTYSBURG."

The band stuck up another transitional hymn before Lincoln rose for his turn. The drained commander reached into his breast pocket and withdrew a single sheet of paper. Unfolding it, he held it aloft and began, "Four score and seven years ago . . . "

The hired photographer fiddled with his lens for an optimum position for his shot. In Everett's two-hour speech, he had had ample time to photograph the speaker; and he assumed he would have the same opportunity now. However, Lincoln's address of only 272 words caught the fellow unready, and he did not snap a photograph of the president before he retired to his seat.

The puzzled audience looked at one another, expecting more. They scarcely focused on the significance of his words before he departed.

The conductor was instructed to play the final dirge for the day, written for the occasion by Alfred Delaney. The somber music ended, and Gettysburg's Lutheran pastor Henry Baugher offered a final benediction. At four o'clock, the consecration ended.

Thomas and the Honor Guard escorted Lincoln back to the waiting locomotive by six, leaving them to disperse and report to their commanders for further duties.

Thomas found Maria and Karl waiting at the fringes of the excitement. "I guess I'm all yours now. Let's go home." He leaned into Maria's embrace.

CHAPTER 36

Besides this you know the time, that the hour has come for you to wake from sleep. For salvation is nearer to us now than when we first believed.

Romans 13:11

ost of the hangers-on for the ceremony dispersed for their homes or boarded Lincoln's train east again. Karl, Thomas, and Maria bought passage on the 7:15 morning express west in hopes of making connections in Pittsburgh for a steamboat on the Ohio River.

Karl advanced on Maria and Thomas as they stared after Lincoln's departure. "Since we don't board until morning, we will need to find a place for the night."

Maria took Thomas' hand. It was clammy, and he was pale from standing so long at the ceremony. "I think Thomas needs a soft bed for the night. He needs to rest." She touched his forehead with the back of her hand to see if his fever returned. Thomas didn't feel overwarm, but she knew he shouldn't take any chances with his health.

"May I help?" A gentleman in a suit and a minister's collar drew close to their party of three and introduced himself. "I'm Reverend Michael Bachmann. My wife and I have plenty of room at our place if you need a place to stay. The farm took a bit of a beating during the battle, and some spots are still waiting on repair. Still, if you don't mind that, we would be glad to have you."

The three looked at each other and back to their unknown benefactor. Maria was the first to speak. "You are so kind. We would love to accept your offer if you and your wife will have us."

*B*achmann turned to Thomas. "I see you've been wounded, young man. Did it happen here?"

"It did, sir. On Cemetery Hill." He shifted to shake the man's hand but winced in his efforts.

"No need for the formalities. We will be honored to take care of you and your friends for the night."

"I'm Private Thomas Krueger, sir. These are my friends, Karl Muller and Maria Neubauer." Maria curtsied, and Karl shook the reverend's hand. "We . . . " Thomas started to divulge their travel plans to the stranger and thought better of it. "We are grateful for your assistance."

At the Bachmanns' home, Mrs. Bachmann was finishing a fine supper of brats and newly brined sauerkraut. The aroma greeted the travelers long before they reached the door, and Thomas' stomach erupted into an echoing growl. All four stepped into the front room chuckling at his wayward appetite. "Sorry, it's been forever since breakfast." Slightly embarrassed, he rubbed his midsection with his good hand.

The feather beds the Bachmanns provided made rising early in the morning difficult. If they had not had tickets for the morning transport, it would have been easy to roll over and snuggle into the clean, inviting sheets again. However, Karl was sure to wake his charges with enough time to catch the train.

Mrs. Bachmann was waiting for them at the bottom of the stairs with rolls she had baked the night before. "Here. Take these and some cheese. You can't leave hungry." She glanced at Thomas for confirmation. "Those rides on the rails can be long and tedious."

Before anyone could respond, each had a small knapsack of provisions in their hands.

"Thank you so much for your hospitality." Maria hugged the generous woman while Karl and Thomas shook the reverend's hand who appeared from a side door.

"Blessings on you both," Karl added.

"You will be in our prayers for safe travels. The world can be a treacherous place these days. Take care." The Bachmanns waved to their houseguests, and the group made their way back to the depot platform to board the westbound express to Pittsburgh.

*M*aria jolted as the whistle blared another intermittent stop as it weaved its way across Pennsylvania. "Does this blasted train need to stop at every burg across the whole state? I had just dozed off, and that screeching siren blasts another ear-piercing scream." Her two companions only smiled at her annoyance.

"It could be much worse. Have you ever ridden a stagecoach across rutted or muddy roads that are not much more than glorified trails?" Karl chuckled. "We are fortunate that we have the Baltimore and Ohio Railroad to hurry us along. A generation ago, that would not have been possible."

Thomas only shrugged. His way east involved marching with his regiment, and he much preferred this to the days and days of forced marching. Explaining that to a pampered Maria would be futile. She would never understand the life of a soldier.

"Can someone at least tell me how much longer before we are scheduled to arrive? I'm getting stiff sitting in the same position for so long." Maria stretched her legs as far as they would extend, knocking into Karl's boots in front of her. "Oh, I'm sorry, Karl. I needed to . . . "

"I understand—sitting still is not your strong suit. Your sister is the same." Karl grinned in remembrance of his early encounters with Lena. "We will arrive by nightfall, and then we will find a steamboat that will take us the rest of the way. I think you will like that better, since you can walk around during the transport."

"I agree. The steamboats are the best way to travel." Thomas touched Maria's hand. "You can lean on my good shoulder to rest. I'm afraid I can't do anything about the whistles, though."

Maria leaned into the offered shoulder and nuzzled her cheek into his uniform jacket. "Thank you. I'll try to keep my complaining to a minimum. Forgive me. You two have been terrific escorts." She closed her eyes and was soon asleep, trying to resume the wonderful dream that had broken up too soon. In it, the daring young soldier rode up on a silver charger and saved her from a fairy tale ogre of her childhood. The image was of the same fair-faced young man she found herself clinging to as she sought to finish her slumbering adventure.

Thomas was amazed that Maria slept through several whistle stops before she woke again. The sun streaked through her tousled hair, and a crease formed across her cheek from his jacket. The otherworldly aura about her sleepy condition stirred his senses. Eventually, she stretched, brushed her hair from her sleepy eyes, and rubbed her temples to rouse herself.

"What are you looking at?" she whispered to Thomas as she noticed his gaze.

"I'm looking at the most beautiful girl I've ever seen." He took one finger and looped a stray strand of hair behind her ear. "You will be happy to know you slept through a few stops along the way."

"I think those whistles became part of a fervent dream I was having. There were too many alarms in it to be a coincidence." Maria giggled and stretched her neck to peer out the window. "Where are we?"

"We will be pulling into Pittsburgh soon." Thomas turned toward her. "I want to hear more about this alarming dream."

"The dream itself was not alarming at all. It was quite pleasant, in fact." Maria returned his gaze coyly. "I was being rescued from perils—thus, the alarms—by a . . . " She smiled, her eyes sparkling. "By a handsome young man on a regal steed. He took my breath away."

"He did, did he?" Thomas soaked in the way she was looking at him. "I hope he was worthy of you."

"In dreams, the hero is always worthy." She turned back to the window to avoid more of Thomas' scrutiny.

"The sky is getting dark. Is it that late?" Maria furrowed her brow at the sight of small dirty houses dotting the hillside.

Karl turned to answer her. "This is a coal mining industrial town. Many of the factories here are keeping the Union supplied with weapons and artillery, plus building ironclads, and other items needed for the war. The smokestacks from the factories cause the dingy air to hang here most of the time. I'm afraid you will have to endure it until we leave."

The once-annoying train whistle was welcome when it announced the Pittsburgh station, and the three disembarked to find night's lodging.

CHAPTER 37

So now I have come out to meet you, to seek you eagerly,
and I have found you.

Proverbs 7:15

PITTSBURGH, PENNSYLVANIA

Karl assisted Maria and Thomas from the train, grabbed their belongings, and stepped out to find transportation. After a long day on the train, only Maria had slept; and Thomas was drained from the train jostling his wounded shoulder.

Adjusting her eyes to the soot-filled environment, Maria asked Karl, "Do you already have a place to stay here?"

"I know a prominent doctor here who helps runaway slaves. I have read some of his work on the Fugitive Slave Act. I am hoping he will have room for us for one night as we head home."

Maria and Thomas tilted their heads at the resourcefulness of their guide. "We are so spoiled to have him shepherding us along," Thomas said to Maria. "I'd have no idea who to contact in a strange city, and I'd be knocking at the door of some seedy tavern or something. I am always at the mercy of the kindness of strangers."

"Karl's not a stranger. He's my brother-in-law and your longtime friend," Maria corrected.

"I don't just mean him. You would never believe my first trip to St. Louis alone. I met many helpful strangers." He paused. "Your kindness was a pleasant surprise, too." He peered through the evening haze at Maria's pretty face, now smudged with a layer of descending ash from a nearby factory.

Karl left to find a porter to speak to and soon rejoined Thomas and Maria. "It's all arranged. A fine fellow happens to be heading that way and is willing to take us to Dr. LeMoyne's."

"A Frenchman?" Thomas was puzzled.

"This country is comprised of immigrants from everywhere, not only Germans, Thomas." Karl guided the two toward a waiting wagon, where a gray-bearded gentleman sat holding the reins of his draft horses.

The driver searched the three travelers from his seat and asked, "Is that all you have with you?"

"That's all," Karl answered. "I told you we would not be much trouble. One trunk for the lady. We fellas travel light."

"I have room for two of you up front, but one of you will have to ride in the back with my freight." The driver motioned to the unlabeled crates and bags of grain weighing down the wagon bed.

"I'll take the back." Karl offered his hand to Maria to mount the front of the wagon.

The driver frowned at the arrangements. "You younger ones should allow your elders the more comfortable seating," he muttered as he made room for his passengers.

Karl appeased him by explaining, "Our young soldier friend here is suffering from a wound he sustained at Gettysburg. Your seat is bound to have more spring to it for its comfort than this buckboard.

I'm fine back here—and I am not that old." Karl settled in among the cargo. "We appreciate your assistance."

The evening sky was backlit by factory smokestacks and fireplace-lit homes on the hillsides to ward off the fall chill in the air. Maria pulled her wrap tighter around her shoulders as they rambled through the streets to the doctor's home.

The wagon stopped in front of a three-story Greek revival style house with two doorways surrounded by ornate pilastered columns. Maria and Thomas stared agape at the opulent home.

"Here ye be," the driver called out. "You okay grabbing that trunk yourself? My back's been giving me fits all week."

"No problem. Just let me be sure the doctor is in before you leave us on the side of the road, please." Karl hopped off the back of the wagon and approached what appeared to be the main entrance when the door swung open before him. "Good evening, ma'am. My friends and I were wondering if you had a place for us tonight. We are on our way back to Alton, Illinois. The doctor and I have friends in common there."

Before the woman answered, an overweight man with a whaler beard appeared behind her. "Who is it, Maude?"

"Someone looking for shelter, sir. Says you know folks in common out Illinois way."

"I'm Dr. LeMoyne. You need a room, do you? My wife is putting down the children at the moment, but I think we can put you up for the night." His eye caught Thomas and Maria making their way off the seat next to the driver. "You're not alone?"

"No, sir. I have my sister-in-law and a wounded soldier with me. We are traveling home after accompanying Lincoln to the Gettysburg Cemetery commissioning."

"Well, that's about the only thing in the papers today. Come in and tell me all about it." Glancing over Karl's shoulder, he said, "That goes for your traveling companions, too. Jubal! Come help these folks with their bags. Let's bring them in from the cold."

A young black man hurried to the door from the back of the house to assist with Maria's trunk. Jubal and Karl locked eyes. "Wait." Karl stayed Jubal's hand. "You from Missouri, son?"

Jubal did not answer. Silence was always the best course of action when the reason for the question was unclear.

"He's a friend, Jubal. It's okay to answer," the doctor encouraged him.

Jubal swallowed hard and checked for any slave catchers lurking in the bushes. While he hesitated, Karl continued. "Is your mama's name Juana, by chance?"

Now more alarmed than ever, Jubal blurted, "You know about my mama?" Involuntary tears began rolling down his cheeks.

"You are her Jubal!" Karl pulled the boy to him and squeezed him in a big bear hug. "I have been looking for you."

Jubal didn't hug him back, stiff against Karl's chest.

"Is Mama dead? Is that whatcha came to tell me?" Jubal stepped back and eyed Karl warily.

"Oh no, no. Not at all. She has been helping my wife and family ever since my wife . . . " Karl paused at the memory of the night he had met Juana hiding behind the wood pile during Lena's labor with the twins. "She helped my wife with a rough baby delivery. She was sent by God that night and has stayed with us ever since. She prays for you every day, and I have been doing my best to find you for her."

"My mama is free?" Jubal almost collapsed from the revelation. "I was so afraid the mastah would beat her after I left, but I couldn't stay no more." He dropped his head in his hands.

"Trust me. She is just fine. She will be so happy the Lord put you in my path." Karl gave Jubal another hug.

"I'm happy for your reunion, but we need to warm these folks up here and get them settled for the night." The doctor regained command; and soon, all parties and belongings were ushered into the house.

Maude fed Maria and Thomas some porridge before seeing them to their rooms. "This'll hold you over 'til breakfast. I'll fix you up something like I do for the family before you go on the road again."

"Doctor? Do you mind if I visit with young Jubal here a bit before I turn in? I'm sure his mother will want a full report," Karl said.

"That's fine. I have some early calls in the morning; so if you don't mind, I will call it a night myself. I'll let you tell me about Gettysburg in the morning before you go." He trudged up the stairs to join his wife.

Turning to Jubal, Karl asked, "How did you end up here in Pittsburgh? Your mama thought you joined the army. I've been trying to find you on some regiment roster, but I wasn't sure what name you used now that you're free."

"I had a mind to do just that when I left home, but the Union wasn't taking no black men at that time. I helped dig some graves after some battles for 'em, though." Jubal averted his eyes. "You mentioned Gettysburg. I was there. Those soldiers had us dig up some of the shallow graves and rebury those boys proper-like. If I never see a dead man again, it will be too soon."

"I imagine. Did you quit following the troops after that?"

"I figured there must be a better way to survive as a free man. I hung around with a few other fellas seekin' safe houses and dodgin' slave catchers. Then we hear'd about work building Fort Robert Smalls here in Pittsburgh. They were using free blacks to do all the work. Me and my friends jumped at the chance for regular work even though none of us knew this Robert Smalls."

"I think I read something about him. He escaped slavery, too, didn't he?"

"Yessir. He captained one of those steamboats right past the rebel guards and took his whole family and some others north to freedom. Can you 'magine?" Jubal chuckled and shook his head. "And now I'm helping build a fort with his name on it. Don't that beat all?"

"The times are changing, Jubal. Are you ready to come back with us and be with your mother?"

"I don't think I can go just yet. First, I need to help finish what I started here, and I hear tell Lincoln is lettin' the freed slaves fight now that the war is goin' on for so long. He needs us."

"I'm sure he does. With the victories at Vicksburg and Gettysburg this year, I am sure we are nearing the end of it now." Karl saw Jubal's earnestness. "You do what you think is right. I will let your mother know you are fine and that I found you doing honorable work. She will be sad I did not haul you home with us, though." Karl held out his hand to shake Jubal's, and he received it with pleasure.

"You travelin' on the river tomorrow?"

Karl nodded.

"Be careful. The Rebs have been attacking steamers. They's taking any blacks, free or not, and sellin' them down the river. The white folks get hurt in the fighting sometimes, too. Don't want your young lady to be mixed up in somethin' like that."

"Thanks, Jubal, for the warning. I traveled most of the way east on the rivers and was fortunate to not have any trouble, but a captain told me stories about attacks. We will stay on our guard." Karl shook Jubal's hand. "Better turn in. We can say our goodbyes in the morning."

CHAPTER 38

The prudent sees danger and hides himself,
but the simple go on and suffer for it.

Proverbs 22:3

KENTUCKY

Jubal volunteered to drive the wagon of travelers to the port in the morning. The mist rose from the water, clouding the riverboats lined along the shore. "You's be careful. This late in the season, the river runs low. Sometimes, they 'most scrape bottom and if'n a cold snap hit, parts can start to freeze before you's make it home."

"Don't worry. These paddlewheel captains have plenty of experience navigating these waters. We'll be just fine," Karl answered as he helped Maria from her perch on the wagon. Thomas refused Karl's hand of help and bounced down on his own accord.

"You're chipper this morning." Maria grinned at Thomas. "You must have slept well."

"I did." He smiled back. "I had some pleasant dreams."

Maria turned away but not before Thomas caught the hint of a blush spreading over her cheeks.

Jubal hoisted Maria's trunk on an awaiting trolley with little effort. Karl purchased tickets to the *Lily*, a sturdy ship in need of a new coat of paint. Returning to his party, Karl announced, "We have tickets on this paddle-wheeler. It is little more than a barge. The army has commandeered her to transport goods. Few passengers are traveling during these turbulent times, so we are lucky to catch a ride down river."

"Will this take us all the way to Alton?" Maria wondered.

"No, we will need to change steamers near Louisville because of the narrow canal around the falls. We will find another ride there."

"Louisville? Isn't Kentucky southern territory? How safe will that be?" Thomas glanced at Maria as if he wanted to reach out and protect her.

"Actually, that may be the safest part of the whole journey. Several federal regiments are stationed at Louisville to prevent Confederate forces from attacking that key position. Ironically, some Kentucky folks want to advocate for the preservation of the Union and keep their slaves. Don't think that's working too well for them. I'm sure you won't see any signs of Rebs in Louisville. All attempts to raid that area have been thwarted thus far."

Relieved, Thomas placed his functional hand on Maria's back and guided her to the awaiting *Lily.* Karl said his goodbyes to Jubal with promises to relay his well-being to his mother once he returned. "If someone can write a note to us in Alton concerning your whereabouts from time to time, I'll be sure to read them to your mother. She has been anxious about you."

"I'll be sure to do that. Tell Mama I have a mind to join up after we got the fort built." With a pause Jubal, added, "Sir, I's so glad God saw fit to lead my mama to you. Thank you so much for looking after her."

"I think she takes care of us more than we take care of her, but I believe you are right. The Lord led us to each other like He sent us to you last night." The two men shook hands in gracious farewell.

Once aboard, Maria walked the deck in silent inspection. "I thought these river boats were grander than this." The rusting railings and pitted planking were dotted with noticeable bullet holes, and a few missing fixtures reeked of wear and tear. "Are you certain it's okay?" She turned her eyes to Thomas for reassurance.

"I've not spent as much time traveling as Karl; but if he says it will get us to Louisville, I'm sure he is right." Thomas pulled her closer as Maria shivered in the morning breeze. Karl walked into sight from around the corner, and Thomas released her and stepped aside enough for daylight between them.

Karl shook his head with a knowing grin. "You two ready to settle inside, or do you want to catch your death of cold out here?" He nodded toward the quarters, and they retreated inside like well-trained pets.

True to Karl's word, the steamboat ride was less jarring than the train ride, even with all the bends on the waterway and dodging floating debris of logs or dead animals. A gentle peacefulness of pastoral scenes and wooded acres gliding past offered a serene window to this new country for Maria. No hint of war dotted the landscape; however, ships that passed them often were loaded with more military cargo and armed mounted guns with sentinel guards.

The towns rolled by on the Ohio River. Wheeling, Marietta, Maysville, and Cincinnati did not entice Maria to explore further. The only port she yearned for was the one where she would find her sister and brother. The days dragged on with no complaints from the young couple, who enjoyed spending more time with each other. To pass the time, the three of them would play the German card game, Skat. The men often allowed Maria to win, even when she played loose with the rules.

Maria wondered if she would be able to see Thomas again once they reached Alton. He was still an enlisted man and would report for duty at the Alton Penitentiary where Karl worked. Maria did not know what expectations lay ahead for her once she arrived either. Would she find another place to sing? She must find a way to contribute to the family without being a burden. *Lord, what will be my future?*

Destined to disembark in Louisville to change boats, Maria, Thomas, and Karl stood in the crisp air as they docked next to other waiting paddle-wheelers. The bustling docks were the gateway to a seedy city that beckoned the young soldiers to empty their pockets.

"Oh, my. You told us about Union troops stationed here, but I had no idea that every other building would be a brothel or gambling hall." Maria's eyes widened at the assault on her innocence. Herr Schroeder and her parents would have never subjected her to such sights. With so many establishments crowded on top of each other, there was no avoiding the corruption that greeted them as they went ashore.

"I'm afraid sordid businesses follow where the men are. I'm sorry. I didn't know we'd be walking into this." Karl sighed. "Let's find a respectable place with a soft bed to stay the night and hop on an early ship out of here in the morning."

"Indeed," Thomas agreed as he searched to find a way around the debauchery before them. A Union general paced the docks inspecting the shipment operations loading onto a barge. Thomas sought him out, saluted, and addressed him at full attention. "General?"

The stout, mustached man turned to the young private in his distinctive Invalid Corps uniform. His eyes softened at Thomas' impaired situation. "Yes, soldier? What can I do for you?"

"My friends and I are looking for a decent place to stay for the night before heading downriver tomorrow," Thomas inquired. "Can you steer us away to more suitable lodgings, sir? We have a lady with us."

"Where is your regiment, young man? Why are you traveling with civilians?" The general furrowed his brow at Karl and Maria, who stood back while Thomas addressed the commander.

"I've been reassigned, sir." Thomas reached into his breast pocket for his signed orders to show his superior. "They are family friends. We are going to the same place, so we are traveling together." He handed him the folded papers to inspect.

The general read a moment, then gave the papers back to Thomas. "These look in order. The Louisville Hotel should be able to accommodate you three. That's where I'm staying."

The three of them followed the general's pointing finger to a formidable Greek revival building. Three columns stood two stories high outside the entrance as if welcoming a giant from one of Maria's childhood fairytales.

Inside, it was no less impressive. More Greek columns connected ceiling arches far overhead. Chandeliers dropped to fill the cavernous openings that illuminated the marble tile floors that well-dressed patrons clicked their polished shoes across. Top hatted men smoked cigars, and bowler men sported canes as they greeted one another with formal handshakes.

Above the registration desk loomed an oversized ornate carved clock that displayed the time from any vantage point in the room. Swaying trees filtered the light through high windows above the fancy clock, causing shifting shadows to bounce across the room. The shadows chased the porters to and fro as they transported luggage and messages about the room. At the end of the lobby, a sign marked TELEGRAPH provided the patrons with the convenience of immediate communication with the rest of the world.

Maria's jaw dropped open as she absorbed the beauty before her. "Can we afford this?" she whispered to Karl. "I never saw anything so beautiful in Bremen or New York, and I have never heard of this place before."

"Louisville has a very prosperous spot on the Ohio. It has become one of the most populous cities in the country." Karl surveyed the opulence further. "I must admit, I'm overwhelmed myself." He then tossed a glance at Maria and Thomas. "If we don't make a habit of it, I'm sure we can swing the price for a night of luxury. Just once."

Maria and Thomas smiled at each other, and Thomas squeezed her hand.

After a night in feather beds, they met for breakfast in the stylish dining hall that served poached eggs, toasted bread, and fresh fruit preserves. Outside, they emerged into the mass of humanity strolling the Louisville streets of trade.

"Today, we board the *Amelia West*." Karl presented them with boarding passes he had obtained through the concierge. "It will be similar to the *Lily* from the past several days. So goodbye to your night of luxury." He grinned.

"I guess if you've seen one paddle-wheeler, you've seen them all," Thomas jested. "It isn't such a bad way to travel, though, I must say."

"Why don't we climb to the upper level for a better view of the city before we leave?" Maria asked. "When we arrived, we were so anxious to find lodging, we did not take it all in. After that marvelous stay last night, I think this city may have more to offer than I first imagined."

⚜

A few more days on the river and the complacency lulled the passengers into a sleepy daze of similar riverbanks and small towns. Each was held by Union regiments along the waterway to keep commerce open. In fact, since the Union victory at Vicksburg, shipping commenced all the way to New Orleans now without a blockade. The war must be over soon.

A whistle split the air before a bullet ricocheted off the railing near Thomas' head.

"Get down!" He pulled Maria to the floor with him as more shots rang out and they realized they were under attack. Huddled together, they scurried behind a barrel secured on deck. Thomas wanted to crawl inside the cabin for safety but knew his one arm would not hold him to drag himself across the opening. Could Maria make it without him shielding her in the open?

"Maria. You'd be safer inside. Can you make it to the door?" She nodded as another bullet splintered the railing above her head. "You must make yourself as small as possible and fast. That means crawl.

You understand?" Thomas turned Maria to look at him to be sure she did.

⚜

*M*aria appraised her voluminous skirt layers and decided they would only impede her escape. To crawl like Thomas told her was impossible in all that fabric. Casting modesty aside, she told him, "I have to take off this skirt if I am to crawl. Don't look, and I'll go." She unfastened the buttons that held her waistband to wiggle out of the incumbrance.

Thomas averted his eyes from her as she shimmied out of the skirt. Her linen undergarments still covered her but allowed her the freedom to move quickly. She heard Thomas' voice in her ear: "Go after you hear the next shot. It doesn't sound like many guns, so they will be reloading."

As Thomas finished, a bullet hit the barrel they crouched behind. "Go!"

Maria wiggled her way to the door faster than a hunted rabbit.

"Now, what about you?" Maria yelled from the relative safety of the steamer cabin.

"My arm won't support crawling like you did. I'm going to have to wait it out here until this is over," Thomas shouted back.

Behind Maria, Karl's familiar voice called her. He had dashed inside from the other side. "Are you fine? Hit?" He tilted his head at her half-dressed appearance.

"I'm fine. The skirts prevented me from crawling, but Thomas is still out there. He says his arm won't allow him to crawl here without raising up above the rails." Her fear rose in her throat at the prospect of losing him.

"Wait here." Karl waited for a shot just as Thomas had warned her; then he ran out and dragged Thomas back inside before you could say Mississippi twice.

Maria wrapped Thomas in her arms. She kissed his cheek and sighed in relief.

"We aren't safe yet," Karl interjected. "Let me see if I can tell where this attack is coming from. You'd think if it were from shore, we'd be out of range by now. Captain Carlson sped up the minute it began." He peered outside before stepping to the rail. "There is a keel boat sidled up beside the paddle-wheeler. It's full of Confederate soldiers, trying to shimmy up the side of the ship. I'll see if I can help." Karl pulled out a gun from his jacket. "Thomas, you keep Maria safe. Here." He handed Thomas the revolver. "You should be able to use it with only one hand."

"Where did that come from?" Thomas wondered out loud.

"Never mind that now. I need to help the captain keep these scalawags off here. They will want whatever we are carrying, and they might hurt Maria if they find her here. Promise me. Don't let anyone hurt her."

"I would never let anything happen to Maria." Thomas held the gun tighter and drew Maria close again.

The *Amelia West*'s crew were already shooting down at the attackers who were trying to scale the hull. One was already bleeding in their keelboat. They had connected themselves with a rope to the *Amelia West*, which was towing them down the river. The accomplices on the riverbank were far out of sight now. Those on horseback could not navigate the forested terrain along the riverbank to give proper chase. Their shore support was gone.

The Rebels cut the cord between the two ships in a desperate attempt to retreat before all in their party died in their failed raid attempt. Soon, the *Amelia West* was weaving her way down the river again without having suffered much harm.

Karl found Thomas and Maria still wrapped in each other's arms when he returned inside. "Ahem." They broke apart as Karl tossed Maria's discarded garment to her. "I think it is time Maria retrieves her skirt and gets decent again."

Both blushed. Maria jumped up and followed Karl's orders.

CHAPTER 39

For this reason, I bow my knees before the Father, from whom every
family in heaven and on earth is named, that according to the
riches of his glory he may grant you to be strengthened with power
through his Spirit in your inner being.

Ephesians 3:14-16

Mississippi River

A couple days later, Karl declared, "We've turned upriver onto the Mississippi now. We'll be home before you know it."

Maria straightened her rumpled dress and sighed. "I'm going to look worse for wear when we arrive. I haven't had a decent bath since our fancy Louisville night."

"Don't worry. Lena and the girls will be happy to see you, no matter what your state." Karl hugged her. "She misses having any sisters around her."

"I don't feel I know her that well. I had only started school when she left. I was just a child."

Thomas interjected, "I think I had the same thoughts about reconnecting last spring. I was only a small boy when Lena traveled with my family to America. I wondered if she would even be happy to greet me? Yet Easter was delightful, and Lena showed genuine interest in me and my friend Stefan." His face fell at the mention of Stefan's name.

"You haven't told me too much about Stefan. You said you joined up together?" Maria took Thomas' hand in hers.

"Yes. I don't think he would have joined if I hadn't convinced him to come with me. I am guilty of his death at Gettysburg." Thomas hung his head.

"Don't take that responsibility, Thomas. The Lord is in control of a person's wellbeing, not us," Karl broke in. "Stefan showed considerable interest in the military tour I gave you both when you visited. I'm sure it did not take too much convincing for him to enlist. If I remember right, he was carrying his own guilt about friends and family who were fighting back home while he was not."

"True, but his real desire in life was to become a pastor, and now he will never have the chance." Thomas shook his head.

The three were quiet for some moments before Karl announced, "The next stop is Cape Girardeau. While the ship exchanges cargo, I'll go ashore and telegram Lena that we will be home in time for Christmas."

"Christmas? Is it that close to Christmas? I have lost track of the days." Maria pressed her hand to her mouth.

"We are deep in the season of Advent, dear. By the time we arrive in Alton, the holiday will only be a week or so away," Karl told her.

"I can't believe it. I will be at your house for all the high holy days this year. First, Easter and now Christmas." Thomas smiled. "I wish I had gifts for your girls, though."

"I think seeing us all home safe and sound will be gifts enough," Karl said. "At least, I hope so because I am coming as empty-handed as you are, and they are *my* girls." He chuckled before the winter breeze sucked the mirth away.

Maria put her arm around him. "Like you said, coming home will be the best gift for them."

"Thank you." Karl returned his sister-in-law's squeeze without looking at her.

As promised, Karl disembarked at Cape Girardeau. It was guarded by several Union forts and occupied by many regiments of bluecoat soldiers. Lads from Nebraska, Iowa, and Illinois marched through the streets in unison.

Karl sought the telegraph office in the three-story brick building of the St. Charles Hotel. Whistling to himself on the way back, he recounted his blessings for this trip. He was escorting his wife's sister home; he had secured the reassigned Thomas to be in his care; and soon, he would be in the arms of Lena and his daughters—and before Christmas! Not only that but he also carried wonderful news to share with Juana about finding her son well and resourceful. The Lord had blessed him beyond measure.

Once he was aboard, the *Amelia West* slipped away from the shore and headed north again. A chill hovered in the air, but the warm spirit of the three travelers embraced it as their due.

"It won't be long before the river won't be navigable again until the spring thaw. We are fortunate to make it home before the full blast of winter descends," Karl mused as the three watched the shoreline whisk past them.

"Boy, I remember what that's like. I had to walk three days all the way to St. Louis from my home last winter, since the river was frozen." Thomas shook his head. "That's the last time I was with my family. I will miss them this Christmas." A cloud fell across his face. "It will be my first Christmas away from them."

"This will be my first Christmas away from home, too," Maria remarked. "I am happy to be with my family here, however. If I'd been left in New York, that would not be the case. Thank you, Karl, for coming to get me."

"It was my pleasure." He gave Maria a side hug. "Besides, if I did not fetch you; your sister would never let me live it down." They all chuckled and sunk back into their own thoughts.

A few days later, Karl stood on deck searching upriver for signs of home through thick fog after leaving St. Louis. "There it is!" he called inside the cabin to Thomas and Maria. "That's the penitentiary on the bluff! That's Alton! We're home!"

The other two searched through the mist for the target Karl pointed out on shore, but it was a few more minutes before the imposing structure emerged, bold and foreboding.

"What a sight." Maria recoiled from the military fortress. "How far is it to your house from there?"

"Not far at all. We live on Christian Hill, where the church bells ring clear as glass." Karl's anticipation of home overshadowed any misgivings of the familiar prison. The paddles strummed to a stop at the Alton port, and Karl almost shouted aloud his delight of returning home. He wanted to jostle himself to be the first one ashore and hurry home, but his manners thwarted his enthusiasm as he waited for Thomas and Maria to gather their belongings and wait beside him.

The ship's whistle pierced the air as it came to a full stop, and Karl hoped that Lena would know it announced their arrival—a silly notion, to be sure, since ships came and went many times a day in Alton. What would make this whistle stand out among all the rest?

Karl paid a porter to deliver Maria's trunk to his home, and he grabbed the first available hack to hurry his charges along. If it had only been himself, he likely would have bounded up the hill on his long legs, leaving everything else behind. Again, he knew that was not the way to approach today and that Lena would scold him for not bringing her sister in after such a long journey.

Thomas' eyes were fixed on the imposing penitentiary that would soon be his new station. "It somehow is bigger than I remember," he said, more to himself than the others. "It's hard to believe that one of my inspirations for joining the army will now be my own obligation."

Following his eyes, Maria remarked, "It looks like a Gothic castle with those chest-size stones jutting out of the fog into the unknown." She shivered under her shawl that she wrapped a bit tighter.

"Goodness, you two. We are finally home, and you are lamenting over the size of the prison? Set your sights on seeing Lena and the girls." Karl's joy was not shaken by their distracted remarks.

Maria straightened up. "Believe me, I am so happy our journey is complete, and I can be with family again. I'm sorry if I sounded ungrateful." She refocused her attention to the fine homes and the Catholic cathedral on the hillside. "Now that is a much better use of stone, I'd say—to build a church." The spires stretched out above the haze.

"Here we are." Karl had the driver stop in front of his white house. The autumn leaves already vacated the trees for the season, but it did not damper the peaceful calm that settled over the home. "The children must be napping. You often find this place a turmoil of giggles and laughter."

Karl burst through the front door without waiting for his guests this time. They could follow at their leisure. He needed his family.

"Lena! I'm home!" The aroma of dinner brewing on the stove drove him into the kitchen, where he found Lena and Juana side by side preparing the evening meal. Lena turned and wiped her hands on her apron to be swept up in her husband's arms.

"Karl! You made it!" He twirled her around the kitchen one more time as the girls emerged from their bedroom for their part in the reunion.

"Papa! Papa!" At once, Karl's arms were full of daughters and wife together, laughing in the pure joy of each other.

At the front door, Maria and Thomas stood smiling at the domestic scene before them. It was fine that no one greeted them for a moment. In time, Lena broke away from Karl's embrace to welcome the guests at the door. She gave him a playful swat on the arm and said, "Why did you leave Maria and Thomas standing in the doorway?"

Without another word, Lena wrapped her arms around her younger sister and hugged her like she would never let her go. "I can't believe you are all grown up." She took a step back to take better inventory. "You are such a beauty. I am so happy you are here." She embraced her again.

Thomas waited for his moment to be acknowledged once the family reunions were complete before stepping into the festivities. The girls recognized him from Easter and offered welcoming hugs but stared at Maria as a new entity they were not sure how to address.

"Come here, girls," Lena cajoled. "This is your aunt Maria. I told you that your papa was going to bring her to us, remember? She is my sister, just like Uncle Herman is my brother."

They came closer and stared up at the pretty lady with blue eyes and silky blonde hair. She did not look much like their mother, who had brown hair; but they were near the same height and figure. "I think our Johanna looks much like you, Maria. Her features are lighter than mine; she could be your daughter."

Maria knelt to the youngsters' level to caress them. "You two are the loveliest creatures I have ever seen. Your grandparents would love to spoil you if they had a chance; but since they are not here, I will have to do it for them, won't I?" She tickled the girls; and they wiggled away to hide behind their mother, still grinning at their new relative.

"Speaking of Herman, when do I get to see him?" Maria wondered.

"I've invited everyone over for Christmas, so they will be coming in a little more than a week," Lena answered. "We will have the most joyous time celebrating your arrival. We have all been waiting for you to come almost as much as the Lord's coming. Juana and I have been planning the best treats to make for everyone." Lena drew Maria to herself again. "This is truly a blessing to have you here with us."

Juana, setting the table for the extra guests, looked up as Lena mentioned her name. "Juana, come here," called Lena. "I want you to meet my sister Maria." Juana dipped a quick curtsey toward the room, and Lena continued. "I don't know what we would do without Juana. She has been a godsend this past year. She has been waiting on news about her son since the war began."

Karl stepped forward. "Juana, I have news about Jubal."

Juana froze as Karl said her son's name.

"Yes, we met him in Pittsburgh," Thomas added.

Juana's eyes grew big and tearful. "You's saw him?" She looked between the two men for reassurance. "He's alive?"

"Very much alive. He is helping construct a fort in Pittsburgh that honors a black runaway hero from South Carolina. When that is finished, he said he'd likely join up with one of Lincoln's black regiments."

As Karl explained, Juana almost collapsed; and Lena grabbed her to hold her steady. "He sends his love, and I told him you were staying with us so he will be able to find you when the war is over. I told him to have someone send us letters about him, and I'll be sure to read them to you when they come."

Juana sank to the floor with her head in her hands, crying out, "Oh, Lord, You's so good to me. Thank You, Jesus. Thank You, Jesus."

Lena embraced her as she rocked back and forth in her blissful thanksgiving.

CHAPTER 40

Blessed are the people to whom such blessings fall!
Blessed are the people whose God is the Lord!

Psalm 144:15

The women in the house busied themselves in the kitchen preparing all the holiday Christmas fare for the upcoming celebration. Juana kneaded extra bread dough; Lena boiled sugar Karl had bought from the river captain's cargo supply to make hard candies; and Maria chopped fruits and nuts for the occasion. They worked in perfect harmony, sharing utensils, dish towels, and kitchen space as they visited through laughter in their Yuletide tasks.

Maria taught the girls to fold colored paper into pleats and make miniature fans for the anticipated Christmas tree. When they tied a small ribbon around the middle, their creations resembled butterflies. Dora insisted on flying her "buttafly" around the room a few times before landing it long enough to make another.

Karl had walked Thomas to the penitentiary to report for his assignment, and he was relinquished to work as a clerk for Karl. With his still near-useless arm, guard duty was not an option; and carrying pans in the kitchen was limited as well. The kitchen already housed enough cooks, and those jobs required two hands to carry kettles of gruel or trays of flatbread.

The position of clerk delighted both Thomas and Karl, who had developed a deep bond over their travels home. Now that Thomas was on active duty again, he was stationed at the Union camp northeast of town with Colonel Kincaid's Thirty-seventh Iowa Volunteers, who now performed all the prison functions. This arrangement did not prevent Thomas from walking home with Karl most evenings—like this one—before reporting to his tent community each night. He stayed better fed than most and sported an everlasting grin when signaling the camp sentinel to permit his entrance.

"You got yourself a sweetheart, Krueger?" a lanky soldier with a beard turning gray at the temples asked as Thomas entered the camp.

"Wouldn't you like to know," Thomas quipped back without the grin ever leaving his face.

The Iowan elbowed his friend, whose beard was longer and grayer yet. "How do you get an assignment like that? You's got family and a girl right here, and we left our kin far away on the farm." Shaking his head, he took another look at Thomas's Invalid Corps uniform. "Guess I gotta get myself shot for a job like that."

Thomas' smile wavered. "Careful what you wish for. I lost my best friend in the battle where I was shot."

The soldier's companion answered, "Don't pay him no mind. He's just pining away for his wife and young'uns."

Thomas bedded down for the night and thanked the Lord for all his situation. Clerking was lighter work than his days at home. He was fortunate to be surrounded by family friends who cared about him, and he had Maria. Well, maybe he did not have her yet; but if she would have him, he wanted to keep her in his life forever. He wondered if Maria would accept him. *Oh, Lord, please show Maria how much I love her and the wonderful life we could share someday.*

❦

*M*aria pulled her fancy Bremen gown out of her trunk to attend Christmas Eve services. Johanna and Dora said they thought an angel glided across the room as she entered. Maria spun around to emphasize the shimmer of the ivory in the glow of the evening sunset.

Lena tilted her head and exclaimed, "My, isn't that fancy!"

"I got it to sing at the Bremen Concert Hall. They called me their Snow Angel. If I don't wear it now, I don't think I would use it anymore. I don't think you have a concert hall in Alton, do you?"

"No. I thought you were done with that now," Lena answered. "I thought you had your sights set on a different life altogether after seeing the way Thomas and you drool over one another." She smiled a knowing grin.

Maria blushed. "Whatever do you mean?" she asked almost playfully. She turned, slipped her wrap around her shoulders, and led the family out the door to church.

The carol singing renewed the story of the Savior's birth and refreshed the family's spirits as they continued a heartfelt "Silent Night" on the way home. The winter gales had not yet found them in Alton, and they were only beginning to see their breath in the evening air.

As they approached the house, Maria worried. "There are lights on inside. Surely, you did not leave the oil lamp burning."

Karl and Lena smiled at each other but did not respond to Maria. Once inside, they found Thomas standing next to a tabletop

Christmas tree he had decorated with the girls' "buttaflies," ribbons, and tapers.

"Did you do this?" Maria asked as she leaned in closer to Thomas.

"I'm not going to give away any secrets." He nodded toward the girls, who were eyeing the bright addition to their front room with marveling attention. Smiling, Maria nodded and asked no more questions.

"Off to bed, girls. It will be Christmas in the morning, and you must sleep." Lena guided the tots to their room, while Karl grabbed a bag of candy and nuts to load into their stockings hanging over the fireplace.

"Do you mind if I take Maria for a short walk while you set things out for the children?" Thomas asked Karl.

"No need to ask me. If Maria wants to be seen with you, that's her business." Karl winked at the two of them.

"Maria? Will you step outside with me for a minute?" Thomas took Maria's arm and led her to the door before she answered one way or the other.

"You are being rather presumptuous, Thomas Krueger," she protested in jest as she willingly exited the room with him.

"We haven't known each other very long," Thomas began, "but we have shared part of every day with each other since summer." He took a deep breath while Maria waited. "I cannot think of another person I would want to spend every day with for the rest of my life than you."

"Are you proposing to me?" Maria tried to look at his face in the light shining through the house windows, but it remained shrouded in shadows.

"Well, I don't know what I can offer you with a lame arm. I can't do manual labor. Although I am learning much about clerking from

Karl, I don't think lawyering is for me either. I've been thinking that I would like to continue my studies to be a minister after I'm released from the army." He tried to gauge her reaction in the darkness. "Do you think you could be a pastor's wife, Maria?"

"I-I don't know. Where would we live? I just now am getting reacquainted with my family." Maria shifted her feet in the evening cold. "I can't leave them now."

Crestfallen, Thomas had few answers for her. "I must finish my studies in order to be ordained. I can't do that while I am a soldier. You will need to wait for me. After that, I could be sent to one of the new German communities out west, like Nebraska or Iowa." Not getting any response, he added, "I can tell I am asking too much. Forget I said anything." He turned to go.

"Wait!" Maria reached out and grabbed his functioning arm. "I didn't say no." Now standing face to face with Thomas, she whispered, "I only said I don't know. This is not how I thought my life would go. When I left Germany, I thought I'd be a star on the stage by now." She took a deep breath, then continued, "I believe that is not what the Lord has in store for me anymore. I think He brought me here to meet you." Maria took his hand. "Like you, I have no idea how long this war will last, but I promise to wait for you, Thomas."

He swept her against his chest and kissed her breath away.

At the window, Karl and Lena watched a moment before saying in unison, "Praise God!"

They were back placing gifts under the table when Maria reentered the house. "What was that all about?" Lena asked as if she had not been watching the scene play out.

Maria absentmindedly slipped her gloves from her hands and tossed an "Oh, nothing" over her shoulder as she continued to bed. Karl and Lena chuckled at each other, amused.

The next morning, the girls were tugging at their stockings and soon spreading sticky candy across their faces. "That's enough for now, girls, or you will upset your tummies," Lena chided as she found a cloth to wipe away the mess.

The happy family opened presents, while the roast turkey filled the home with appetizing aromas. The girls each received carriages for their dolls and stuffed animals to cuddle at night: a curly-haired dog for Dora and a floppy-eared bunny for Johanna. Juana had made them new doll blankets to go in the carriages; and later, Aunt Dagmar brought whole new wardrobes for both girls and dolls she had sewn. Maria gave them pastel hair ribbons she had acquired in New York for special occasions.

Soon, the house was full. Uncle Herman and Aunt Dagmar came in with cousins Hans and Katie from the farm. Herman picked up his youngest sister and spun her around the room with ease and then introduced her to his family. Hans was already taller than his aunts and was a reliable worker. Katie and Johanna were the same age and inseparable when they had the chance to see one another. Both were showing each other their new treasures, and Dora was sure not to be left far behind.

Thomas arrived before dinner, and introductions were made around the room again. As the house was beginning to be filled to capacity, there was another knock at the door. Thomas asked, "How many people do you know?" before Lena opened it to find the rest of Thomas' family on their doorstep.

Thomas ran to the door at the revelation and hugged everyone. "I had no idea I'd be seeing you. I've missed you all so much." He tried without success to keep the tears from his eyes as he tried to wrap everyone in his arms at once.

Next to Thomas' mother and father at the door was his brother Tobias, who was about the same age as Hans. Where Hans had grown taller, Tobias had grown broader; but the two farm boys formed an immediate connection and began comparing their prowess in all things outdoors. Sister Stella must have sprouted a foot in the last year herself. Her blonde hair framed ringlets about her face.

Lena shook her head. "I can't believe this is the same baby I held on my lap over the Atlantic. It seems like only yesterday you were in diapers." Stella blushed at the image of herself in diapers but smiled and rustled her two brothers into the front room.

"These two must be the twins, Henry and Herman." Lena bent to distinguish between the identical seven-year-olds. "Your brother told us all about you when he was here at Easter."

They shrugged at one another and bounded over to admire the Christmas tree.

Uncle Herman followed them and asked, "Which one of you is Herman?"

One pointed at the other.

"Hi. My name is Herman, too. Glad to meet you." He reached out and shook Herman's hand. "Glad to meet you, too, Henry." He repeated the greeting with the other youngster.

"How did you get here?" Thomas asked his parents as he shook his head in disbelief.

"Karl telegraphed us from Cape Girardeau and asked us to come. The winter has been mild enough to travel, so your mother insisted we accept." His father smiled broadly.

Thomas turned to Karl. "You are full of surprises, aren't you?"

"I knew you were missing your family, and I thought that would be the best Christmas gift of all for you."

Thomas' mother eyed him up and down as if to make a full assessment of his injuries. "How hurt are you? Why didn't they let you come home?"

Before Thomas could answer, Karl interjected, "Actually, I have another surprise for you." He pulled out a folded paper out of his breast pocket.

"I don't know how you could top this," Thomas wondered.

"I spoke with the prison doctor about you. He and Colonel Kincaid have written discharge papers for you. This says you can have an honorable discharge from the army based on your injuries."

Karl pulled the papers out of his breast pocket to present them to Thomas and the Kruegers.

"What?" Thomas took the paper and wiped his eyes to be sure the documents agreed with what Karl said.

Maria wrapped her arm around him and read over his shoulder. "That means you can go back to school faster than you thought," she whispered.

"School?" his mother repeated. "You want to go back to school?"

"Yes, Mama. I can't manage farm labor very well like Tobias or Hans. I want to become a minister like my friend Stefan who was killed at Gettysburg. I'd like to carry on his legacy, especially after I've seen all the blessings the Lord has bestowed on me. You only need to look around this room to see how blessed I am." His eyes landed on Maria, and he pulled her closer to him. "Maria said last night that she would wait for me to finish school to be my wife."

The room erupted into cheers of well-wishing and toasts to the young couple. With all the commotion, no one heard the knocking at the door until Juana opened it.

Lena followed her and said, "Who could that be? Almost everyone we know is already in this room."

Opening the door, Juana stepped aside. Standing before them was Stefan.

❄

After Thomas' strong embrace to be sure Stefan was real, the whole house sat down to listen to his tale.

"You fell. I thought you were dead, and they would not let me go back to you." Thomas was eager to hear Stefan explain.

"I did fall. I think I stumbled over these long legs of mine trying to dodge all the shooting. Before I knew it, a gray coat yanked me up by the collar. He pushed me into a house where other captives were being held. Some were wounded, and I tried to tend to them as we sat waiting for whatever came next.

"The burly oaf at the door kept a steely eye on us and did not allow us to speak to one another. But with signs and whispers, we comforted each other; and it helped us stay calm. Of course, that first day, the Rebs thought they were winning since they routed our regiment out of town; but soon, we were moved back by the Lutheran Seminary out of range of Union forces. By time the tide turned, the Rebs were already marching us south."

"South?" Karl interjected. "Did they take you to Andersonville?" An audible gasp escaped the listeners; the horrible conditions at that camp were rumored to be unbearable.

"No, we ended up in the burg of Salisbury, North Carolina." The exhaled sigh echoed in the room. "For a prison, we lived in relative comfort. We passed the time making trinkets, playing baseball, and even doing a little theater. They allowed us to worship and sing hymns."

"My, I think I'd wait out the war in a place like that." Thomas interjected as he remembered the mangled men on the battlefield.

"Things changed when too many prisoners filled up the place. Conditions soured, and some prisoners escaped north. I joined them."

"So you came straight here?" Lena asked.

"We hid with a Union sympathizer for a while; but I was afraid if I went home, they'd drag me back to the fighting. I thought no one would look for me here." Stefan's glance around the room pleaded for acceptance of his plan.

"You're welcome as long as you like," Lena offered.

Karl stepped forward. "Stefan, I don't think I can justify housing a deserter with my current position with the government. Why don't you go back to school with Thomas if you don't want to return to Indiana?"

Thomas jumped up and hugged Stefan again. "That's a wonderful idea. Thanks to Karl, I've been given an honorable discharge and will be returning to Concordia as a student right away." He turned to Maria and pulled her into the circle of friends. "I want you to meet Maria. She is Lena's sister, and she has agreed to be my wife after graduation."

Stefan smiled at his friend's fiancée and bowed a formal greeting. "My pleasure." He turned his grin on Thomas. "I let you out of my sight for a few months, and you find yourself a girl."

"That's right. The Lord has been generous to me. He resurrected my friend from the dead and found me an honorable wife who will follow me into the ministry."

"Ministry? I didn't think you were planning on that." Stefan looked at Thomas in surprise.

"At first, I thought it was to honor you, Stefan. I wanted to follow the path I knew you wanted for your life once you were gone. I know now it is *my* calling, too, to honor all God has done for me."

Touched by Thomas' proclamation, Stefan conceded. "If I am to be a man of honor, I cannot be a deserter. I need to report to duty again and not run away." He turned to Karl. "Can you help me with that?"

"My pleasure." Karl clapped his shoulder.

EPILOGUE

The War Between the States finally ended. Maria and Thomas were married at Trinity Lutheran church near the St. Louis campus after Thomas graduated from Concordia. It was time to celebrate. Not only was the war over and these two were starting a new life together but Stefan and Jubal had also returned to the fold. Stefan resumed his ministerial studies, and Jubal worked construction, capitalizing on the many skills he had learned while away. Jubal and his mother found a place to share near the river, but she and Lena stayed close.

The two newlyweds departed for a small town near Lincoln, Nebraska, where many newly arrived Germans had settled. Thomas felt it was providence to live near a city named for the great emancipator. Thomas became the pastor he had foreseen, and Maria started a small church choir to thank and honor the Savior for her good fortune. She also taught the children folk songs in the church school, to everyone's delight—all for the love of honor and blessings of God's grace.

AUTHOR'S NOTE

*T*he Civil War battles and incidents cited in the story are taken from the pages of history. Generals and other leaders were real people, but their interactions with the fictional characters are fabricated.

The Ladies of Alton really did host a Thanksgiving dinner for the Grey Beard troops stationed at the Alton penitentiary. Their thank you was printed in the local paper.

Frederick Douglas did speak at the Brooklyn Concert Hall to encourage black enlistees to join the Union cause. Those in attendance are unknown, although he did, in fact, have a German journalist, Ottilie Assing, assist in promoting him.

The names and titles of the women in the Anti-Slavery Activists are historically accurate. These black women likely did not include someone like Maria; however, the Germans were sympathetic to their cause.

The Manhattan Colored Orphan Asylum did burn down during the 1863 New York riots. The impromptu concert with Maria is fiction, but German members of the Turner Hall did assist in caring for the orphans after the riots.

Places the characters visited on their travels are depicted as they were in 1863. For instance, the Robert Smalls Fort was being built in Pittsburgh by freed black men at that time, and Louisville had a grand hotel for visitors.

I hope you enjoyed their adventures.

Terri Bentley

CITATIONS BY CHAPTER

Chapter 2

Neumark, Georg. "Lutheran Service Book 750. If Thou but Trust in God to Guide Thee." In Lutheran Service Book 750. Hymnary.org. Accessed May 23, 2024. https://hymnary.org/hymn/LSB2006/750.

Chapter 3

Eggert, James R. "The Origin and Diffusion of the Common Table Prayer 'Come, Lord Jesus.'" Accessed May 23, 2024. https://www.lutheranquarterly.org/wp-content/uploads/2023/03/03_LUT_37-1_Eggert_049-072.pdf.

Chapter 19

"Speech of Frederick Douglass at the Annual Meeting of the Massachusetts Anti-Slavery Society at Boston." n.d. https://www.lib.rochester.edu/IN/RBSCP/Frederick_Douglass/ATTACHMENTS/Douglass_What_the_Black_Man_Wants.pdf.

Chapter 20

Wesley, Charles. 1195. "Christ the Lord Is Risen Today." Hymnary.org. 1195. https://hymnary.org/text/christ_the_lord_is_risen_today_wesley.

Chapter 21

Kleen, M. A. "Civil War Ballads: I'm Going to Fight Mit Sigel." September 21, 2017. https://michaelkleen.com/2017/09/21/civil-war-ballads-im-going-to-fight-mit-sigel.

CHAPTER 24

"Dante's Inferno." *Full Text Archive*, 3 Sept. 2023, www.fulltextarchive.com/book/dante-s-inferno/#CANTO-3-4.

CHAPTER 28

Wikipedia. 2023. "Die Gedanken Sind Frei." Last modified November 17, 2023. https://en.wikipedia.org/wiki/Die_Gedanken_sind_frei.

CHAPTER 35

"Edward Everett, 'Gettysburg Address (19 November 1863).'" Voices of Democracy. June 17, 2016. https://voicesofdemocracy.umd.edu/everett-gettysburg-address-speech-text.

Coming Soon

FOR *Love* OF HOME
IN A LAND SO STRANGE, BOOK THREE

CHAPTER 1

*M*artin slammed the letter down on the paper-strewn desk, which appeared more like a ransacked crime scene than a professor's stacks of ungraded essays. The sudden rush of turmoil caused by the letter wadded in his hand rustled some unattended papers to the floor in a white flurry.

Martin cursed and leaned across the clutter of pens, paper weights, and notebooks to retrieve the wayward assignments before they further escaped. The last thing he needed was to have a student claim he had lost their work. The pile of end-of-term assignments was growing exponentially each day as his classes prepared to return home for the summer.

Returning to the unfolded missive crumpled on his desk, he shook his head. He blamed Von Bismarck, trouncing through the German countryside rounding up soldiers, for his parents' distressful letter. The commoner did not care who made treaties with France, Austria, or Denmark. Why not let the peasants live their simple lives the way God intended? The Good Book says in Ecclesiastes, "There is nothing better for a person than that he should eat and drink and find enjoyment in his toil."[3] Why march the young men off to war leaving mothers and loved ones to worry about their return?

---

3   Ecclesiastes 2:24

The country was not under attack by anyone but their own soldiers gathering more fighters in every village.

The student population at Leipzig University had felt the sting of Von Bismarck's aggression, too. More seats remained empty every term because of the depletion of young men relegated to fight political wars. They were fresh meat for the ambitious war machine.

Martin read the lines of the letter again. Mother's handwriting was shaky but discernible. "I'm sure this news breaks her heart," Martin whispered. "How do you allow your youngest son to go to war? His younger brother Thomas may have been an eager participant with his outdoor proclivities and yearning to fight American Indians like the cowboys from the stories he read as a boy. But Mama and Papa cannot be happy about this."

At least, their older brother Herman was raising a family in America and had somehow remained unharmed during the American Civil War. Thankfully, news of an armistice meant that their country could start healing from the stain of war and his siblings remained safe.

A second letter with an American postmark peeked out under a few stray student papers. Martin slipped it out from beneath the debris. This letter had not been sent by family but was an offer to teach in America. He shifted the spectacles slipping down his nose and touched the return address: C. F. W. Walther. The man and his nephew had visited Leipzig a few years before in an effort to recruit new pastors and teachers. Walther had impressed Martin, and they had talked long into one night about the need for instructors in America. So many immigrants dotted the American West in new settlements, there was a shortage of pastors for their growing communities. The Concordia School in St. Louis, Missouri, intended to equip as many pastors for the German newcomers as they were able. The German-speaking school enticed Martin at the time, but he did not intend to walk into a civil war overseas.

Martin's brilliant mind and insatiable reading had led him to an instructor's position upon his own graduation from university. Relating to the students was easy, since he was so close to their age; and his literature courses were popular on campus. His enthusiasm for his stories would draw extra students to sit in the lecture hall to listen to his examinations of classic or contemporary texts.

Only two years older than his brother Thomas and being of healthy fighting age, he could be conscripted into service by Von Bismarck as easily as the others. He did his best to sport a beard to help distinguish himself as older than the students he taught, but it was not difficult to discern his unwrinkled blue eyes behind his reading glasses.

Martin loved the Greek classics. Sophocles, Homer, and Euripedes all held a special place in his heart. When contemporary authors like Mary Shelley used classic concepts such as the myth of Prometheus and original sin in her writing of Frankenstein, he had almost swooned. If only he could get his students to weave ancient concepts and modern ones together so well.

Deep in thought, Martin jumped at the insistent pounding on his office door. "What is it?" he called to the door, annoyed at the disturbance.

A diminutive colleague in a gentleman's cape and top hat to provide a few inches of height burst through the door, out of breath. With a gasp, he called out, "Neubauer! You might want to make yourself scarce! Von Bismarck's men are on campus rounding up more recruits!"

"I don't think recruit is the right word here, Grau. What he is doing can't be called recruiting. It's more like abducting." He sneered down at his disheveled desk but did not move to retreat from the room.

"Who cares what they call it? Do you want to be swept along with the army or get yourself out of here?" Professor Grau handed Martin his cloak, and the two of them raced to a nearby hiding place behind a large bookcase.

The storm of boots rushed up the stairway, and doors swung open and slammed closed on every floor of the four-story building. A commander remained on the ground floor shouting orders overhead. "Do your duty, men. Do your duty!"

It was uncertain whether he was shouting at the soldiers searching the rooms or if this was his way of encouraging the sought-after recruits to join his ranks. It did not take long for the whole sweep to be complete, and then they were off to terrorize other parts of the town with their sword rattling.

Dr. Andreas Grau and Martin Neubauer eased the closed bookcase open and assessed the damage. Martin chuckled to himself. "The desk looks the way I left it. They could have at least had the decency to straighten it up before they retreated."

Grau shook his head. "You may be a brilliant professor, but how you keep track of anything in this mess is beyond me." He patted Martin on the back goodheartedly.

"That's what assistants are for, and mine has been missing the last few days." He shrugged. "I do need to tackle these essays, though." He straightened one of the stacks that threatened to tumble off the edge.

"You just came out of hiding from those military goons, and your only thought is to grade papers? I can hardly catch my breath, and

I'm not sure I can keep doing this." Grau slid into the nearest chair, dislodging another stack of assignments.

Martin nodded at his friend. "I was considering going to America. I have a job offer to teach in St. Louis, Missouri. It's next to the Mississippi River in the middle United States." Grau leaned forward to listen to Martin's revelation. "Were you here a few years ago when Dr. Walther visited campus? He was educated here and now heads a university in America. His school needs more German teachers to facilitate the growing influx of German settlers. I already have family over there; and since their war is over, I think it may be time for me to accept his offer." He stared at Grau, but his friend only tilted his head like a dog trying to understand a command. "I don't intend to be sent to the frontlines for one of Von Bismark's border disputes."

Grau leaned back in his chair again and stroked his chin. "How long have you been thinking about this? It's the first I've heard you mention it."

"It's been on my mind for a while. But I just received a letter from home, and my younger brother is now part of the Von Bismarck regime. I think my parents will understand me going to America. Half the family is there already—two sisters and a brother, anyway. I think it is time I join them. Home can be wherever I choose it to be."

"You think Dr. Walther might have a position for me, too? I'd come with you. I don't have anything holding me here, and that spot behind the bookcase is a bit crowded." Grau brushed the dust off his cape.

"As small as you are, you could squeeze into my travel bag." Grau was not amused at the poke at his height. "Don't worry. I'll write and ask, but I'm sure you could find employment in either case. The term here is almost over. Let's finish it out and book the first ship sailing to America before we find ourselves marching around with a gun in our hands."

Martin turned back to his paperwork. "I don't want to disappoint my students by not getting their essays graded." The sarcasm was not lost on Grau. "I hope I have enough ink to mark all of these ridiculous attempts at literary analysis." He slumped into his desk chair and grabbed the top assignment, even though his mind rested on escaping to America.

About the Author

Terri Bentley writes in the Idaho mountains, where she lives with her husband and two big dogs. After raising three children and retiring as an English teacher, she is now a national speaker and Bible study leader for women's groups. She is also the successful writer of articles, devotions, and church programs. When she is not writing or assembling jigsaw puzzles in her beautiful cabin retreat, she spends time with her grandchildren in the Boise valley.